D1547802

THE PRIEST

This is a volume in the
Arno Press collection

THE AMERICAN CATHOLIC TRADITION

Advisory Editor
Jay P. Dolan

Editorial Board
Paul Messbarger
Michael Novak

See last pages of this volume
for a complete list of titles.

THE PRIEST

Joseph Caruso

ARNO PRESS
A New York Times Company
New York ● 1978

Editorial Supervision: JOSEPH CELLINI

————◆———

Reprint Edition 1970 by Arno Press Inc.

Copyright © Joseph Caruso 1956

This edition is reprinted by arrangement
with Macmillan Publishing Co., Inc.

THE AMERICAN CATHOLIC TRADITION
ISBN for complete set: 0-405-10810-9
See last pages of this volume for titles.

Manufactured in the United States of America

————◆———

Library of Congress Cataloging in Publication Data

Caruso, Joseph, 1923-
    The priest.

    (The American Catholic tradition)
    Reprint of the ed. published by Macmillan,
New York.
    I. Title. II. Series.
[PZ4.C329Pr 1978] [PS3553.A787] 813'.5'4
ISBN 0-405-10821-4   77-14629

THE PRIEST

THE MACMILLAN COMPANY
NEW YORK · CHICAGO
DALLAS · ATLANTA · SAN FRANCISCO
LONDON · MANILA

BRETT-MACMILLAN LTD.
TORONTO

THE PRIEST

by

Joseph Caruso

THE MACMILLAN COMPANY
New York, 1956

Library of Congress catalog card number: 56-11865

This book is fiction and the characters and incidents portrayed are imaginary, but if there is truth in the story as well, the author wishes to thank the priests who have helped him to find it.

. . . every high priest taken from among men is appointed for men in the things pertaining to God, that he may offer gifts and sacrifices for sins. He is able to have compassion on the ignorant and erring, because he himself is also beset with weakness, and by reason thereof is obliged to offer for sins, as on behalf of the people, so also for himself. And no man takes the honour to himself; he takes it who is called by God.

HEBREWS 5:1–4

As the falling snow dwindled, the morning sun, shining feebly, rose out of the cold water of Boston Harbor. The planking and the piles of the old wharf were covered with ice and snow. Fishermen squinted at the rising sun, furrowing the wrinkles that were carved on their swarthy, weatherbeaten faces. Draggers and beam trawlers, glistening with iced ratlines and dragnets, unloaded catches of redfish, cod, and halibut. Sea gulls, screaming at black-tipped terns, winged through the sparse grove of masts and dived into the oil-slick water, gulping down discarded bait and small fish.

Farther inland, the city began to stir and grow noisy, but around the waters of Boston Harbor the city sounds seemed unreal. The whir and horns of automobiles, the shrill cries of newsboys, the rumbling of trailer trucks faded and died at the lapping edge of the sea.

The Honorable John H. Whitney slowly removed his glasses. His movements were precise, unhurried. He watched the jurors file back to their seats. There were twelve people, eight men and four women, who had been endowed with a power by the State—the power of deciding guilt or innocence; the power of being able to free, incarcerate, or kill a fellow human being.

Whitney watched the note leave the head juror's hand and arrive at the bench. The word *Guilty* leaped at him, and he relaxed. There was no recommendation for clemency. He passed the note to the clerk, who read it out loud.

After two hours and twenty-six minutes the jury had arrived at a verdict. Joseph Shannan was guilty of murder in the first degree. Now it was Whitney's duty to pass judgment on the criminal.

It was not often that the task of sentencing a man to death confronted Judge Whitney. He derived no pleasure from sentencing a man to die. But on this occasion he would have no difficulty in doing his duty. He knew that Joseph Shannan should have been penalized in some way long ago.

Whitney's knees began to tremble, and he forced them to rigidity. He had been troubled for some time by a nervous condition. His head ached dully, and he closed his eyes for a moment. The murmuring in the courtroom subsided. The judge looked at Shannan gravely, then asked him if he had anything to say before sentence was passed on him.

Joseph Shannan got up. He was a squat man, with broad, sloping shoulders. His face was pale and his hands were clenched tightly. He glanced at the jury.

"What's there to say?" Shannan asked harshly. "I been saying I didn't do it."

The judge frowned and tapped the bench with nervous fingertips.

Shannan continued to look at the jury. "There's one thing I want you to remember," he cried. "I didn't kill Ellen Greer. On my mother, I didn't kill Ellen Greer!"

The foreman of the jury scowled and turned his head away.

Then the Honorable John H. Whitney condemned Joseph Shannan to death in the electric chair, at a time and place convenient to the State. For the State, he said, has the task and duty of protecting its citizenry from such chronic criminals as Shannan so that it shall be able properly to function and produce . . .

On T Wharf the fishermen had finished unloading their draggers and were walking to their homes in the North and West End. They wore smelly caps with twisted and crumpled visors, and their trousers were baggy and patched. They were not troubled by the cold, and the younger men laughed and winked at the pretty women who passed by. When the group of men who lived in the West End passed St. Dominic's Church, they touched the visors of their caps.

2

II

When the alarm went off, Father Octavio Scarpi was already awake. He reached over and pushed back the lever. He listened to the rain for a moment, looking up at the small circular window above his cot, then got up. He tapped the small radiator beside the bed, but the gesture was automatic; he knew it would be cold. The pastor had notified the custodian not to stoke the furnace after the first of May.

As he started to put on an undershirt, he saw that it was torn, changed his mind, and put it aside. It wasn't the first time he had gone without an undershirt. Slipping into his trousers, he palmed his cheeks, feeling a slight stubble of beard. But when he looked into the mirror above the washstand, he decided not to shave.

Placing a basin within the bowl of the washstand, he filled it with water from a pitcher, which rested on an old scarred bureau, and laved his face vigorously. After drying himself, he peered into the mirror as he squeezed toothpaste onto the bristles of a brush. As he brushed his teeth, he gazed at the streaks of gray daubing his brown hair, and grimaced at his crooked, broken nose. As a young man his nose had been broken several times in street fights and in the prize ring, and most of the cartilage had been removed. Once, during a period in which he fought six times in two weeks, a blow had so complicated the breaks in his nose that he couldn't breathe properly, and he had gone to a doctor who had removed most of the bone.

Octavio Scarpi was a strong-looking man, in his late thirties, but because of his bulk and height and the gray in his hair, he looked older.

After washing, he shrugged into his cassock and slipped his collar on backward. He didn't try to fasten it, for he knew that it wouldn't

3

fit around his broad neck. Father Scarpi hoped someday to have special Roman collars. He had been ordained three years before, and because he had taken a personal vow of poverty he felt that he should not buy articles that would make him comfortable. He could accept such things as gifts, but none had been offered him and he never spoke of his discomfort.

After making his morning offering, he glanced at his alarm clock and saw that it was time for morning Mass. He put on his biretta and, fingering the stubble of his beard, gazed into the looking glass again. Gray eyes, below swollen lumps of scarred eyebrows, looked back at him. Shaking his head sadly, he murmured something about vanity being in the ugliest of men, and descended to the sacristy.

Two altar boys were in the small space behind the altar of the lower church. They were chattering to each other and putting on their surplices. As the big priest entered, the boys smiled and hastened with their dressing, straightening each other's gowns. A moment later they were ready and helped Father Scarpi with his vestments. Then the priest followed the acolytes to the altar without glancing at the pews. He knew there would be only twenty or thirty parishioners in the church, mostly old women, and the sparse attendance would sadden him. He heard the people rise, and as he started the early-morning Mass someone began to cough.

" 'In Nomine Patris, et Filii, et Spiritus Sancti,' " he intoned the opening of the Ordinary, adding, " 'Amen.' " He paused, then went on, saying in Latin, " 'I will go to the altar of God.' "

And heard the parishioners' response: " 'To God, the joy of my youth.' "

The Introit for the day, the second Sunday after Easter, was from the Thirty-second Psalm, and, fixing his eyes on the pages of the altar missal, Father Scarpi said, " 'The earth is full of the mercy of the Lord, alleluia: by the word of the Lord the heavens were made, alleluia, alleluia.' "

After the Mass he removed the ceremonial robes and went into the dining room, where the housekeeper placed a breakfast of two poached eggs and a cup of coffee before him. Then he entered the outer office and opened his tattered breviary. He started to read the matins, pacing up and down. He was reading: " 'Domine, labia mea aperies. Et os meum annuntiabit laudem teuam,' " when he heard the rapid tapping of heels in the vestibule.

4

A young woman entered the office. Her coat was wet from rain, and her hair was tied back clumsily with a kerchief.

"I'm looking for a priest," she said breathlessly. "My name is Theresa Spinale. My brother Vincent is dying."

Father Scarpi hesitated. "The pastor isn't here." He added uneasily, "I'll call him."

"Aren't you a priest?"

"Yes." He looked down at his hands, at his long, protruding wrists. He felt too proud to tell her that the pastor liked to restrict all such calls to himself or Father Lazzini.

"There isn't time," she said earnestly. "Why won't you do it? My brother may lapse back into a coma at any moment."

"I'll come," he said quickly. "Wait just a moment." He walked into the inner office and snatched up Father Lazzini's anointing cruse from its place in the desk. His own cruse and stole were in the trunk in his cubicle. The big priest saw Father Sconnetti's coat hanging on the coat tree in the corner. He draped the coat about his broad shoulders like a cloak, knowing it was too small for him. Clapping on his biretta, he hurried down the flight of steps leading to the street.

Theresa Spinale was waiting impatiently at the rectory door, standing in the rain. As soon as the priest appeared, she began striding up Allen Street. He caught up to her in a few long steps. Her kerchiefed head bobbed up and down beside the spear-tipped shafts of the iron fence which enclosed the church. The rain, cold and driving, smacked into the cement walk. The girl trembled in her sodden coat. She faltered in midstride, and the priest, towering by her side, took her arm gently.

"Thank you, Father," she murmured.

Holding the cruse in one hand, the priest guided the girl with the other. They passed through Lyman Street and down Staniford, up South Margin and into Hale Street. As they walked, it seemed to the priest that he was retracing the course of his green years. They passed the synagogue where he had seen long-bearded rabbis on the Sabbath; the viaduct, old when he was only a child; Lyman Street, where Don Calcedonio Giordano, a long-maned, mustached old poet, had recited from Dante with the singsong Arabic dialect of Sicily choking the Tuscan words; Hale Street, the crowded cradle of his birth, with its rounded façades and the wrought-iron handrails and massed pushcarts with their mounds of fruit and vege-

5

tables. Refuse littered the cobblestone street where the peddlers, arranging the wares on their carts, would sing *C'e 'na Luna Menzo Mare* as they prepared for market.

At last the young woman led him up a flight of stairs into a dimly lighted flat where they walked into a bedroom.

People were clustered together in small silent groups. A man lay on a bed, a wasted, wan-faced figure, grimacing with pain. Pity overcame Father Scarpi so that he could scarcely speak.

He opened Father Lazzini's oil-stock burse, lighted the twin candles, placed the crucifix between the flickering lights, and draped the purple stole about his neck. The young woman asked the others to leave and tried to take an old woman, who had been hovering beside the bed, with her. But the old woman whimpered and made inarticulate noises.

The girl began to weep. "She won't leave, Father. She is our mother. She's deaf and dumb."

Father Scarpi looked at the old woman. Her face was seamed and her hands were knotted. She seemed to be trying to take her son's pain upon herself. She would hear nothing that was said, Father Scarpi reflected. "Let her stay," he said.

The girl left the room, closing the door behind her. The man's eyes opened and gazed at the priest. He stretched out a trembling hand and grasped the priest's cassock with wasted blue-veined fingers.

The old woman at the foot of the bed uttered a short cry and began to sob.

"Where's God, Father?" the man asked. "I suffered enough. Tell Him I suffered." He lapsed into an incoherent murmur.

"Have you anything to tell me?" Father Scarpi whispered, leaning closer.

"I have sinned," the dying man murmured. "I killed a woman, Father." Startled, the priest leaned nearer to the bed.

"God forgive me," the dying man said.

The old woman came forward and took the man in her arms. He gasped, "Mother." The woman wept silently. Breathing quickly, the man gripped the priest's wrist and begged him for absolution for his sin.

"Greer. I killed Ellen Greer. Save me, Father!" he cried, and fell back on the bed.

6

"Ego te absolvo." Father Scarpi anointed the man's eyes, ears, nostrils, lips, hands, and feet, saying, " 'Through this holy unction, and His most tender mercy, may the Lord pardon thee whatever sins thou hast committed, by sight, hearing, smell, taste, word, touch or step.' "

"Save me, Father," the man repeated. Then his breathing became shallow, and he lay quiet, unconscious again.

Father Scarpi blew out the candles, put away the stole and closed the cruse of oil. The words of the prophet came to him: "The groans of death were about me, the sorrow of hell encompassed me; and in my affliction I called upon the Lord."

Shaken by the confession, the priest stumbled into the kitchen. The relatives and neighbors of the family who were crowded into the little room would not let the priest leave. He remembered some of them from his boyhood.

"Have a cup of coffee, Father." A tall man pressed a mug into the priest's hand, and introduced himself as Vincent Spinale's brother, Al.

"It's cold out and the rain beats hard," an old woman said. "Today foxes married, for the sun shone bright while the rain fell. I know you, Father," she continued, peering at the priest through the hatchwork of wrinkles about her deep-set eyes. "Don Beneditto Scarpi. The fisherman, the father of the eight shoes." She cackled. "And you are the eighth shoe, and the last one."

Father Scarpi smiled, for in the dialect of Augusta *scarpi* meant shoes. He had been the eighth born and had been baptized Octavio.

"Ma tu non me ricordi," she said, looking shrewdly at him. "You don't remember Rosa Mangacabri."

He did remember her, however. She was a seamstress he had known all his life. She had gold in her teeth, and a grin that made her look like a female Punchinello. He nodded.

Spinale's mother came into the kitchen. Shadows were in her eyes. She sat beside the stove. Her son Al went to her. "Okay, Ma. Take it easy," he said. "It's better this way. He's suffering too much." The woman continued to weep silently.

Rosa Mangacabri murmured, "Poor Christian."

An old man with pink cheeks and a bald head whispered to the priest. "Do you remember me? Nunzio Scalpone. U ganghere. The butch'?"

7

Father Scarpi nodded. He recalled the times when his father had been unable to work because he was bothered by a gunshot wound in his leg, an old wound from his youth in Sicily. It had troubled him usually during the winter or in rainy weather. His father's leg would swell and he would be unable to walk. After Octavio's mother had used whatever money she had, she would send Octavio to wait in front of Nunzio Scalpone's shop until the butcher closed for the night. Just before closing, Scalpone would come out of the shop and give Octavio scraps of meat and big chunks of bone wrapped in wax paper. "I know," Scalpone used to say. "I know. Your father's leg is sick again." Then the butcher would shake his head. "Cia darri 'a carne a tu madre!" he'd order in the dialect.

After unwrapping the meat, his mother always cleaned the wax paper, folded it, and put it into a drawer full of bags and wax paper and string. Then she would make broddo, a thick soup with potatoes and carrots and onions, out of the pieces of meat and bone. Octavio and his brothers would dip their black bread in it and chew the delicious crust.

"Sì, me ricordo a Vossia," Father Scarpi said to Scalpone. "You used to give me meat when I was a little boy."

The old butcher blew his nose into a red handkerchief, and wiped his rheumy eyes; he was proud that the priest had called him "Your Honor" in the style of the Old Country. "It is best you do not bring to mind an ancient hunger," he confided. "There are deep scars that sometimes do not heal."

"I can only recall the warmth of my belly with your meat in it," Father Scarpi said gently.

Theresa emerged from the sickroom. She signified to her mother that Vincent was asleep. "He's in a coma," she murmured to the priest.

"He sleeps within God's arms," Father Scarpi said.

Theresa shrugged, but the butcher said, "Amen."

"Amen," Father Scarpi echoed, and made the sign of the Cross.

Rosa Mangacabri crossed herself with gnarled hands. She sipped her coffee, burying her hooked nose in the cup; then she licked her lips. "The son of a fisherman is a priest," she said. "And the son of a stonemason is in jail. That is destiny."

"What?" the priest asked.

"She speaks of Nino Schianno's son," Scalpone explained. "You

8

do not recall him? But then he was older than you are. Peppino Schianno."

Al Spinale tried to pour more coffee into Father Scarpi's cup, but the priest refused it. "They mean Joe Shannan," Al said. "He's convicted. He killed a girl named Greer. You should remember him. One of your brothers was a friend of his."

The priest half rose from the table, looking at the closed door of the sickroom. Then he sat down again, heavily.

"This house has no luck," Rosa Mangacabri said. "Do you know why? Why? It isn't blessed. In Augusta all the homes were blessed. First Vincenza becomes deaf, then her daughter-in-law dies, and now her son is ill. The house should be blessed," she repeated piously, peering at the priest.

There was silence for a moment, except for the subdued clatter of spoons and crockery. Then old Rosa said: "Blessed is a blessed house. Evil cannot enter a blessed house." She crossed herself again.

"Do you think we should bless the house?" Theresa asked the priest, goaded by the old woman's insistence.

But Father Scarpi was too disturbed to pay attention. "Call me when he comes out of the coma," he said to her. "Call me."

Theresa nodded. "Thanks, Father," she said.

"Tell him to bless the house," Rosa whispered to Theresa. "He has to bless the house."

As the priest started down the wooden staircase, he heard Rosa say: "Why didn't you ask him? Why not?"

He walked on outside, down the cement steps, grasping the wrought-iron railing. The rain had stopped, but a thick mist rolled through the little street.

Sister Ann Louise, the convent laundress, was ironing the last batch of wimples. She took one from a clothesbasket and sprinkled it with starch. Then she ran the electric iron deftly through its folds. She finished it quickly, and took out another.

Some years before the pastor had conferred with the Mother Superior about sending the clothes out to a special laundry that did work for religious orders. When Sister Ann Louise had been approached for an opinion, she had wept, asking if her work did not please. She had begged the Mother Superior not to send the clothing out. The subject had never come up again, but Father Ferrera, the

9

pastor, had bought two automatic washers and a dryer and donated them to the convent.

The convent attached to St. Dominic's Church was actually under diocese supervision, and was not an integral part of the church. The sisters were in the order of Notre Dame and had been billeted there at a time when housing was an acute problem.

Each morning the sisters would eat their frugal breakfast in their own dining rooms and then file across the street to the parochial school where they taught. Only Sister Mary Catherine, the cook, and Sister Ann Louise, the laundress, were not teachers.

Years after they had come to St. Dominic's it was suggested that they should be moved to a new convent outside the city. But the diocese did not reckon with the peppery Mother Superior who liked St. Dominic's and who refused to be moved. After a while the bishop gave up trying to move them, and the new convent was converted into an orphanage.

Now, as she passed the hot iron over the last wimple, Sister Ann Louise heard the creaking of basement steps through the locked door that separated the convent laundry from the church cellar. As she listened to the heavy tread, she knew it to be Father Scarpi's. The sister had great respect for the big priest; she liked him better than Father Lazzini, who, it was said, walked through the corridors of the parochial school with a cigar concealed in the cup of his hand; or Father Sconnetti, who spent more time singing and playing the organ than he did in praying. In many ways Father Scarpi reminded the little sister of her father. She glanced at a glass of milk and a thick slice of freshly baked bread that Sister Mary Catherine had brought down to her a little while ago. Then she shut off the iron, pulled the plug from its socket, and coiled the wire about the handle of the iron.

Father Scarpi was slumped in an old chair in the cellar, still dressed in his wet cassock, when he heard the door leading to the convent laundry being unlocked.

Sister Ann Louise came in carrying a glass of milk and a slice of bread. When she saw that the priest seemed to be in prayer, she placed the food and drink silently on the desk behind him and turned to go.

"Sister," the priest said, "please don't leave." He had an impulse to tell her of Spinale's confession; it would have been a comfort. But of course that was impossible. "Just for a moment, Sister," he added.

Sister Ann Louise straightened her slumped shoulders and paused. She wrung her hands; her fingers and palms were stubby and red from constant work in the laundry. She was ashamed of them, and would conceal her calloused fingers when near a priest or another sister. She peered through the small-lensed spectacles that slid down her button nose, and waited. Her pale face was wet with sweat, and she wiped her cheeks with the rough apron fastened about her waist.

"Will you say a De Profundis with me?" he asked. "It's for someone who is dying in great pain."

It was an unusual request, she knew, but Sister Ann Louise could see that Father Scarpi was distressed.

" 'Out of the depths have I cried unto Thee, O Lord: Lord, hear my voice. . . .' " The little sister's presence helped the priest. Rising, he dared not offer her a helping hand for fear of offending her. She got up herself and hurried down into the convent basement. Father Scarpi could hear her habit rustling like muted vespers.

St. Thomas Aquinas writes of our lives sweeping through the lives of other men and women like the wind over the waters of the sea, whipping up the foaming waves, and hurling them unto faraway shores. In such manner did Sister Ann Louise affect the big priest, healing his anxieties by her faith and humility.

Sipping the milk that the sister had brought him, Father Scarpi thought of Shannan. He remembered accounts of the trial that had been held the winter before only vaguely.

Shannan had been tried for the knife slaying of his mistress. The scandal sheets had made much of the trial, for more than a mere crime of passion was involved. Joseph Shannan had been a witness for the congressional committee investigating organized crime in the United States.

The priest sighed. He hoped that Vincent Spinale would come out of his coma. Then the priest might ask the dying man to give himself up.

He ascended the winding staircase to the corridor. There the housekeeper met him and told him that the pastor had been asking for him. He tapped on the door and heard the pastor's familiar, "Come in, come in."

11

Father Ferrera was standing behind his desk. He was wiping the thick lenses of his glasses. He squinted myopically in the direction of the big priest.

"Is that you, Scarpi?" he asked gently.

"Yes, Father."

The pastor sighed tiredly and put on his glasses. "Ah," he said, "the blind can see. Sit down, Octavio."

He fussed with the papers on the blotter of the desk nervously. The pastor's hands were long and thick, and his eyes swam behind the lenses of his glasses. His face was lean, and his pale cheeks were hollowed beneath high cheekbones.

He looked at Scarpi out of the corners of his eyes. The big priest was tired, he decided. And he needed to shave. As blind as I am, I can see that he is tired, the pastor thought. Why should he appear tired? A giant of a man. Or was he himself so weary that others looked as tired?

Earlier that morning Father Ferrera had said his private Mass and had gone to breakfast. Inquiring for Octavio, he was told that the priest had been seen leaving the rectory with a young woman. Young woman? He had wondered. What young woman? Sconnetti had gently suggested that it might be a mission of office, and Lazzini had admitted that his anointing cruse, stole and candle were missing from the outer office. Father Ferrera had eaten little. At one time during the breakfast, he had asked, "Is the brother not aware of our rule concerning punctuality?" Father Sconnetti had suggested that the early-morning hour had perhaps made it inconsiderate to disturb the pastor.

But the pastor knew that a rule was a rule, and that he should make Octavio aware of his peccatum; a sin was a sin, and differed only in degree. Most of all, the pastor decided, he must show harshness. It was his duty to register disapproval at the deliberate breaking of a rule. Father Ferrera loved Octavio; it was never easy for him to enforce discipline.

Now he cleared his throat, looking away from Father Scarpi.

"Father Lazzini says that his anointing burse is missing. Have you seen it?"

Father Scarpi flushed, remembering that the burse was still in the pocket of Father Sconnetti's coat, which he had hung on the coat hanger in the vestibule.

"Yes," he said. "I have it. I used it this morning to administer the last rites."

"Without notifying me?" the pastor asked.

"Yes," Octavio admitted. He neared the desk. "I was late for breakfast. Won't you forgive me?"

"No, no." Father Ferrera shook his head quickly. "As a man one may not withhold forgiveness. But you have transgressed a parish rule. A small rule, yet a large one, for to break one rule is to break all rules." The pastor paused and turned away, wishing that Father Scarpi had not asked for forgiveness.

"I want to do what's right," Father Scarpi said.

The pastor protested. "Parish rules are always right. And rules are made to be obeyed, no matter how senseless they seem to be. Must I instruct you in matters of discipline? Have you forgotten that obedience is an integral part of your vow? Obligare ad peccatum."

Father Ferrera grew angry. He rose and paced up and down behind his desk.

"Then again," he went on, "is it possible that you were cramped by our rule? Did you not deliberately disregard it? Tell me that. Tell me."

Father Scarpi nodded slowly. He gazed at his hands and put them behind his back.

The pastor's anger dissipated before the priest's guilt. Father Scarpi troubled him. It was unusual for a priest to be assigned to serve in the neighborhood where he had spent his childhood and youth. The pastor had been uneasy about Father Scarpi ever since his return to the West End as a priest a year before.

"Perhaps," Father Ferrera said, "we are both in error. I for making the rule, and you for disobeying it, and thereby showing arrogance and pride. Perhaps we share in the same sins."

"No," Father Scarpi protested. "What you say is true. I'm arrogant and proud. Not you, Father. Not you."

The pastor smiled sadly. "Oremus pro invicem," he said quietly.

Father Scarpi was aware that the pastor was having difficulty with his breathing. He wanted to ask the older man if he felt well, but he could not. Father Ferrera gave Octavio Scarpi house duty for the day. As Father Scarpi turned to go, the pastor called him and gave him Capecelatro's life of St. Filippo Neri.

"So the time shall not hang heavy in your mind," Father Ferrera explained.

"Thank you, Father." The curate turned and walked slowly out of the office.

As a boy, Octavio Scarpi was attracted by the gamblers and bookies that hung around Kelly's gym where he worked out. Old Hambone would sit behind a battered desk chewing an unlighted cigar; on the wall behind the desk hung an 1860 drypoint of Heenan squaring off against Sayers. Hambone would jerk a thumb over his shoulder. "Strong guys they were."

One day after a workout, Dominic Manatza, a bookie and gambler who had been named after his father's patron saint, said that he was willing to wager even money that Octavio could knock a horse senseless with one blow. Octavio, lounging on the corner of Howard Street and Scollay Square with his trainer, Andy Martin, grinned at Manatza's challenge. But Dixie Lansone, a rival gambler, thinking Manatza was muddled by the few drinks they'd had, immediately put up $500.

"The only man I ever heard of could do that was Max Baer," Dixie grunted, "and I think it was a stunt."

"Listen, kid," Manatza said, "would you be willing to try? I'll give you a finiv just to try and a double sawsky if you can do it."

"Nothing doing," Andy Martin said. "The kid's hands are his living."

Manatza offered to cut Octavio in for a fifth of the wager if he knocked out the horse, and Andy relented. "Okay, kid, it's up to you."

Octavio thought he needed the money and agreed. It was a Saturday night, and Manatza, knowing there would be a number of horses in the market place, suggested they go there. They waited for Octavio while he ran up to Kelly's and got his gym bag. Then they trooped down Hanover Street to the market; other bookmakers and gamblers joined them and began betting actively.

Manatza and Dixie agreed on a Percheron harnessed to a wagon loaded with apples. They spoke to the fruit peddler who had hired the horse and team, but he shook his head. "What if he knocks the horse cold?" he said. "What do I do then, eh?"

"Don't give me that," Manatza said. "You can always say he got sick. And if it's a handout you want, I'll slip you a few bucks if the

14

kid hurts the nag. Jesus," Manatza growled, "even if the kid does knock the horse out I lose money."

The arrangement satisfied the peddler, and he agreed to let Octavio try.

Octavio knew he'd be slamming his fist into solid bone, and for a moment he wondered if it was worth the effort. But he felt it was too late to back out. He told Andy Martin, who was taping his right hand, to bind it tightly. Andy nodded and wrapped the tape around the boy's hand and wrist and between his fingers. Then he worked Octavio's sandbag glove on the taped hand.

"How's it feel, kid?" he asked. "How's it feel?"

"Good," Octavio grunted, looking at the dingy white draught horse. The crowd that had gathered around grew quiet. They gazed at the huge youth as he sized up the horse. Octavio had stripped down to his jersey, and his huge shoulder muscles rippled.

"Another hundred says the kid does it," Manatza yelped. But there were no takers.

He's an animal, Octavio decided, gazing at a spot between the Percheron's eyes. He hasn't any feelings. He stepped back a little, and then smashed a straight punch between the horse's dull vacant eyes.

The beast's eyes clouded, and he slumped in the traces, dazed by the blow. Then the right side shaft splintered under the horse's dead weight, and the animal fell to its knees and rolled onto the broken shaft.

For a moment there was complete silence. Then a swift murmur rose and the bookies and peddlers began to shout. They felt Octavio's shoulders and tried to shake his hand. But he shook them off and gazed at the fallen beast.

A little fat man who had been shopping nearby got on his knees beside the horse.

"What's the matter?" Octavio asked.

The fat man got up, brushed his hands together, and looked at Octavio. "The animal is dead," he said slowly. "He's dead."

Octavio Scarpi had confessed this incident a hundred times, but no matter how many times God may have forgiven him he never was able to forgive himself. Time and time again, a flashing picture of the Percheron would come before him, the dull eyes clouding, the shaft breaking as the beast sank to its knees and rolled over.

15

The priest climbed the stairs to his cubicle. He sat on his iron bedstead and gazed at the book the pastor had given him without seeing it, thinking again of the helpless horse. He got on his knees.

" 'Pater noster,' " he murmured. " 'Qui es in coelis, sanctificetur nomen tum . . .' " The words comforted him and gave him a measure of peace.

III

St. Thomas wrote that faith is necessary to attain the vision of God, and that all infidelity causes men to lose God. It is difficult for those who are blind and yet have the gift of sight to envision God in the affairs of men.

As a boy, blowing soap bubbles from his window on Hale Street, or waiting for his father to come home from the sea, Octavio had seen many sights, but as a camera sees them, without thought. It was only now, since becoming junior curate at St. Dominic's, that he beheld the marvelous sights to which he had been blind: the narrow, twisting way of the cobblestone street; pushcarts on the walk, piled up one against another, like a stacked deck of cards standing on end.

When he was a boy, Octavio had flushed with shame as the fishermen of the North and West End paraded on the feast day of the Blessed Mother or Santa Lucia or St. Dominic. He felt ashamed because the men marching in time to the blaring brass and the pounding drums seldom went to church, rarely confessed their sins, and had an intense dislike for the clergy.

Octavio, hearing the Roma band long before the procession was in sight, would run to his mother crying: "They're coming, Ma! They're coming!" His mother would fling the windows open and he and his brothers would look out, waiting for the parade to turn the corner at Green Street.

First came the little girls with their papier-mâché wings, and the gilded, twisted coat hangers rising in circlets over the heads, like halos. Their proud, anxious mothers fluttered breathlessly after them. Then came the squat, powerful fishermen, red-necked, with brown weather-lined faces and flashing eyes. They wore open-neck white shirts; their sleeves were rolled up, revealing muscle-corded forearms.

17

Eight of them carried the statue of the Blessed Mother on their shoulders.

Octavio's father would lead the way before the statue, carrying a box, and limping a little. He would weave from one sidewalk to the other, picking up the money thrown from the windows by his neighbors. He would pass dollar bills to Don Turrido Bellino, who would pin each greenback to one of the ribbons about the Virgin's neck. Then the procession would halt in the center of Hale Street while the sweating musicians played a lively tune and the dollar bills fluttered from spokes of bright silk ribbons entwined about the collar of the statue.

Father Scarpi was alone in the dining room when the phone in the outer office rang. The priest had just finished saying the early-morning Mass. He was slowly stirring his cup of coffee, reading from Father Scaramell's *Directorium Asceticum,* absorbed in the chapter dealing with religious poverty. He laid the book aside, and went into the office to the telephone.

"Father Scarpi speaking."

"Father, this is Theresa Spinale. You know—my brother was sick. You told me to call."

"Yes, yes," he said. "Is he conscious?"

"No." She hesitated. "He's dead." The priest could hear her sobbing.

"It is God's will," he said.

"Will you come to say the Rosary? The wake is being held at Nenni's Funeral Home."

"Yes. I'll come tomorrow night and the final night."

"Thank you, Father. Thank you." She broke the connection.

Father Scarpi returned to the dining room. Joseph Shannan was again in his mind. Though Shannan was innocent, Father Scarpi realized that he could not help him. He drained his cup of coffee; it tasted bitter.

Father Scarpi was filling his pipe when Father Sconnetti came into the dining room.

"Good morning, 'Tavio." Father Sconnetti smiled.

He was a thin priest with a birdlike tilt to his head, and as he bustled about, gesturing excitedly, the folds of his short cloak flapped up and down like wings. He was often afflicted with painful headaches, and at such times he wore huge, horn-rimmed glasses that made his small face look smaller and wan. This morning he had put on his glasses. He spoke with a heavy accent, and when he became excited he would lapse into his native Italian.

"Morning, Joe," Father Scarpi said. He pushed the coffeepot toward the thin priest, and Father Sconnetti filled his cup. He ladled out two teaspoons of sugar and slowly stirred his coffee.

"Does it hurt much?" asked Father Scarpi.

"A minor pain." The dark-eyed little curate fingered his temples and shrugged. "Would that all pain were that little," he added.

Father Sconnetti was not of the Diocesan priesthood, as were the other curates of St. Dominic's. He was in the order of the Pious Society of the Missionaries of St. Charles Borromeo, and had been sent to the parish by the Chancery to minister to the Italian immigrants. He conducted four weekly Masses in Italian and was supposed to hear the older people's confessions in their native tongue. But the older parishioners spoke a Sicilian dialect that Father Sconnetti could not understand, and it was Father Scarpi who heard their confessions.

Father Sconnetti sighed and adjusted his glasses.

"I was wondering how the pastor would react to a suggestion that we use the Gregorian chant at high Mass at the next holy day," he said.

"It's worth discussing," Father Scarpi agreed cautiously. He knew that any great enthusiasm on his part would so inflame Father Sconnetti that the little priest wouldn't be able to eat.

"The Mass was meant to be sung," Father Sconnetti said, "not droned. We've been over this before, I know. But I think I can use, say, the Holy Name Society to lead off on the responses; then even a choral repetition is possible. Who knows? Maybe we can even start a hymn for Terce and for Compline. Man was meant to sing. God so created his vocal cords that he has the greatest possible musical range. The soul of man—"

"Your coffee. It'll get cold, Joe."

"Ah, the coffee." Father Sconnetti sipped from his cup.

The other curate, Father Dante Lazzini, came into the room. He was tying the stock of his *rabat* around his full paunch; his vest was still unbuttoned. Father Lazzini was stout and balding; he had a bulbous nose, and his lively brown eyes were half hidden by his rotund cheeks.

"How much time left?" he asked.

Father Scarpi glanced at his wrist watch. It was 7:43. "Two minutes," he said.

"Made it, by heaven!" Lazzini said. Just as he sat down, the pastor walked across the threshold. Father Scarpi and the others started to rise, but the old priest held up his hand.

"Keep your seats, gentlemen," he said.

The housekeeper brought in a breakfast of poached eggs, toast, and coffee. The pastor said morning Grace slowly, and after a hasty "Amen" from Father Lazzini they began to eat silently. It was an unwritten rule that conversation began only over the coffee.

When the time came for conversation, Father Sconnetti said, "The old Jews used to call this the Shema."

Father Lazzini gazed sourly at the little curate. "Pass the cream, please," he said.

"They used to eat a piece of bread, a bit of cheese, and some olives," Father Sconnetti went on.

"It's an adequate breakfast," the pastor said. "Quite adequate." As a boy, the pastor had eaten such breakfasts and dinners. His father had been a laborer, and sometimes, especially during the winter, there had been little employment. During such periods Father Ferrera had eaten sparsely. That had been many years ago. The pastor pushed the thought from his mind and placed a lump of sugar in the coffee.

Father Lazzini glanced at Father Scarpi. "What do you think of the Red Sox this year?" he asked. "Think Williams is good for another season?"

The big priest shrugged but made no reply. He knew that Lazzini was trying to interest him in sports so that he would help him organize a parish team, but Father Scarpi didn't think that sports should become a major factor in the parish. He was not opposed to athletics, but baseball would give way to football, and football might lead to boxing. The priest had made a secret vow years before, when he was a seminarian, to discourage body-contact athletics. He would rather help Sconnetti organize a band, or stage an operetta. He knew nothing about music, however, and he knew a good deal about body-contact sports.

"The Poles in the parish are going to erect their own church," the pastor said quietly.

"Their own church?" Father Sconnetti asked.

Father Lazzini gave a forced laugh. "Your proposal to include a Polish-speaking priest in our rectory was turned down?"

"Yes," Father Ferrera admitted. "It was turned down."

Conversation became awkward and everyone seemed relieved when shortly afterward the pastor left the dining room.

"Why wouldn't they allow a Polish priest into St. Dominic's?" Father Sconnetti said.

"That means we lose about 20 per cent in collections," Father Lazzini pointed out.

In the suburbs and in rural parishes priests went from house to house making annual or semiannual collections, or eliciting oral promises for contributions, but not so in St. Dominic's. First of all, a good bit of the money that appeared in the parish had just been handed out by a social worker. Then, too, most of the Italian parishioners were anticlericals, who would often simply refuse to speak to priests.

A priest, to these people, was equivalent to the governing powers abroad who had subjected them to many indignities. In Sicily, on Sundays and holy days, while the men played cards in the village squares in open contempt of the archpriests behind the church doors, the women would file into church and attend Mass. But they would walk out without giving any money to the Church. God doesn't want money, they would say; He wants love, and that is all we can give Him, love. The men would say: "God is a tool of the landlords. The landlords and the Italian investors pay Him; He is on their side." Secretly, though, they were religious. The Lord had suffered for them at the hands of the wealthy landlords, too; He had made the world, had put the fish in the sea; His Bleeding Heart was a sign of His love of the poor. The men did not attend the churches, but on feast days they paraded. And they attended funerals, had their children baptized, confirmed, and married by the Church. Priests are no good, they said; it is a shame that the only place you can reach God is in their Church.

Father Lazzini had been born in the North End of Boston. He had not, as had Octavio Scarpi, grown up in an anticlerical family. As a boy, however, he had attended public schools because his father did not believe in parochial upbringing. His father had owned a pharmacy on the corner of Fleet and Hanover streets. He was a pompous man, and Dante Lazzini could still remember how he had derided his wife for her attendance at Mass.

Once, when Dante was twelve years old, his father had failed to come home for some days. His mother had sent him to the pharmacy to look for his father.

The place had seemed empty, and Dante had slipped through the curtain to the rear of the store. There he had seen his father sitting close to a fat woman with bright red lips; they were murmuring words that were sick with love. Dante had slipped back into the front of the store, shocked, his stomach churning. After a while his father had found him, given him $10, and sent him away. His father had never returned home. Dante would go to him once a week for money, but they never spoke together of what the boy had seen.

Sometimes Dante Lazzini's mother would place a big dish of pasta in front of him and say: "Only two things are important, my son. To believe in God and to eat well." She herself had eaten little, but wept most of the time, cursing her husband for his infidelity.

Father Lazzini sighed. He left the breakfast table and went into the kitchen. The cook, Bridget, an old Irish woman, was peeling potatoes.

"Can I help you?" Father Lazzini asked. It was a game they played.

"Teach me part of the Divine Office, I'll show you the magic of my kitchen," Bridget said with a wink.

"How about Prime?" Bridget nodded, and Lazzini began to pray. After he had finished, she went to the stove and fried a plate of ham and eggs. Father Lazzini began his second breakfast.

Bridget picked up her paring knife again, and caught Father Lazzini's grateful smile. At noontime she might exchange a piece of chicken or beef for a prayer. She was, to Father Lazzini, a woman of great understanding.

Father Sconnetti sipped his coffee in the dining room. His hand trembled, and he replaced the cup carefully in its saucer. Then he shifted his horn-rimmed glasses. He was thinking of a woman, Elena Mare, the soprano in the choir, and was ashamed.

This morning, when she came to sing, Father Sconnetti planned to keep his distance. He had adapted Compline to chant in the vernacular, and he wanted to prove how effective it could be when sung

22

by a good singer. Elena was a good singer, but she was more than that.

The day before, he had pointed out the error of holding a certain note for an extra measure and she had thanked him, her graceful neck arched, her lips smiling. Her brown eyes had seemed to mock him, however, and later, as she was leaving, she had held his feverish hand for a moment in her own cool one. He had watched her as she walked slowly down the winding staircase from the organ loft.

Elena was a widow, and she seemed to understand him better than anyone—better than he understood himself. He had told her of his plan to have the school children exercise in time to music, and she had shown great interest. She had looked at his charts, coming so near to him that he could smell her perfume. But today he must keep a proper distance. He adjusted his glasses again and shook his head.

In the afternoon Father Ferrera got a glimpse of Father Scarpi in the vestibule down the corridor from his office. He watched the big priest for a few moments, and could see that he was troubled.

"Are you restless, Father?" the pastor asked.

"A little." Father Scarpi glanced away.

"Take a walk. Take a long walk. That's what I used to do." The pastor smiled. "What troubles you?" he asked.

"Nothing, Father."

"Go for your walk," the pastor said gently.

He watched as Father Scarpi took a gilt-edged breviary from the bookcase in the hallway. The big priest squeezed into a black topcoat but was unable to fasten the buttons. His biretta was too small and the hem of his cassock was too high, and the ankle-high laborer's boots the priest wore were exposed. Father Scarpi clasped the breviary in a huge hand; his long, thick wrists protruded from the sleeves of his topcoat. He nodded to the pastor and went out into the street.

"Dominus vobiscum," Father Ferrera murmured. A sudden weakness seized the pastor and he sat down heavily. He began to cough violently. He wiped his lips with a white linen handkerchief; flecks of red streaked the cloth. His stomach tensed.

Father Ferrera had been subject to fits of weakness, and had occasionally coughed up blood, for the last three months. A week before he had gone secretly to the City Hospital, where he was put through a long and tiring examination. Afterward the doctor had told him that if anything was wrong the Health Department would have to be notified. It was like a final confirmation. Father Ferrera had murmured his thanks and left.

Father Scarpi counted the cracks bordering the cement squares of the sidewalk. He remembered stepping on them as a boy and saying, "If I step on every one I'll find a thousand dollars." He had never found any money at all. Once, however, at night, when his father had sent him to Prince Street to buy a loaf of black bread, a passing truck had jounced over a hole in the street and dropped a carton from its tailboard. Octavio had rushed into the street and dragged the cardboard box into a darkened doorway. He had ripped it open, and found dozens of shoes. He had run home for his brothers, and they had lugged the carton back to the house. And there, with great disappointment, they had discovered that all the shoes were for women.

Father Scarpi walked for a long time. At first, as he walked, he was angry—angry at his inability to help Joseph Shannan. But he grew calmer at last, and soon he was aware that he was walking past the prison where Shannan was being held. He turned back, then, and went through the gate. A guard directed him to the administration building. It was a low structure along the inner wall of the prison yard.

Father Scarpi spoke to the assistant warden and asked to see Joseph Shannan.

"It's against the rules, Father," the assistant explained. "The inmates have a chaplain who sees them. You'll have to take your chances at the regular visiting time." As Father Scarpi turned to leave, however, the man stopped him. "Why don't you see Father Henry, the chaplain? Maybe he could make some special arrangement for you."

Father Henry was walking behind the administration building. As Father Scarpi joined him, he saw that the chaplain was reciting his Rosary. They walked back and forth for several minutes before Father Henry turned to the big priest and smiled inquiringly.

"I'm Father Scarpi. From St. Dominic's."

Father Henry grinned. "How's Father Ferrera?"

"He seems to be all right."

They shook hands. "What can I do for you, Father?"

24

"I'd like to see Joseph Shannan."

"Do you know him personally?" Father Henry asked slowly.

"No."

Father Henry drew a package of cigarettes from the blouse of his cassock. He ripped it open. "Cigarette?"

"No, thanks."

Father Henry inhaled, and then let a stream of smoke sift slowly from his nostrils. He looked at the sun, sinking below the elevated structure leading to Lechmere Station. Then he asked, "Any special reason for seeing Shannan?"

"No," Father Scarpi said. "I want to pray by his side."

"Do you think he's innocent?" Father Henry asked.

Father Scarpi said nothing.

"I thought he was innocent," Father Henry said slowly. "Now, somehow, I have the feeling, the intuition, perhaps the grace of sharing God's knowledge, that he *is* innocent." He stripped the paper from his cigarette stub and rolled it into a tiny ball which he flicked away with his thumb.

Father Scarpi smiled. "Army?"

"Army?" said Father Henry absently. "Oh, you mean the field stripping. No, Marines." He grinned. "You too?"

"I was in the ETO," Father Scarpi said.

An awkward silence developed. Automobiles rumbled on the Prison Point Bridge.

"You're wasting your time," Father Henry said. "Joseph Shannan doesn't believe in God."

"Will you arrange an interview for me?"

"All right, I'll call your rectory sometime tomorrow."

The next morning Father Scarpi said his usual morning Mass. He listened to the subdued murmur as the parishioners echoed the litany. Afterward, he went to the sacristy where the two altar boys, still in their snowy white cottas with hand-trimmed lace, helped him unvest. He thanked them and, in cassock with biretta, wandered outside the church.

It was a mild spring morning; the bushes beside the church were beginning to bud, and the sun cascaded on him. He glanced up at the staid structure of St. Dominic's. It was square, and of red brick, except for the front, where two huge fluted columns supported an unadorned pediment. Behind an iron fence, a long series of granite steps mounted to the three-door entrances of oak.

The church was old; more than a century had passed since it was erected; and it had had an unusual history.

At first, the church had been Episcopalian, but as more and more Irish Catholics had come to Boston, the Anglicans had moved from the neighborhood and left the church to the Irish. Even in Father Scarpi's own generation, the Irish had still worshiped there. His brother Anthony had married an Irish girl named Agnes. Agnes told of lessons she had learned in the basement of the church. The old men would gather their children there to tell them the history of Ireland, to instill in them their traditional hatred of Cromwell. They would speak of the harshness of the men in orange. Agnes's father would speak to her, too, of Dublin; of O'Connell Bridge and the Sinn Fein. He would speak of trips to Blackrock, Clonskea and Connacht, and Agnes had loved the roll of the names on his tongue. Her father would thunder stories of Irish persecution. "Crux fidelis!" he would boom. They had been robbed of their land; their God, the one God, had been defiled. In the basement of the old church, Agnes's father, and men like him, had told the old stories of Ireland.

But in that generation there were changes, and the old Church was abandoned by the Irish. The Sicilians who moved into the neighborhood bewildered the Irish. In Ireland the clergy had sided with the people against the Protestant landlords and the English laws; in Sicily the landlords *were* the clergy and the laws, and Sicilians believed that the priests had defiled God and His Church. In Sicily it was a man's duty to hate the law and to obstruct it, for the law was Italian and it penalized the Sicilian. In Sicily it was a man's duty to hate the clergy, for the clergy and the landowners made the law. Because the landowners and the clergy used God to confuse the peasant and the fishermen, it became a man's duty to join secret societies that were intent on obstructing the law and the clergy. They carried their traditions with them when they immigrated, just as the Irish had.

Eventually, most of the Irish left the neighborhood, and Fleet Street, Salem Street, Prince Street, and Copps Hill resounded with Sicilian yells and Neapolitan songs. The Sicilian men avoided the church, and were probably not aware that it had a basement; they played boccie and three-seven and drank chilled wine. The women

26

patronized the church, however, sent their children to Mass, and eventually the church was taken over by the new parishioners. They renamed it St. Dominic, after the patron saint of their native town of Augusta in Sicily.

Father Scarpi liked the neighborhood where he had been born, and he was glad to have been assigned it. He liked to walk away from St. Dominic's to the old North Church, from whose tower a lantern had swayed to signal to Paul Revere. In the summer evenings he liked to watch the Sicilian fishermen in the courtyard behind the church. They would rig an electric light near the statue of Paul Revere by running extensions from their houses nearby. Patrolmen on the beat would pretend not to see the card players; they were merely playing for drinks. And occasionally, on hot nights, the policemen were offered chilled wine or beer, which they drank with relish.

Father Scarpi would watch the old men playing their game of three-seven, while young children romped about the lighted courtyard. The sight would bring back to him the noises, the color, the faces of his youth. He would reflect that all over the world were similar squares and streets, in cities or in towns, where people laughed and found some pleasure. And somehow as he watched, his gilt-edged breviary in his hand, he would feel that he had caught a glimpse of every street in the world.

Father Joseph Sconnetti was listening to Elena Mare singing. Her blue-black hair brushed the shoulder of her coat, and the feather in her hat tilted back as she hit a high note. She had a rich, warm voice, and there was a tenderness in it that disturbed the little curate. His spirits soared as she sang. Then the song was over, and he was breathing rapidly.

"That was beautiful," he said, forgetting his morning resolve to keep his distance from her. She looked young, only thirty or thirty-one, young and poised. Then he realized he was repeating, "That was beautiful."

Elena said nothing but continued to look at him. The organist, a tall long-nosed man named Clotti, began shuffling sheets of music. He gathered them and placed them in an old brief case. The priest scowled, but Clotti, who was putting on his topcoat and humming, paid no attention to Father Sconnetti.

The curate followed them downstairs to the floor of the church.

27

At the entrance, Elena took his hand, pressing it gently, talking rapidly. Father Sconnetti was too conscious of the pressure of her hand to hear what she was saying. He forced himself to listen.

"When are you going to come to dinner?" she asked.

Father Sconnetti cleared his throat. She had often invited him to dinner, but he would always murmur an apology and they would part with sad smiles. He wanted to summon up the courage to say, "Tonight," or "Tomorrow," but he could not.

"Someday," he said awkwardly, blushing. They were still holding hands, and suddenly, without thinking, he found himself squeezing her hand. Stammering a goodbye, he backed away and hurried down the narrow staircase to the lower church. His heart was pounding.

The little curate knelt before the niche containing the statue of St. Joseph. Three banks of votive lamps flickered before the statue. Father Sconnetti struck his breast. "Dear St. Joseph," he whispered, "help me. Dear Lord, I am unworthy. Dear Lord, I am unworthy," he repeated. Long after he had grown weary, he forced himself to remain kneeling, repeating the same words over and over again.

In his cubicle Father Scarpi was reading the *Summa*. There was a tap at his door, and the housekeeper said, "Phone for Father Scarpi." He placed a ribbon marker in his book.

It was Father Henry calling. "Would you like to see Shannan today?"

"Yes," Father Scarpi said, "When shall I come?"

"Any time after eleven o'clock this morning."

Father Scarpi felt suddenly tense. "Thank you, Father," he said.

"Father, if you've got a thin skin don't come. Shannan doesn't think much of the clergy."

Father Scarpi smiled wanly. "I'll come," he said. "I'm used to that."

The connection broke and he cradled the receiver. The priest wondered what kind of man he would meet. Shannan was alleged to be a kingpin of organized crime in the country. The priest wondered how a man acquired such a title.

He shook his head slowly. He knew only that Shannan was innocent of the crime he was condemned for. "Almighty God," he whispered, "cast your infinite mercy and grace on him."

IV

The convicts in the old Crabtree building of the State Prison watched the guard lead the two priests through the steel door which opened onto a flight of steps that led down to the Death Block. The curates walked silently, their lips moving in prayer, until the guard stopped before Shannan's cell.

Shannan was seated on his cot leafing through a copy of *Life* magazine with short, stubby fingers. He failed to rise when he saw the priests, and looked at them through the bars of the cell without change of expression. The sleeves of his blue prison shirt were rolled up above his elbows, and his forearms were thick and heavily muscled. His jowls were blue with stubble.

Father Scarpi did recognize him, and he remembered Al Spinale's words: "He was your brother's friend."

Shannan and Onofrio had gone in partnership with a horse and team. On Saturdays they would rent the rig from the livery on Pitts Street, load it with fruit or vegetables at the Terminal on Commonwealth Pier, and take it to market. But his name had been Schianno then, not Shannan.

Onofrio was proud of Schianno's friendship.

"He just got out of the can," he would say, "and he wants to peddle as my partner until he gets his bearings." He wanted Octavio to help him on Saturdays, but Octavio hated Onofrio then.

Octavio was ten or eleven years old at the time. Though he refused to help Onofrio, on Saturdays he looked for work elsewhere in the market district. Shivering in the early-morning cold, hoping the sun would rise quickly behind the Custom House and warm him, he would run up and down the street. If he saw a peddler arraying his

29

cart and making ready to go into that part of North and Blackstone streets which the City of Boston had designated as the market place, he would approach the huckster and begin helping him without comment. If the peddler did not drive him away, Octavio knew that he was hired for the day. Then he would work for ten or fourteen hours, running errands and shrilling the peddler's wares, his voice becoming hoarser and fainter as the day wore on.

Octavio vividly remembered the first Saturday he had seen Schianno. It was on a day of the Immaculate Conception Octave, and Octavio was casting about for a peddler to hire him. He threaded his way through the horses and teams that were lined up waiting in front of North Street. At a signal they would break into a run. The signal came from a policeman who stood at the corner of North and Blackstone streets and blew a whistle. Whoever got into Blackstone Street first got the choicest position.

That day, as the whistle sounded, the peddlers gee-hawed their Percherons and coach stallions. A chestnut gelding of Clydesdale breed broke out in front. "It's Joe Schianno!" a pushcart peddler near Octavio cried.

Schianno stood on the platform gee-hawing, giving the gelding its head, with Onofrio beside him, lashing the beast's flanks with a length of clothesline. They plunged into Blackstone Street, the other teams behind them. The other riders spewed oaths and laughed at one another as the massive, steel-rimmed wheels clattered over the bulky cobblestones.

Father Scarpi looked at Shannan, remembering Onofrio, who was now dead. The priest turned away, shutting his eyes for a moment.

"Hello, Joe," Father Henry said.

Shannan nodded but did not reply. However, he rose when a guard unlocked his cell door.

"This is Father Scarpi," Father Henry said. "He'd like to speak to you."

Shannan looked at the curate; his hazel eyes flicked over the priest's huge body, but he said nothing. Then Father Henry left. They heard him striding through the corridor. The guard locked Father Scarpi in with Shannan and remained outside the cell.

Shannan clenched and unclenched his stubby fingers. He looked down at his hands. They were trembling. "Ever been nervous?" he asked. His voice grated, as if he weren't used to speaking.

"Very often," Father Scarpi admitted.

There was an awkward silence. Shannan turned to a small radio that lay on his cot. He made a movement toward it but seemed to change his mind.

"Portable," he said. "Mine. They let me use it." He paused. "Couple a hours a day."

Father Scarpi felt the restraint the man imposed upon himself. The priest murmured, "That's nice of them."

Shannan was peering at him. He passed his hands over his eyes with a weary movement. "Don't I know you?" he asked. "I met you somewhere."

Father Scarpi remembered the time they had met. It was the night he had injured Onofrio. They were at a wedding, and Onofrio had been drinking. Octavio's older brother, Victor, had tried to stop Onofrio. "You had enough," Victor had kept saying. "You had more than enough." Finally, Onofrio had pushed Victor away and tried to strike him. Octavio had run toward Onofrio, grasped him by the shoulder and spun him around. Octavio had thrown a fast left, and followed up with a hard right. He had put all his strength in the right cross; shoulder and side, stepping in at the same time. A one-two combination. A hook and a right cross. And Onofrio, without a sound, had smashed into the wall and gone down, poleaxed.

A few weeks later, Onofrio had become ill. He had died by inches. First his hands had withered and become useless, then his arms and limbs, and last, his heart. Many times in the night Octavio had been awakened by the sound of Onofrio's voice screaming in pain.

Octavio had asked the doctor what had brought on the disease. But the doctor had shaken his head.

"Could it have been a punch?" Octavio had asked. "A hard punch?"

"Perhaps." The doctor had shrugged. "Who knows?"

Octavio had meant to hurt Onofrio. As his brother had fallen to the floor, Octavio had lifted him to hit him again. His brothers, Victor and Anthony, and Onofrio's friend Joe Schianno had restrained him. Schianno had kept saying: "Big bastard, hitting his own brother. Big bastard."

31

A few months later, while Octavio was on a liberty ship heading for Great Britain, Onofrio had died.

"I'm sure I know you," Shannan repeated.

"Onofrio was my brother," Father Scarpi said quietly.

"Onofrio?"

"Oni Scarpi. He was my brother."

"I remember you," Shannan said thoughtfully. "The big bastard. You knocked Oni dead that night. How many years ago was it? Eighteen, twenty?"

The priest winced but said nothing.

"So you're a priest. What do you know," Shannan said. "What do you know. A priest." He snorted. "What do you want to speak to me for? You want to tell me how to punch my way out of here?"

"I want to pray with you," the priest said. He spoke quietly, as if he were afraid of his own words.

Shannan laughed bitterly. He sat down on his cot. "What's your gimmick?"

"No gimmick," the priest replied slowly. "I want to pray by your side. God will hear our prayers."

"Go to hell," Shannan said.

There were several moments of silence then, except for the radio, which was playing a Strauss waltz. Shannan stared at the priest.

"God!" Shannan cried harshly. "Look who's talking about God. God is dead. He died when I was a kid in the North End. You guys are just percentage men working a shakedown." He looked at his hands. They were still shaking.

"Everything is an act," he went on. "That investigating committee, the guys who gave me a hard time on TV—all else they needed was a stripper. It would've run on Broadway forever. How they needled me! That old bastard, when the mikes were off he kept saying I should be deported 'cause I was a wop foreigner. I was brought over here when I was eight months old, but he'd like to deport me for being a wop foreigner." He snorted. After a moment he got up and walked over to the priest.

"Jesus!" Shannan said. "I don't have to tell you everything's an act. You knew me when I was with Oni. Do you think they found me guilty of murder? Like hell. They found me guilty of being a thief when I was a kid. They found me guilty because my name used to be Schianno and I changed it to Shannan." He turned away. "I got a couple a bucks now, and they don't like it. You and God," he sneered, and whirled back to Father Scarpi.

"Do you know how God treated me?" he asked. "Listen. When I was a kid, my father died. I was the oldest of five kids. It was up to me to support us all. So I went into a church for a handout. And the priest asks me, 'What's your name?' and I say, 'Schianno.' And he looks at me and says, 'Well, we can't help you.'

"That was when I knew I was on my own," he went on. "Always before that I was figgering God was my ace-in-the-hole, but when I flipped over the hole card I found a joker instead."

Shannan sat on his cot. He shut his eyes, as if he were ashamed of his outburst. Seeing that Onofrio's brother had become a priest had shaken him. He had wanted to strike out at the huge man in some way, and now he felt angrily apologetic.

"You want to pray," Shannan said, "and I don't want to pray. That finishes our talk. I'm ready to die if I have to, but I don't need any prayers."

"Death is the beginning of eternal life."

"You think Onofrio is still living?" The priest bowed his head and looked down at the cement floor. Shannan laughed bitterly.

There was a sound of footsteps in the corridor.

"I think Father Henry is returning," the priest said. "May I visit you again? Is there anything I can do for you?"

Shannan looked at the priest, measuring him. "You're a sucker for a beating," he said.

The light in the corridor flooded the cell as the door opened. Father Henry stood outside, waiting.

"Do me a favor, then. Will you do me a favor?" Shannan asked suddenly. "Will you go see my wife? Tell her she can have the works. Everything. But I want Ellen's diary. I'd like to read it. Everybody's read it but me."

"All right, Joe," Father Scarpi said. "I'll try. I'll come back when I get the diary." He looked at Father Henry, and the lanky priest nodded.

Father Scarpi remembered reading about a diary that had been mentioned at the trial. It had belonged to Ellen Greer.

"I'll get it, Joe." He extended a pad and pencil to Shannan. "Give me the address."

33

"I'll probably never see you again," Shannan said.

The priest shook his head. "Pray to God, Joe."

Shannan did not reply, but frowned. For some reason he wanted to tell Octavio Scarpi to forget what he had said about God. And about Onofrio. He had to restrain a sudden unaccountable impulse to jump up and embrace the priest. His hands trembled as he reached for the paper and pencil and wrote down his wife's address.

The guards closed and locked the cell door. Shannan watched the two priests walking down the long, dark corridor. The radio on his cot was tearing out a rock-and-roll tune.

V

Father Ferrera watched the children march into St. Dominic's from
the side door of the baptistry. Parishioners were seated in the church,
watching the procession. Father Lazzini, in benediction cope, and
followed by two acolytes bearing incense, brought up the rear of the
little parade. The little girls and boys trooped toward the sanctuary
with white robes draped over their left arms.

In the loft Father Sconnetti nodded and Mr. Clotti began to play
the organ. The curate raised his hands to direct the children's choir.
They sang a processional hymn.

The pastor blessed them from the altar. He spoke about Baptism,
what an important sacrament it was and how it should be a constant
reminder to those baptized in Christ. He said: "I hope that this
ceremony among children who were baptized on the same month
shall continue as long as St. Dominic's Church endures. Baptism is
the first sacrament, and perhaps the most important." He went on
to thank Sister Superior who had instituted the ceremony. He
blessed them again.

"In the name of the Father, and of the Son, and of the Holy
Ghost," he prayed.

Then the sisters nudged the children and they recited the Pater
Noster and the Apostles' Creed. Afterward, the girls and boys who
were celebrating the anniversary of their baptism proceeded to the
baptistry of the church.

In the baptistry Father Lazzini arranged them in a semicircle.
Then he read the questions for the renewal of vows, and the children
answered in unison. The stout priest sprinkled the children with
holy water. He reached for the white robe that one boy was carrying

and pulled it over the child's head, murmuring the ritual of Baptism. At the same time the other children put on their own robes.

Afterward, the children walked out of the baptistry bearing candles. They marched, two abreast, to the altar and knelt before it and sang the anthem to the Blessed Virgin.

At the rear of the church, the pastor whispered. "The Childlikeness of Christ." He made the sign of the Cross.

Later, as Father Lazzini was unvesting, the pastor asked for Father Scarpi. The stout priest said he had borrowed his car for a drive. Father Ferrera said, "It's a shame for him to miss such an inspiring procession." Suddenly he began to cough, and excused himself.

As Father Scarpi drove Father Lazzini's old Ford down Rutherford Avenue and turned right on the Warren Avenue Bridge, across the channel he could see the Registry building on Nashua Street.

Years before, in the summertime, he had run across the railroad yards from Nashua Street, while the wind, blowing out of the sea, tumbled tattered newspapers over steel tracks and wooden ties. He would scramble down the moss-encrusted wooden planking fastened to Pisan-canted piling.

His brothers John and Nick were nearly always with him. After their mother died the three youngest boys were almost inseparable. Wriggling out of sweat-stained denims, they would stand, naked, on a channel pile and dive into the sea, cutting through the scum and flotsam of the oily green water.

One summer day they clambered out of the cold channel water and lay on their backs on the rotting timbers of the pier. They could see Old Ironsides anchored off the Charleston Navy Yard. The planking beneath them was hot and the sky was a deep blue.

" 'Tavio," John said.

"What?"

"What're you going to do when you grow up?"

"Don't know. Go fishing with Pa. How 'bout you?"

"I don't know."

"What'd you ask for?" Nick snorted.

"I'm going to be an artist," John said fiercely.

"Don't get sore about it." Octavio laughed.

"Someday I'm going to paint a picture of Mama. Just like she was," John blurted out. He had tried to keep the words back, but he couldn't. John was always saying things that made other people uncomfortable.

The three boys fell into an uneasy silence.

The drawbridge above the channel opened, halting traffic. A motor launch, its Wolverine Diesels chugging at quarter-speed, churned through, drawing in its wake iridescent patches of oil and a motley following of gulls.

The three boys stood on the pier. They could see a number of people on the launch, among them several poised, well groomed women.

"Look at them!" John cried, his voice trembling with rage. The three boys ran along the pier, still undressed, following the launch. They began to shout obscenely to the people on the boat, flipping their genitals up and down. The women turned their backs, but the three boys jeered and shouted until the launch was out of sight.

Father Scarpi remembered their anger and envy with a surging sense of shame. He could remember looking at other women who had led seemingly untroubled lives, and hating them fiercely. For his mother's life had never been easy.

But that had been long ago. Now he felt only shame, for now he knew that the women he had hated would die, as he would die, as all would die. For the very breath of living is the belated breath of Death blowing on Heaven's door.

Father Scarpi drove through the Arborway into Route 3 and followed it into Dorchester and from there to Milton.

The address he wanted proved to be that of a sprawling, expensive modern house. An Irish setter was lolling on the front lawn. He pressed the doorbell. A moment later, the varnished oak door opened automatically and he found himself in an elaborate foyer.

A tall, handsome woman was descending the staircase.

"Are you Mrs. Shannan?" he asked.

"Yes." She nodded. "I'm Marie Shannan." Her face was expressionless, her voice tight.

"I'm Father Scarpi," he said.

She nodded again. She was a slim, graceful woman in the bloom of life. Her eyes were cold gray and her dark brown hair was combed severely back from a smooth white forehead into a chignon at the nape of her neck.

"Please come in, Father."

She led the priest into a living room. He sat down on the edge of a low couch. His huge hands twisted his black felt hat and, feeling uncomfortable, he brought out his pipe. He fingered the smooth wood of the bowl and looked at her.

"I saw—I saw Joseph Shannan this morning," he said.

Marie had just finished school when she met Shannan, and she had found him amusing. He was polite; he tipped his hat solemnly. She never dreamed that she would marry him. But when he suggested it, she had accepted at once.

In the early years she was sure she loved him. Joe had money and had freely helped her family after her mother died and her father was ill. He sent her brother Robert through Boston University and, later, through Harvard Law School. Then, when Robert was campaigning for State senator, Joe was put in front of the television cameras by the investigating committee. By that time Marie had grown to despise him, and she was glad when he was forced to testify. Yet, she was sorry. It had been like looking at herself and a stranger in the same instant. The publicity had spoiled Robert's campaign, and he was defeated. His advisers told him to forget about politics until Joe Shannan was forgotten.

Shannan had wanted children, but they had none. Marie could not understand it; she blamed her husband for it, as she had come to blame him for everything. She knew he had begun to be unfaithful to her. Finally, before his arrest, she had let her brother begin the arrangements for a divorce. Though her family was Catholic, Robert believed that in this case he could get an annulment, even though the marriage had lasted for ten years.

Marie was aware that the priest was looking at her uncomfortably. "How is he?" she asked finally.

Father Scarpi hesitated. "Bitter," he replied.

"That's Joe," she said. The sunlight streaming in through the window splashed on her hair. "He won't see me," she burst out. "Did he tell you he won't see me?" She stood up nervously. "That's Joe, all right. Bitter."

Father Scarpi reflected on Marie's own bitterness but said nothing. His hands fumbled with the bowl of his pipe.

"If you want to smoke, Father, go ahead. I smoke myself. I don't believe it's a sin to smoke." She laughed nervously. "When I was a little girl I went to a parochial school. A priest used to give the best behaved girl a bag of jellybeans every week. I got it many times. I began smoking because I was nervous—" She broke off abruptly.

Father Scarpi filled his pipe carefully, crimping the tobacco into the bowl with a nicotine-stained thumb. He lighted the pipe and then took the stem from his lips.

"Even though Joe is bitter," he said, "we must not feel the same."

"Ah, Father, those are words. Do you know what my life is like? Every week a man comes to the door. He leaves a thousand dollars in a sealed envelope on the desk in the foyer. He doesn't say anything—just leaves it on the desk and walks out. It's from Joe's lottery operations. How do you think I feel taking it?" She pressed her hand to her forehead. "And now God is punishing him. For his crime and for not believing!"

Father Scarpi wanted to help her, but he could find nothing to say. At last he asked about the diary.

"I haven't got it," she said. "My brother hired a detective agency to get evidence for the separation. I think one of their men stole the diary a few days before the girl was—before she died. But then the agency turned the diary over to the Courts. I didn't turn it in. It wasn't my idea at all." She looked at the priest, her eyes brimming with tears. "Do you believe me, Father?"

"Yes, I believe you." Then Father Scarpi said: "I may see your husband soon. Have you any message for him?"

"What good would it do, Father?" she asked wearily.

The priest looked at her sadly and shook his head. "I'll leave now," he said.

Abraham Abrams, District Attorney, was preparing a brief, dictating it to a competent-looking secretary. Finally he said: "That wraps it up, Ruth. Type it and let me see how it looks."

In a few minutes the intercom buzzed and he heard his secretary's voice, "A Father Scarpi is here, Mr. Abrams."

Abrams shrugged. "All right," he said. "Send him in."

A moment later a huge priest with great shoulders and a thick neck came into the office. He seemed hesitant.

Father Scarpi had come to ask for the diary. He looked at the fleshy man whose glasses were perched on a generously endowed nose. Abrams's pale blue eyes were humorless behind the thick lenses, and his long fingers twirled an unlit cigar as he listened to the priest's request.

"What parish are you from?" Abrams asked.

"St. Dominic's, in the West End."

"Are you the pastor?"

"No." The priest blushed. "Only a curate."

"Does your pastor know you're interested in Shannan?"

"No."

"Is this an official visit?" Abrams asked.

"No," the priest said again, but this time his answer came quickly.

Abrams smiled to himself. Priests always wore the same clothes, he thought. When could they act unofficially? He speculated about the man before him. What a waste of strength! he thought. Why had such a huge man become a priest? From the look of him he didn't need security. Abrams was convinced that men became priests and rabbis and ministers because they lacked security.

He said: "I can't let you have the diary. It's State property. If Shannan wants to read it, I'll let you copy as much of it as you want." He strode into the outer office and returned a few moments later with a black leather-bound book. As the lawyer chewed his unlighted cigar, he kept flicking it absently, as if it were burning and tipped with ash. "Use that desk there." He gestured to a desk beside a window. "I don't know why I'm doing this," he added before he left Father Scarpi alone.

The priest opened the diary. The first entry made by Ellen Greer was dated September 1 of the previous year. The script was slanting and almost illegible:

Work again. It's about time, too. I wrote a letter to Dana because he has fallen down on his promise to write at least twice a week. His letters are weak. No thought. Just a few lines: "I'm fine, am eating well." As if food were what I want to hear about! Men are horribly weak. Dana keeps getting more like his mother every day.

40

The priest thumbed slowly through the pages.

October 2. At the office they are beginning to look at me with secret smiles. Let them stare and whisper all they want. I haven't got any mail from Dana for two weeks. No spine. If he doesn't want to write, why doesn't he say so?

Father Scarpi was struck by a later entry:

October 18. A date I shall always remember. Laura died two years ago. I can scarcely believe it has been two years. And Dana telling me he loved her. And that fat policeman twisting my words around, making me stammer. Damn him! "Dreadful accident," he said. And: "You came after her, yes, miss? You were outside her door, miss? Why "miss"? "Miss" this and "miss" that. Staring straight through me until I was ready to scream: "I was there—I heard her crash through the windowpane, and fall!" Lovely Laura.

Shannan was first mentioned three days later:

October 21. I met a horrible man at the Turf Bar. He's stilted, and has old-fashioned attitudes, like tipping his hat politely. And his words are, oh, so proper, like: "I wish to call on you on to-morrow night, in the evening." And: "Woncha say yes, please?" He doesn't say much, though, and seems bitter. He said his name is Shannan. I was broke, so I let him take me to a show at the Plymouth. Afterward he bored me by saying how much he enjoyed it. What a fool! But then men *are* fools!

All through the month of November she wrote of telephone calls from Shannan and her constant refusals. The next month:

December 2. I'm down to my last few dollars. Dana has stopped sending money. I can't get a job. Good God, are we supposed to starve? I'll see Shannan. What else can I do?

December 4. I despise Shannan; he's stupid and dull. But I'm able to keep him at a distance by reciting poetry and discussing religion. These topics seem to fascinate him. Last night he blurted out that he was in love with me. I wanted to laugh in his face. I told him the story of Dante and Beatrice, and he ate it up. He says he's a contractor but he carries too much money to be that. He's such a fool! Just the thought of him—or any other man—near me sets my teeth on edge.

41

December 8. What a night! Nightmares, one sprouting out of the other. Is there no peace? God, if there is a God, let me be what I should be. Don't make me feel like a woman when I'm a man, or like a man when I'm woman. Turn and turn, and there's nowhere to go. Laura, my love, Laura! Where are you?

Father Scarpi got out of the chair and walked to the window. "No," he said to himself. "It can't be true." He felt a surge of outrage. But instantly he thought: What of your own failings, Scarpi? What of your own sins?

It was early spring of 1945, somewhere between the Roer and the Rhine, in a country of monasteries and winter-nude, gnarled vineyards. The regiment was being held in reserve. Lieutenant Scarpi's platoon was lost. They had broken into a house which had wide staircases and filigreed ceilings, and they had raided the wine cellar. Octavio was drinking brandy from a bottle, and listening while Branson, the company commander, played a piano. Octavio watched for a while, drinking steadily until at last his head swam so that he mumbled, "Going out," and lurched through the door.

Alone, he had gone walking in the potato fields, through the shell-scarred woods and vineyards, carrying the brandy bottle and drinking from it. When he had emptied it, he laughed and threw it away. The trees stood twisted and bent, their branches torn by fragments of shells, and burned by fire. War had passed over the landscape like the breath from a blast furnace. The forest was still now, almost dead. But life appeared here and there: in the young shoots springing from scorched stumps, and in the tentative sounds of a few night insects.

At the first streak of twilight, Scarpi arrived at a clearing. It was a potato field pocked by shellholes. At the far end he saw a farmhouse.

A young girl was washing the stone steps, dipping her brush into a pail of water. The steps were of red cement, and the water splashing on them darkened them and seemed to turn them blood-red. Soundlessly, Octavio approached. The young girl was on her knees, her pale gold hair falling over her shoulders as she worked. As he looked down at her, she sensed his presence, and turned, fear darkening her eyes. She stood before him, pale and delicate, and seemed to shrink beneath the heat of his gaze.

"Guten abend," he said hoarsely.

She could see that he was drunk, and she made no answer.

Then he said, "I'm 'Tavi. Du?"

She understood his gestures. "Johanna," she whispered. Suddenly she darted for the heavy door of the darkened farmhouse and attempted to close it behind her. But the heavy latch caught her dress and arrested her. As she ripped the dress loose, he was upon her, pulled her toward him savagely, and lifted her in his arms. He carried her away from the house and toward the woods. All the way across the field she struggled to get free. But she was powerless against him.

Octavio's senses reeled into focus at the sound of a piercing scream. He shook his head sharply. The girl lay twisted on the ground before him in the moonlight, rigid with fear and pain, and looking at him with stricken eyes. As he kneeled clumsily before her, his clothing disordered, his breathing heavy, he saw that her dress was stained with blood. He rose heavily to his feet, looked down at her in panic, then turned and ran. He stumbled through the woods, clutching at branches to save himself from falling. He paused for a moment, panting; he thought he had heard the girl cry out again. He ran on, blindly.

He heard the sudden sound of a burp-gun and saw tracers flashing by. There was a numbing blow on his arm and he fell unconscious.

He found himself lying in a meadow, his cheek against cool stubble. He fumbled for his automatic, groping almost unconsciously. But he seemed unable to move or to think clearly. The moon paled and disappeared behind a cloud.

As he lay there, still unable to move, he saw the outline of a figure approaching him. He glared, and tried to speak, but the sound died on his lips. The figure seemed suddenly illuminated in the moonless meadow. He blinked, shook his head, and tried again to rise.

Though the figure was tall, Octavio could make out only the outline of the face. He heard no sound, yet words seemed to penetrate the night: "Don't you know me, my son?" Then a profound stillness fell upon the meadow. The figure beckoned to Octavio, but when he tried to lift himself from the ground the figure disappeared.

As Octavio fell again, he thought he heard once more the anguished scream of the girl. And somehow, he heard the anguished, dying cries of Onofrio as well.

43

Father Scarpi turned back to Ellen Greer's diary, shaking his head. He had never forgotten the girl, or her name. Nor had he forgotten the figure he had seen in the meadow, although he spoke of it to no one. In a few weeks he had made vows of continence to himself and had begun to think of joining the Church as a brother or a priest. He was sure that it was God who had reached out to him.

The priest read on in the diary. Ellen Greer described meeting a pretty child who reminded her of Laura. The writing seemed urgent, and was nearly illegible. She wrote of being deeply aroused by the child.

Father Scarpi shook his head and skipped to the last page of the diary.

January 4. I can't endure Shannan any longer. Tonight I'll tell him to stop bothering me. To hell with his money—I'm not afraid. The little girl is coming to see me soon. I'm going to have her up here. She is so lovely, so like Laura . . .

He closed the diary and went into the outer office where he found Abrams. The priest caught a flicker of understanding in the lawyer's eyes.

"All through?" Abrams asked.

"I didn't copy it," the priest said.

"No? Well . . . naturally not. That is, I shouldn't have let you read it without telling you. . . . You can't read something unless it has an imprimatur. Isn't that right?"

"We are allowed more freedom than that," the priest said absently.

"Is that so? Well, I thought you had to have permission."

"Why wasn't the diary introduced into the trial?" Father Scarpi asked abruptly.

Abrams looked at him. "Why should it have been?" he said quickly. "It wouldn't have helped the defense. The truth is, I tried. It would have helped me, don't you see? Possible motive. I brought it before the court as evidence. But when White went through it, he objected. Judge Whitney agreed with him. He told me that the witnesses I already had to prove that the girl and Shannan had quarreled furnished enough motive. 'Why introduce something that would confuse the issue?' he asked. So, with the permission from the defense, I withdrew the diary as evidence. Naturally, White would have liked to use portions of the diary, but it was all or nothing. And—well, I objected to his putting emphasis on the sex life of the victim. I mean the theory that she was a deviate. Actually, she was to be pitied. Isn't that so?" He compressed his lips.

"And Shannan? Is there no pity for Shannan?" the priest cried. "No mercy? How could the jury be so sure of his guilt? How could twelve people calmly sit down and judge a man guilty, and refuse him clemency from a death sentence, in two hours and twenty-six minutes? In two hours and twenty-six minutes," he repeated sadly. "Were they trying for a record?" The priest was trembling, and his huge hands gripped the edge of Abrams's desk.

The lawyer was startled by the curate's outburst. "Of course I pity Shannan," he protested, waving his unlighted cigar. "Do you know how many witnesses appeared for the State? More than thirty people testified against Shannan. And the exhibits: there were more than fifteen of them. Cigars that Shannan smoked, two suits in her closet—evidence, all evidence pointing to him. Time element, means, possible motive. It was overwhelming," Abrams said sharply. "Circumstance after circumstance. Incident after incident. He was seen entering the building; he was seen leaving the girl's apartment without notifying the police. An innocent man doesn't act like that, does he?" He shrugged. "Well, I can understand your attitude. You're a priest—"

"All the evidence was circumstantial," the priest interrupted.

Abrams was irritated. "The pattern of all criminal acts is circumstantial, Father," he explained patiently. "Circumstance forces the criminal to commit the crime in such a way that it falls into a recognizable pattern. The police apply the pattern to all suspects—two suspects or two hundred. The person who most nearly fits the pattern is almost always guilty. Unless a crime is witnessed, or confessed, all the evidence is circumstantial. It has to be. Sure, there's a possibility that the pattern may best apply to an innocent man; but the exceptions are so rare that they prove the rule we go by."

"How about the particular pattern of violence in this crime?" Father Scarpi asked. "Is Shannan the kind of man that would repeatedly stab a woman?"

"In a fit of rage; yes, he would. Perhaps, even I—"

"Rage?" the priest broke in. "What rage?"

"You read the diary," Abrams said, frowning.

45

Father Scarpi sighed. "Shannan asked me to get the diary for him. He loves the memory of Ellen Greer. He doesn't know of her sexual perversion."

"What's your interest in Shannan?" Abrams asked.

"I've already told you." The priest hesitated. "I went to see him. He's a human being. One of God's children."

"Permit me to contradict you, Father," Abrams said quickly. "Joseph Shannan is an atheist."

"That's a harsh word," the priest replied.

"Why are you so interested in Shannan?" Abrams repeated. "Why did you go to see him? What do you know of the crime?"

After a long while the priest said, "Mr. Abrams, I cannot tell you what I know."

Abrams closed his eyes. What did this priest know? he wondered. When the Shannan case was laid before him, Abrams had prepared the whole case around the testimony of Ellen Greer's younger brother. The boy had seen Shannan enter and leave the apartment building. After preparing a brief, Abrams had laid his finger on the weakness of the State's case. If the Greer boy had received no answer from the door buzzer, wouldn't the defense point out that the woman could have been dead before Shannan entered the building?

This glaring weakness in the brief had sent Abrams on a personal visit to the apartment building, where, to his relief, the custodian admitted that the buzzer had been out of order for the entire week of the killing. Abrams got the man's affidavit and informed him that he might be called as a witness. Then he reviewed the evidence again and felt that the brief was strong enough to bring to Court.

Abrams was convinced the verdict had been just. The summation for denial on the appeal to the Supreme Court had strengthened that conviction, for the justices processing the appeal had found insufficient evidence for a mistrial. The mass of evidence fitted Shannan's hand like a glove. The pattern was perfect. Only the motive was missing. But who looks for a motive in a crime of passion? Now, however, this priest had appeared.

"If you know something," Abrams said angrily, "you must tell me. It's your duty."

Father Scarpi prayed silently. "No," the priest said. "No!" He stared out the window; the day was ending in a brilliant burst of sunlight.

Abrams watched the priest cannily. "Withholding evidence from the Courts is punishable by law," he said.

"Goodbye, Mr. Abrams," Father Scarpi said. "And thank you."

"Wait, Father." Abrams sounded weary. "I'm sorry."

"I'm to blame," the priest said. "The sentence seems so harsh—"

"Why don't you see Larry White?" Abrams said swiftly. "You understand that as far as our office is concerned the case is closed. But see White. He was chief defense counsel. Here, I'll give you his address. Go see him. White, Fisher, and Aaronson. And don't say I sent you. He hates my guts."

At the end of the long corridor outside, Father Scarpi looked back. District Attorney Abrams was gazing at him from his door. The distance between them seemed symbolic.

VI

In his essays on human happiness, St. Thomas enjoins us to partake of the beatitudes, for they are the keys to happiness. Elsewhere he wrote that the tragedy of man is not that he cannot find happiness but that he looks for it in the wrong places.

Father Ferrera was a priest of modest wants and simple joys. Happiness, to him, was sitting down to the evening meal with all his curates present. This trivial pleasure was almost an obsession to the old priest, and no curate could absent himself from supper without first obtaining permission.

After the meal the pastor would lean back in his tall chair listening to their talk. Though he rarely spoke himself, he derived great pleasure from their banter. In those moments he felt a kinship with the younger curates. Sometimes he would reflect on the day that had passed and smile, thinking himself one step closer to God.

The pastor went into the rectory dining room. Sconnetti and Lazzini were waiting for him. He motioned them to remain seated when they started to rise.

"Where is Father Scarpi?" he asked.

"Didn't you give him permission to go out earlier today?" Sconnetti stammered.

"I don't believe so," the pastor said quietly. "He also missed the procession, didn't he?"

Silence enveloped the room. The housekeeper entered with their suppers on separate trays. Father Lazzini gazed at the baked ham, the lyonnaise potatoes, and the sweet peas; then he looked at Father Ferrera, waiting for the old priest to say Grace.

The pastor had removed his glasses and was wiping the lens with his handkerchief. He turned his head aside and coughed, his whole body shaking. "We'll wait—" He coughed again, wiping his lips. "We'll wait for Father Scarpi," he repeated.

Father Lazzini stared at him. "The food—ah—won't the food get cold?" he asked. "That is, it does seem a shame for . . ." Without finishing what he was saying, he looked at Sconnetti for approval. But the thin curate, head bowed, was praying silently. The fat priest looked at the meal ruefully but remained silent. .

A half-hour passed before Father Scarpi arrived. He entered the dining room and saw that the supper lay cold and untouched before the curates. They were sitting stiffly and silently at their places. Father Lazzini looked at him reproachfully, and Sconnetti smiled.

The big priest murmured an apology and sat down.

"We can eat now," Father Ferrera said. He had scarcely finished Grace when Father Lazzini plunged into his meal.

Father Scarpi looked at the cold food before him. "Father," he said abruptly, turning to the pastor, "please forgive me. I was troubled. I—"

"Satis, Frater," Father Ferrera murmured, holding up his thin hands. A sudden weakness overcame him. "I cannot eat in any case. It is I who should be forgiven—for holding up the cena." He rose from his chair. The other curates stood up.

"Keep your seats," he said weakly. "Father Scarpi, a member of St. Dominic's Fraternity was here earlier. They"—he coughed— "they want you to attend a meeting concerning the statue of St. Dominic which they are going to donate to our church. I believe eight o'clock was the hour. Perhaps you can help in the confessional up to that time."

"I've been asked to say the Rosary at a wake," the priest said quickly, recalling his promise to Theresa Spinale.

"Fit it into your schedule somewhere," the pastor said quietly. "Forgive me, my brothers," he added and, putting on his biretta, left the dining room.

"Don't worry about hearing confession, 'Tavio," Father Sconnetti said. "Dante and I will hear them. All right, Dante?"

Father Lazzini nodded with his mouth full. He gulped. "Sure," he said. He stood up and winked. "I'm going to see if I can get a bottle of that dry burgundy from the cook."

Nenni's Funeral Home was crowded with mourners. At the entrance, Vincent Spinale's brother shook the priest's hand. "Thanks for coming, Father."

"My sympathies," the priest murmured.

He could see the bier, surrounded by flowers, in the inner chapel, and he heard the subdued murmur of voices. He repeated the rote words of sympathy to Spinale's mother, who sat mute and forlorn beside Theresa, near the coffin.

"Tessie," Al Spinale whispered, "I can't find the kid."

"Find her," Theresa said harshly.

Father Scarpi gazed at the dead man. Black Rosary beads were twined about his lifeless fingers. "Be merciful," he murmured. "Be merciful, dear Jesus, to this man and to me."

When the priest entered the chapel, he saw many fishermen in the room. Some he recognized from his childhood, when as a boy of fourteen and fifteen he had gone to sea with his father. Now they began edging out of the chapel. He knew it was because he had come to pray there. It wouldn't do for them to be seen in prayer with a priest, oppressor of the workingman. Nor could prayer bring the dead back to life!

Once, when he had worked for Don Turrido, Octavio had heard the question of prayer discussed between Don Turrido and Don Cicco Testa. They were on board ship, and it was during a lull between times of hauling up the nets.

"This business of prayer," Don Cicco said, "is taken from the ancient Romans. Incidentally, a professor told me this: he said that in the old days, in Rome, when the people complained, they were given bread and circus. Now they give them prayers and tell them it's better than food. So, instead of bread and circus, now they get only the circus."

"But how about the time we were on the rocks?" Octavio's father asked. "You prayed harder than any of us."

"But that was different," Don Turrido explained. "When we pray by ourselves there is a chance that God will hear us. 'Blood of the saints,' God says, when he hears us pray. 'Something is up; these boys never pray,' and so he listens."

"True," Don Cicco cried out, "true! But when the thieving priests

50

pray, He says: 'Here's that old song from these scoundrels. Who wants to listen to them?' Eh, Turrido? Is it not true?"

Don Turrido had laughed until tears ran from his eyes.

The priest watched the men making a mass exodus from the chapel, leaving the women behind. "You stiff-necked anticlerics," he murmured, but he smiled at their pride.

"Let us pray," he said to the kneeling women. He recited part of the Canon of the Mass and said the Rosary to the dead. After the last Hail Holy Queen, he intoned, " 'Eternal rest grant unto him, O Lord.' "

The mourners answered: " 'And let perpetual light shine upon him. May his soul and the souls of all the faithful, departed through the mercy of God, rest in peace.' "

Then, for some reason, he added the rest of the Introit from Psalm Sixty-four of the Mass for the Dead: " 'A hymn, O God, becometh Thee in Zion and a vow shall be paid to Thee in Jerusalem: O Lord, hear my prayer; all flesh shall come to Thee. Eternal rest grant unto them O Lord; and let perpetual light shine upon them. Amen.' "

He heard the echoing, "Amen," and made the sign of the Cross. Then he left the hushed chapel.

Outside, the men gathered around him. Puddo Nenni, the embalmer, shook his fat jowls solemnly. "Ah," he whispered, "a difficult corpse. Frail, emaciated. Is it a good job, Father? Lifelike?"

"Very good," Father Scarpi said. "Very . . . lifelike."

"Lu povero suffrio a sai," a thin man said sadly. "Don't you remember me?" he asked in the dialect. "Gianni Nuzzo? U musicanti? You had a brother who loved music, and he'd follow me around all day."

Instantly the priest remembered the old hurdy-gurdy man. "Yes," he said. "I remember Your Honor. That was my older brother Onofrio who accompanied you. He is dead now."

"It is life," another old man said loudly. "Is it not better to die than to suffer pain and humiliation? Ah, you priests."

Father Scarpi smiled at the white-haired old man who turned away and walked toward the front door, holding a white cane before him.

"That was old Frank Testa," someone said. "He's blind. He became blind when he was caught aboard Molino's barca. He was in the hold, and a fire broke out."

"Don Cicco Testa?" the priest said. He tried to follow the blind man, but another man gripped his cassock.

" 'Allo, parrino, me ricordi. Eh, me ricordi?"

The priest stared at the trembling old man who had spoken. Memory stirred. Who was this shivering ancient? He shook his head.

"Ah, ha," the old man cackled, feebly striking his thigh and grinning triumphantly. A nicotine-stained mustache swept over the old man's toothless mouth.

The Sicilians circling the priest all grinned. "But how can the priest remember?" Gianni Nuzzo, the organ grinder, laughed. "Twenty years have gone by."

"More," the mustached old man cackled. "Tu—Turri," he hinted.

"Don Turrido Bellino!" the priest exclaimed, remembering the blue eyes, the sweeping mustache.

"Guisto." The old man nodded. "Me ricordasti."

Fragmentary scenes flooded Father Scarpi's mind. The fishing boat, and the sun beating down, and the cold numbing his fingers. He could remember the nets being winched in and the strong arms hauling in the flat drag-weight and the hollow glass spheres. The fish writhing in the net, as a fisherman slit the outlet, and the whiting, redfish, hake, the flounder and the freak monkey fish, and the hungry sand sharks gulping down food while they themselves were caught. The fish cascading down the iced hold, fiilling it and sprawling on the deck up to the coamings.

"I worked on your dragger, the *Nina Bella*. I was a boy. Sí, me recordo a Vossia." The priest smiled.

"Old I am now," Don Turrido blew his nose and shook his head. There were tears in his eyes. "Do you not recall how we would anchor off York, in Maine, to hunt rizzi?"

The priest nodded, remembering that he and the old man would lower the dinghy and row to the rocks at low tide, hunting sea urchins and sea eggs. The old man would stand on a flat rock and direct Octavio to one lagoon or another.

"Sutta pedri!" he'd shout. "Under the rocks!"

Octavio would run his hand beneath the rocks, feeling for the stiff spines of the urchins. Once a lobster, caught in a lagoon at low tide, had snapped at Octavio's finger, and the old man had shouted:

"What are you wasting time with lobsters for? You know my heart desires a few rizzi."

Now Don Turrido peered at him eagerly. "Will you say the Rosary over me when I marry the earth?" he asked.

The priest saw that the old man was in earnest. "It shall be as the good Lord wishes," he replied.

The old pescatore took off his cap. "Thank you, Don Ottavio." He blew his nose again. "One of these days I shall go to church," he said. "Priests can't all be fools if you are one of them."

Father Scarpi smiled at the Old Country speech. He knew he had been paid a great compliment, and when the fisherman embraced him the priest returned it warmly.

"Extend my regards to your father. Tell him Turrido Bellino was asking for him." Then Don Turrido turned away and walked into the chapel. Vincent Spinale had once worked on his dragger.

As the priest was leaving, he saw several women grouped about a little girl at the doorway.

Theresa Spinale was saying: "You are his only child, his daughter. You must pray over him. At least look at him."

"No, no," the child whimpered. "I'm afraid. I'm afraid."

"That's silly," Theresa said. "There's nothing to be afraid of. Is there, Anna?" appealing to a stout woman.

"Nothing," Anna said. "Nothing at all."

"I'm afraid," the child repeated. "I hate him. I'm glad he's dead," she sobbed. "I'm glad."

In a flash of anger, Theresa slapped the little girl.

"Theresa," Anna cried. "Vergogna! Lower your hands."

"It's her father," Theresa said, wringing her hands. "Her own father. God in heaven, I wouldn't mind if it wasn't her father!"

"What have you done?" The fat woman sighed. "Child of mine, little niece, come to za Anna." She held out her arms.

But the child saw the priest and ran, instead, into his arms. The priest held her to him and comforted her. He turned his face aside so that she would not see the ugliness of his broken nose.

"Shush, shush," he said gently, wiping her tears with his handkerchief. "Come. We'll go for a walk." And nodding to Theresa, the priest took the girl by the hand and led her outside. After a while, her sobs subsided.

Father Scarpi led the child to a store and bought two ice-cream cones. Then they walked along the darkened streets of the West End.

She looked at the priest shyly. "I go to St. Dominic's School," she said. "I'm in the fifth grade." Her eyes were a deep blue. She was a beautiful child, with light hair. She seemed tall for her years.

"What's your name?"

"Mary Spinale. I'm in Sister Marie Ann's class."

She was very grave. The priest looked at her tenderly.

"Mary, Mary, quite contrary, how quick your tears do flow."

She laughed and licked her ice-cream cone. " 'How does your garden grow,' " she corrected.

"With crocodile tears and shadowy fears—"

"Oh, no," she interrupted. "I never heard it that way."

"What are you afraid of, Mary?" he asked quietly. "Why wouldn't you see your father? Didn't Sister Marie Ann tell you that dying is like being born all over again?"

"Oh, I'm not afraid, Father. Well, maybe just a little. It's his ghost. When somebody dies, his ghost haunts the house he lived in and his soul goes to heaven." Suddenly she was sobbing again. Her ice cream fell on the sidewalk and she swung away from the priest. He reached after her and grasped her wrist. "But he's going to hell!" she sobbed.

"Mary," he sighed. "Mary. He was your father. He *is* your father. You shouldn't think that way of him."

"He beat me," she explained, speaking with difficulty, "if I went out without permission. Or if he wasn't feeling good. He always beat me. Once I said, 'If you hit me again I hope you die.' And now he's dead, because I wanted him to die and I prayed he would die—and—and I don't care! I hate him! I hate him!"

Father Scarpi stood beside her, holding her hand. "Veni, Domine Gesù," he prayed. "O Lord, come to this child and remove her fears. Come, O Lord, and dry her tears."

After a while she dried her eyes and, looking at him with her head lowered, said: "I'm sorry, Father. But Aunt Tessie doesn't understand. No one does. Nana might—she loves me—but she can't hear me."

Mary fell silent as they retraced their steps to Nenni's funeral chapel.

Theresa was waiting outside the entrance. She offered her handkerchief to the child, but Mary refused it and clung to the priest.

54

"Did Vincent beat the child many times?" he asked Theresa.

She nodded. "He was hot-tempered."

Theresa looked at the child. "Go along now, Mary," she said. "Go to Aunt Ida's. You won't be alone there."

Mary ran to her aunt then, and kissed her. "Good night, Aunt Tessie," she said. "Good night, Father."

Theresa burst into tears. "He had a bad temper," she said. "Ever since his wife died—Mary was only six—he'd come home from a fishing trip and get drunk, and Mary would get on his nerves. He used to say, 'Get her out of here.' We knew he said that because she reminded him of her mother. Mary looks just like her. She was very lovely. I don't know how to handle her either," she added. "I don't know."

At five minutes past eight, Father Scarpi ascended the stairs that led to St. Dominic's Fraternity. Don Peppino Messana, the vice chairman, escorted him to the front of the hall. On the right side of the chairman's chair was the flag of the United States, and on the left, the flag of the Italian republic. Don Peppino wore the ribbon of the fraternity for the occasion, a white and green ribbon strapped over his shoulder. A miniature Stars and Stripes was also pinned to his shirt front.

Don Peppino was a fat, florid-faced man with a shiny bald head. He was a fishmonger, and no matter how often he washed, the odor of fish always clung to him. Whenever one of his sons reproached him for the odor, Don Peppino would say: "But the money doesn't stink, does it? When I hand you five or ten dollars, you don't say the money stinks. You shove it in your pocket as quick as a wink. All right, I stink. But the money doesn't stink, does it?"

Now Don Peppino looked over the hall at the members who had taken their seats, and his heart sank. There were too many women. In a weak moment the men had allowed women to join the fraternity, and now, whenever the fishermen were at sea, the women outnumbered the men.

Don Peppino waited until the priest had been seated; then he said bitterly, "We wish you to be present at the death of the fraternity."

"Die and be done with it!" a woman shouted. "The women will accomplish more without you dead weights."

Don Peppino picked up a gavel and began pounding on a little desk in front of him. "Silence!" he roared. "Silence! I have the floor."

"Take the floor and get out," the same woman cried.

"I know that it is Concetta Spitoli who talks so loudly." Don Peppino wagged his finger at the woman. "When the cat's away, the rats will play. Your husband will be interested in your conduct when he returns from sea."

"Take him, too." The woman laughed.

"Why is the fraternity going to die?" Father Scarpi asked patiently.

"Because these women are going to donate the Sicilian statue of St. Dominic under their name and not in the name of the fraternity!"

A fat woman lurched to her feet. "I want the floor," she said. "I insist on having the floor. Why should the men get credit for the statue?" she asked. "It was the women who collected the money for it. The men didn't want us to get a statue; they wanted a bar with whisky and wine. Deny that, Peppino Messana. I dare you to deny that." She sat down, and the women applauded wildly.

"True," a lean black-haired woman cried, rising from her seat. "It was we who told the professor to send letters to the Sicel sculptor asking him to make the statue, and when we sent the money the men called us fools. They said they washed their hands of the affair. But when they found out we were going to donate the statue without including them, they cried they had been betrayed and called us traitors."

Don Peppino forced a laugh.

"Women," he gestured scornfully. "What can a man expect of an inferior race. They are not civilized yet."

Concetta Spitoli got up. "Why do the men insist on being included?" she asked Father Scarpi. "Why should they be included? They never go to church." She winked slyly. "Starting with my husband, most of them haven't seen the inside of a church since they've been married. Every time I mention church or a priest they regale me with stories of their childhood; about how evil priests are, and how many women bore a priest's bastard." She paused and flushed, as everyone stared at Father Scarpi. "Well, I'm sick and tired of their stories. If they want to be included in the donation, let us see how much like Christians they can act."

Don Peppino was aghast. He felt that the priest was insulted. In

56

Sicily it was all right to assume that priests were liars, thieves, and adulterers. But this priest was the son of Don Beneditto Scarpi. He leaned over to the big priest.

"Did I not tell you that they were uncivilized?" he whispered. "Whenever they get out of their kitchens, or stop bearing children, they go insane. It is a woman's malady, insanity. And a lot of men catch it from them."

The priest shook his head and stood up.

"Gentlemen," he said. "Lords. The lady has a point. She feels that if you don't think enough of St. Dominic to attend the Mass, why should you concern yourself over this affair?"

"That is not the issue!" Don Peppino howled. "The issue is: Shall the women exclude the men from participating in this affair?"

"That is not the issue," Concetta Spitoli cried.

"I pray," Father Scarpi said, "I pray you to remain calm." He looked at the gathering. "I'm sure," he went on, "that if the men would show interest in the Mass, the women would donate the statue under the name of the fraternity."

"But how can we?" Concetta asked. "They're pagans. They never attend the Mass."

"This is foolish," a lean black-browed man said. "Some of us don't attend church but we're all Christians. Is that not so?" he inquired in a loud voice. The men in the hall applauded noisily. Then, as if by common agreement, they clustered together in the center of the hall and conferred quickly.

A tall thin man with sloping shoulders stood erect. "We must tell you that many days ago the men had agreed that when the statue came we would attend the Mass."

Don Peppino cocked his head and looked shrewdly at the speaker. "Yes, that is so," he lied loudly. "That is so. Not only shall we attend the Mass but we shall bear the statue of St. Dominic through the streets of the West and North End."

At that moment another man jumped to his feet. "Now that is settled, and I, Nunzio Rao," he cried, "make a motion that we open membership in the fraternity to the other Sicels!"

"And I, Nino Quatrocchi," a man who wore thick-lensed glasses on the tip of his nose shouted, "second the motion!"

"It is a conspiracy," the fishmonger roared. "I, Peppino Messana, refuse your motion. I discard it. I destroy it. I spit on it!"

"That is not the way the democracy works," Rao bleated.

"A motion can not be refused in the democracy," yelled Quatrocchi.

"You dare mention the democracy?" asked the fishmonger, clutching and clasping his hands as if in prayer. In a hasty aside to the priest he explained, "These two are socialists and cobblers."

"Basta!" Rao said, sneering. "I do not bandy words with ignorant fishmongers."

"Ignorant?" Don Peppino shouted. "I'll show you—"

"Cavaliers!" Father Scarpi stood up and placed a restraining hand on Messana's shoulder. "Cavaliers. We forget there are ladies present. What is the difficulty?"

"Ah, well . . . it's an inside affair," Don Peppino muttered. "These two radicals say we should extend membership to other Sicels, instead of only to Augustans."

"Why not?" Rao, bristling with anger, inquired. "Perche no?"

"Silence! I'm talking to a priest. Have respect."

"And who asked the priest to come?" Quatrocchi retorted. "As an American citizen, I protest his presence—"

"O! Sta zittu, ignoranti," Concetta Spitoli cried out.

"Why do you deny their motion?" asked the priest.

"They are trying to push it through while the fishermen are out to sea," Don Peppino explained. "The traitors!" he added vehemently.

"Why not shelve the motion until the fishermen are present?" Father Scarpi suggested. "Then it can be acted upon immediately."

"What wisdom!" the fishmonger exclaimed. "A capital idea."

After a few more shouts of protest, the cobblers, Rao and Quatrocchi, agreed and resumed their seats.

A beetle-browed, heavily bearded man dressed in a red shirt and a bright yellow necktie tugged at Don Peppino's shirt.

"Later," the fishmonger growled. "Later." He turned to the priest and eloquently invited him to partake of the refreshments that were to be served by the ladies.

Father Scarpi smilingly made his excuses and hurried out of the hall.

"I know," Don Peppino hissed, swiveling around to the bearded man. "I am aware, professore."

Carmello Poverello, the professor, glared at Don Peppino, his formidable beard quivering with indignation. Poverello's beard was carefully maintained and worn in the style of Umberto I. Poverello was a bachelor, and could flaunt a banner of independence. He was a much respected member of the fraternity, as it was said that he had attended the University at Syracuse and was able to read and write in English as well as in Italian. He seldom labored, and made a precarious living writing epic poems which he mailed to Italian-language periodicals all over the country. Sometimes he would borrow a pushcart and, getting a load of blemished tomatoes known in the idiom as "specks," he would sell the fruit up and down the streets of Boston. When irate policemen chased him, his beard flapped like a flag as he ran. But because he always wore a necktie, and was a scholar, he was admired and respected. Then, too, the professor's beard was said to resemble that of the prophet Moses.

As the fishmonger and the professor retired to one corner of the hall, a bulbous-nosed man hurried toward them.

"Here comes Santo Cuniggio," Don Peppino grumbled. "He'll complain, too."

"We are undone," Cuniggio cried softly. "Finiu a schifiu. A big, veritable mess."

"Pianissimo," the professor murmured. "They'll hear." He gestured to the other members, who were creating a mild uproar by talking, arguing, and drinking coffee that Trinasci, the caterer, had lugged up in a five-gallon container.

"What is to be done?" Cuniggio persisted.

"Don't annoy me," said Don Peppino. "I'm sick. I thought this meeting would confuse the women for weeks, until we had the bar installed. Once the bar was set in place and we served the women cordials," he said, "they would have forgotten their silly ideas about getting a statue."

"It's my fault," the professor lamented. "The women trusted me and gave me the money to order the statue, and then I listened to your scheme of getting a bar and whisky instead."

"This meeting to break up the fraternity temporarily not only didn't work, but you, Messana, you also were the one to say we would carry the statue around the streets. What statue!" Cuniggio exclaimed. "It doesn't exist!"

"Shut up!" Don Peppino said fiercely. "Let me think."

"With what?" Cuniggio wanted to know. "What are you going to use for a brain?"

"This is no time for an argument," the professor wailed.

"All right," muttered Don Peppino. "The women gave the professor $1,500 to send to a sculptor in Sicily. After talking it over, we agreed that the women were crazy and we needed a bar. Right?"

"I didn't agree," Cuniggio said coldly. "I said that it would be nice to get a bar and whisky instead of a statue."

"What does that mean?" the fishmonger asked in disgust.

"Gentlemen, gentlemen," the professor said wearily.

"How much did we give the carpenter as a retainer to build us a bar?" Don Peppino inquired.

"Four hundred." Santo Cuniggio cleared his throat. "It was to be made of solid mahogany."

"And how much did we give that salesman for the whisky and the wine?"

The professor took out a soiled notebook and peered into it. "Three hundred and forty dollars," he said.

"How much do we have left?"

"Oh . . . about $800," Poverello estimated.

"Ebbene! What is there to worry over?" Don Peppino asked triumphantly. "We'll just go out and buy a statue, and we'll have the liquor as well."

The professor looked up to the ceiling in despair. "For that little money," he said, "a sculptor would not tie his shoestrings, let alone create a statue of St. Dominic. It's impossible. Don't forget, we've had the money for two months. I have been telling the women that I correspond regularly with the sculptor, and that he says the statue will be finished in time."

"I shall never be able to hold up my head," Cuniggio groaned. "My honor is gone."

"Time! Time!" Don Peppino cried. "We have more than two weeks." He stood up, his paunch shaking. "A nation can be destroyed in two weeks," he orated. "Courage, companions! We'll think of something."

"There is hope!" Poverello cried suddenly. "There is a possible chance." He lowered his voice and spoke cautiously, glancing toward the group of noisy, laughing women clustered around Concetta Spitoli.

Arriving at the church, Father Scarpi found Father Lazzini seated in the outer office of the rectory. The stout priest seemed tired, and Father Scarpi offered to take over his box. Taking Father Lazzini's stole, he draped it about his wide shoulders and entered the lower church through the sacristy.

A long line of parishioners stood before Father Sconnetti's confessional, but when they saw the big priest many of them veered toward Father Scarpi's box. The priest took off his biretta and entered the enclosure. He murmured a hasty prayer and listened to the first confession from a slow-speaking woman. She told him of preventing birth. After she had finished, he admonished her. Money was nothing, he told her; security was senseless. What greater security than having eternal life was there? He directed her to say the Rosary twice, hoping she wouldn't sin again.

A young man stooped into the box. Father Scarpi could not see him, but his youth was evident in his voice.

"Bless me, Father, for I have sinned," the young man said hastily, and recited accounts of adultery and lying.

"My son," the priest murmured sadly, "my son, what have you done? Do you take pleasure in these things? Do you?"

"No, Father."

"Then why do you do them? Don't you realize that our Lord sees these things? Do you think your actions cause Him joy? Go to the altar; think more fully of your sins; then return to me. By then you will know more clearly how evil your sins are."

The young man hurried out of the confessional.

Father Scarpi shut his eyes. "Forgive me, O Lord," he prayed. "Make me not lacking in mercy."

The confessions continued: lying, theft, jealousy, anger, hate, doubt, adultery. There was little variation in sin.

After a while the young man returned. The confessional was stifling; sweat beaded Father Scarpi's face and neck. The young man recounted his sins; he was nervous, hesitant. The priest gave him severe penance and dismissed him.

Father Sconnetti had been hearing confessions in the box on the opposite side of the church. After the parishioners had left, the two priests met in the sacristy and looked at each other. They were both hot from the closeness of the confessional box.

"How about a long, cool walk?" the little curate asked.

"Let me clean up, first," said Father Scarpi.

As he was washing his hands, he reflected on the faith of the parishioners. When he was a little boy, he had asked his father what faith was.

"Faith?" the old fisherman echoed. "Faith is like a book written in air and bound by the seven seas." Then his father had smiled sadly, adding, "You do not understand, do you?"

Octavio had shaken his head, and his father had said, "Perhaps, someday, you will."

VII

Joseph Shannan gazed dully at the magazine spread out on his cot. It was open to an article describing an average American family. The average family, the article stated, consisted of the parents and 3½ children. The height of the male parent was 5 foot 8½ inches; he was a high-school graduate and owned a home that he had bought on an installment plan. He owned a car, and his hobby was baseball.

Shannan threw the magazine aside. He wondered, vaguely, where the remaining half of the fourth child was. He was seized with an absurd desire to laugh. Suddenly, it seemed very necessary to him to laugh. But he could not, and he felt helpless and confused.

After a while the light in his cell was turned off, and he watched the two guards stationed outside his cell playing clabbyash by the corridor light.

When Shannan had been placed in the State Prison, the trusty who brought his meals had whispered, "Frank says, if you want out give the nod." If anyone could arrange an escape for Shannan it was Frank O'Meara. But Shannan knew that a break was risky, and he had been convinced that the death sentence would be revoked. He thought that then he'd be able to secure enough evidence for a retrial. He had been too sure; he had depended on his innocence. I should have known, he thought, that once a man is off his feet the wolves are at his throat.

He had refused to give the sign for a break. Whenever the trusty came with his food tray, he'd look at Shannan and Shannan would shake his head, pushing the thought away. Now, as he lay on his cot, he heard footsteps in the corridor. A moment later the warden was standing before the bars of his cell. A lean, tall man was with him. The door was opened and the two men entered the cell.

"Hello, Shannan," the warden said. He was a short bald-headed man with a paunch.

Shannan said nothing and gazed at the stranger.

"All right," the man said quietly, "there's no sense stalling. I got a proposition. We know you're waiting for a reprieve. I can't tell whether you're getting it or not. But if you sign this affidavit your chances to save your life are good."

The stranger placed a typewritten sheet of paper on the cot. Shannan saw that it was sealed and notarized; only the signature line was blank, but the document had already been witnessed.

"Who's we?" Shannan asked softly.

"That doesn't matter." The stranger waved his hand. "After you sign, I'll tell you anything you want to know."

Shannan got up from the cot and took the paper to the bars of the door. The light from the corridor slanted down on the notarized affidavit.

He read: "I, Joseph Shannan, do swear that for the fiscal year 1946–1947, the income of Francis Dennis O'Meara was in excess of $50,000. This I know, by intimate business dealings with the said Francis Dennis O'Meara, to be true and accurate—" Shannan stopped reading. He looked at the stranger.

"We know that the income was greater than that," the stranger said, "but we're willing to let it go at that."

"It's no evidence," Shannan said harshly.

"Your testimony will make it convincing."

"You mean in front of television cameras, for instance?"

The stranger shrugged. "Maybe," he said.

Shannan laughed shortly. Then he tore the affidavit in two and flung it at the stranger.

"Go to hell," he said. He lay down on his cot and turned his back to the two men.

Father Sconnetti and Father Scarpi were walking along the Esplanade. The night was cool and filled with the murmur of the passing, restless day. High in the heavens, stars glimmered. They watched the placid waters of the Charles River, and saw the headlights of automobiles crawling, like mobile Japanese lanterns, on the dark arch of the Longfellow Bridge.

The little curate glanced at the black inverted bowl of sky. "I wonder how it is, up there," he said.

"Airless," Father Scarpi replied, "and dark."

"More airless and dark than a confessional box?" the thin curate said, "or the human soul?"

Father Scarpi glanced at him quickly. The little priest flushed with regret at his remark.

"Forgive me 'Tavio," he sighed. "You know I didn't mean that. I was thinking only of myself."

"I understand."

" 'Tavio, 'Tavio," Father Sconnetti murmured, "sometimes I sit in the confessional, and wonder if I'm worthy of the honor. I watch them dragging up their sins and hear the uncertain words, the awful pauses, and my heart is torn. Do you understand, 'Tavio? Have you had the same feeling?"

They had stopped walking and were sitting on a park bench. Father Scarpi looked at the little priest beside him and fumbled in his coat pocket for his tobacco pouch.

Once, in the confessional, a sad old Sicilian had said, "They pinned Jesus to the Cross with his arms outstretched like this." And in the half-light the priest had watched the old man trying to spread out his arms in the cramped quarters. "I feel that way now," the old man had said. "But while poor Jesus was nailed by others, it is my sins that are crucifying me."

As he had wanted then to embrace the old man, Father Scarpi, now, wanted to embrace his little friend. He said only, "Yes, I've felt that way."

"You know, 'Tavio, I wonder why we, above other men, are chosen for the priesthood. There's a priest I know who went blind when he was a young man, and during his blindness he made a vow that if God restored even a portion of his eyesight he'd minister His words; he'd become a priest. The Lord in His infinite mercy did restore much of his sight, and the man became a priest.

"You know what I wonder, 'Tavio?" the little curate went on. "I keep wondering, if he loses his sight again, will he withdraw from the Church?"

"Why did you become a priest, Joe?" Father Scarpi asked.

Sconnetti mulled the question over. "I guess"—he smiled—"I'm

65

one of the few men who are born into it. My uncle was a bishop in the province of Calabria. My father, like a good landowner, meant me to go into the Army. You know, protect the regime, and all that. But I was a sickly child and spent more time with the sisters of the parochial school than a boy normally does.

"Things kept staggering along from year to year, my father hoping I'd go to a military school, my mother hoping I'd join the priesthood. Finally, when I was sixteen, my father took me around his wheatlands. I guess he wanted to impress me with my responsibility and importance. But somehow I shied away from his ideas, and the following year I entered the Seminary of St. Francis in Piacenza."

Father Sconnetti, however, did not tell the whole story. His father had taken him to the village square where the overseers were recruiting contadini for the harvesting. The peasants, men, women, and children, were lined in single file before the portals of St. Peter, the provincial church, which served a large area. The peasants were tired and dusty. Some had traveled forty or fifty miles on foot. They had brought bedding and their belongings. Some of the women were pregnant and some were breast feeding hungry infants. Joseph Sconnetti had flushed as he saw a young woman calmly expose her soft white breast and place it to her wailing baby's mouth.

He watched his father's overseers inspect the peasants, feeling their arms and legs. One overseer poked the breast of the nursing mother, and everyone laughed. But the woman's husband became angry and struck the overseer, knocking him down with a single blow. The overseer sprang up, knife in hand, and stabbed the peasant in the flesh of his arm. At the same instant Joseph's father spurred his horse forward and clouted the overseer with a club he carried.

The bleeding peasant was taken into the church, and Joseph's father sent for the family doctor. Meanwhile, the other overseers continued choosing workers. When Joseph's father thought enough had been hired, the workers were led into the wheatlands. The remaining peasants, including the man who had been knifed, began walking to the next patch of wheatlands, hoping to find work there.

That night Joseph told his father he had decided to become a priest.

"Why?" his father asked. "Because of what happened in the square today?"

Joseph nodded, saying that what had happened had something to do with his decision. He went on to say that no man had the moral right to treat another man as a work beast. His father laughed, and told him that Don Paolo, the village pastor, had a share of the wheatlands.

Joseph was shocked to discover that a priest was deriving profit from the labor of poor peasants, but he did not despair, thinking that Don Paolo did not represent the priesthood.

Two years later a horse threw his father, and the strong man died of a broken neck. Joseph was the only heir. He sold half the wheatlands to Don Paolo; the other half he distributed among the poorest peasants. The money he derived from the sale he turned over to his mother.

His uncle, the bishop, berated him for his stupidity, telling him that the land he had parceled out would revert to Don Paolo sooner or later, because the contadini did not have the capital necessary to develop the land.

Joseph replied slowly, "Then I can only hope and pray that Don Paolo will give them the capital."

Three years later all the wheatlands were owned by Don Paolo. Joseph's mother died, and soon he accepted a post in America, where priests who could speak Italian were needed to minister to the immigrants.

Father Sconnetti sat on the park bench, looking at the placid waters of the Charles River.

"But you, 'Tavio," he said, "why did you become a priest?"

"Me?" the big priest asked. He shrugged. "I guess it was kind of like your friend, the priest who was blind. A man I knew was dying, and I made a vow that whether he lived or died, I'd become a priest." He held the bowl of his pipe tightly.

It was in the summer of 1945, in a little town in Czechoslovakia. A husky GI in his platoon was fighting against a Third Army boxer named Hugger, who had been a professional prizefighter. The boy from Octavio's platoon sprained his ankle and was forced out. Someone asked Octavio to replace the GI so that the match wouldn't have to be canceled. Somehow, eleven-ounce gloves couldn't be found, but there was a pair of six-ounce gloves.

Octavio tried to withdraw, saying that the six-ouncers were money gloves. He knew that fourteen- and eleven-ounce gloves were standard for army fighting, and that the professional ring seldom used six-ouncers. Even championship bouts were staged with eight-ounce gloves.

The prizefighter, a quick-moving heavyweight staff sergeant, was contemptuous. "What's the matter, Lieutenant?" he asked. "Afraid of a couple of gloves?"

Scarpi looked at Hugger, who was shuffling his shoes in the rosin. Octavio could have said that he was an officer, and that officers weren't allowed to fight with noncoms. But he remained silent.

Hugger said quietly, "Yellow wop."

Several officers at the ringside heard the remark, and looked at Scarpi. Octavio knew that he was caught. No matter what he did he'd be in the wrong. He took off his overseas cap and shrugged out of his khaki shirt. While a kid from his platoon laced on the gloves, he kicked off his army brogans.

He went through the ropes quietly. The referee was a lieutenant.

"I don't know the regulations on a deal like this," the officer said. Octavio shrugged and rubbed his feet in the rosin. Then somebody rang the bell and Hugger moved in.

The sergeant flicked a jab, but Octavio neither moved away nor blocked it. He wanted to get the job over and done with. Hugger came in bobbing, throwing hooks to Octavio's belly. Scarpi caught the hooks and sidestepped. Hugger spun around and caught him with a right-hand blow that opened old scar tissue over Scarpi's eyes and caused the blood to stream down his face. Anger began to work in him, but he restrained himself and caught gloves. The bell rang and the round was over.

The referee asked Octavio if he wanted to call the bout off and get his cut attended to, but Scarpi laughed, shaking his head.

In the second round, while they clinched, Hugger grunted, "Yellow bastard." The sergeant stepped back and hooked. The officers around the ringside laughed. Octavio heard the laughter, and went to work. As Hugger threw a jab, Octavio went under it, and hooked a blow to his opponent's heart that hurt. Before Hugger could get set, Scarpi hooked twice, trying to stack the noncom up for a knockout. Hugger dumbly shook his head and bored in. Octavio faded to his own right, slammed a left to the sergeant's belly and crossed a right to the side of the noncom's chin. Then, while Hugger hung slack against the ropes, Scarpi smashed a wicked left and a final crushing right to the man's face. The sergeant sank down on the canvas; but Scarpi, beside himself, pushed away the shouting referee, lifted Hugger, and hit him again.

He was trying to pull Hugger to his feet for the second time when he became aware of what he was doing and of the sudden silence around the ring. He released the senseless man, and watched him sprawl limply on the floor of the ring.

Major Delnicki climbed into the ring and examined Hugger. "Bring a litter and get a weapons-carrier," he said to a youth at the ringside who wore a medical corps brassard. The sergeant was lifted to the weapons-carrier that was used as an ambulance and taken to the closest field hospital.

Scarpi followed in a jeep driven by Captain Branson, who kept telling him he shouldn't have lost his temper. When they reached the hospital, a pair of orderlies ran with Hugger into a tent. Octavio looked at Major Delnicki.

"He'll be all right, won't he?"

Delnicki shrugged.

A strident-voiced colonel appeared abruptly and, looking at Octavio, cried, "My God, the man's too big!" He slapped Octavio on the back. "You're too damn' strong, Lieutenant. Samson pulling down pillars, Hercules breaking a lion's backbone." He laughed, snorting through his nose, and strode off.

Octavio went outside where cold stars shone in a black sky. He looked at his huge hands in the dark. "God," he prayed, "let the man live! Don't let it be Onofrio again. Let him live, and I'll follow you forever!"

About an hour later Hugger regained his senses. The doctors wired the noncom's broken jaw and removed slivers of bone and shreds of cartilage from his smashed nose.

On the way back to the company C.P., Octavio was silent. Branson drove without saying a word, occasionally shifting a gear viciously as they jounced on the dirt roads. That night Octavio lay awake, tossing and turning, until at dawn he fell into a fitful slumber.

At breakfast the other officers were cold toward him. Octavio refused powdered eggs, and sipped at a mug of coffee. After the coffee he asked the battalion jeep driver to take him to the field hospital.

He found Hugger in a cot, face swathed in bandages. His muddy eyes stared sullenly as Octavio asked for forgiveness.

"Forget it, Lieutenant," Hugger said. "I was too cocksure. I deserved it." But he didn't sound friendly, and he turned his face away.

Late that night Octavio wrote to several seminaries, asking for admission. From these first letters grew a correspondence with the rector of St. John's Seminary.

Scarpi returned to the United States in the late summer of 1945. In the fall he was admitted into St. John's. He had already sent in his medical certificate and had packed a footlocker containing two black cassocks, three black trousers and a pair of black shoes, bedding, stationery, towels, toilet articles, and a tattered copy of the New Testament he had carried around for some time. With these articles of property and an intense desire to be close to God, Octavio began his new life.

For the first two years, he took normal college courses at St. Clement's Hall. Here and in the first year of philosophy at St. William's Hall, the clerical teachers were able to determine the faith of the seminarian and his mental balance. Octavio's class dwindled until only a few of those who had started were left.

In spite of having a difficult period of adjustment and a more difficult time keeping up scholastically with his younger and more adroit fellow seminarians, Octavio felt a great happiness for the first time in his life.

Each day became a delight, starting with the moment the porter pounded on the dormitory door and cried out, "Deo gratias!" Stubbornly dogging the heels of his classmates, Octavio drudged through two years of philosophy, wrestling with syllogisms, and then went on to four years of theology at Theology House. In his third year of theology, at the time of his subdiaconate, Octavio assumed the vows of a diocesan priest. He presented himself in the seminary chapel wearing an alb and a cincture with an amice swathed about his thick neck. He carried a tunic and maniple on his left arm, and in his right hand he bore a burning candle. He heard his name called and he responded, "Adsum." After prostrating himself to signify his sense of humility, Octavio heard the bishop say that each of them was accepting the burdens of his office of his own free choice and of his own accord.

Then the bishop extended to him an empty chalice and a paten, saying: "Behold what ministry is entrusted to you. . . . Conduct yourself as to be pleasing to God."

Octavio Scarpi, gazing straight into the bishop's eyes, mentally accepted the necessary vows of celibacy and the privilege of reciting the Divine Office daily. Then, suddenly, he whispered: "I vow before almighty God to remain celibate, to say the Divine Office—and—and to embrace perpetual poverty."

Smiling, the bishop said, "You are a step closer to God; thus you must come closer to me." He beckoned to the new subdeacons lined before him.

Wondering how he would be able to keep his vow of poverty, a vow that a diocesan priest almost never assumed, Octavio Scarpi took a step closer to the bishop.

Soon after that he was plunged into the core of Thomist philosophy and theology. At night, bleary-eyed, he read the works of the Dominican. It was difficult for him. Sometimes, in despair, he would be convinced that he was stupid, and he prayed to God to extend him enough intelligence to learn what he had to know. Perhaps, he thought later, his prayer had been answered, for eight years and some months after entering the seminary he was ordained.

Now Octavio Scarpi, a priest, sat grim-faced on a park bench, puffing on his pipe, remembering the fight with the sergeant and the days in the seminary.

"Shall we start back, Joe?" he suggested. "It's rather late."

Father Sconnetti stood up, and they began their walk back to the rectory.

"What were you thinking of?" Sconnetti said.

"Processus peccatorum," Father Scarpi replied quietly.

"Ah, yes. You could. But not I." The little curate shook his head. "I shall never be able to review the sins of my life." He sighed, thinking of Elena. And of life without her and without music. A schola cantorum, and he would make the choir practice psalm-toned propers. His head began to ache. He blinked his eyes. He had left his glasses behind. He wanted to say, "I feel halfway between heaven and hell." But he didn't want to distress Father Scarpi; besides, it sounded like a line from a melodrama, so he said nothing.

When they arrived, Father Lazzini told Octavio that his brother

Victor had called. Father Scarpi glanced at his watch and, although it was late, he decided to return the call.

When his brother answered the ring, Victor sounded tense and irritated.

"Vic," the priest said, "you sound worried. Pa is all right, isn't he?"

"It's not Pa," Victor said. "It's my daughter Rose."

"What's wrong?" There was no answer. Father Scarpi asked, "Vic? Are you there, Vic?" He could hear Victor sighing.

"Will you come down tomorrow?"

"I was thinking I might before you called."

"All right," Victor said. "I'll expect you about noon."

"What's the matter with Rose?"

Victor hesitated. "It'll keep until you get here."

Father Sconnetti, who stood at Octavio's elbow, smiled. "Are you going to your brother's place?" he asked.

"Yes. Why don't you come along?"

"Perhaps it'll be a good day for boccie," Sconnetti said. He was an expert player of the Italian version of bowling on the green, and he liked to play with Scarpi's father.

"It won't be an imposition?"

Father Scarpi grinned at the little priest. "Of course not," he said.

VIII

Father Scarpi groped for the alarm clock and turned it off. He sat up on his cot, looking at the sun breaking through the clouds.

He thought of the introit for the week. It was from Psalm Sixty-five.

" 'Shout joyfully to God,' " he murmured.

All through the years of his life he would feel humble every morning when he said the Mass, for at that time he was closest to God. He thought of the time, some two thousand years ago, when a young Jew was the host-guest at a simple banquet held in the home of a sympathizer near the city of Jerusalem. The tired Jew spoke gently of dying, and broke bread, calling it His Body, and poured wine, calling it His Blood. A few hours later He was a man alone, shunned and denied by His followers, jeered and taunted by policemen and soldiers. He forgave them, and allowed them to crucify Him as a common criminal, between two mocking thieves.

Today he, Octavio Scarpi, junior curate of St. Dominic's Church, would celebrate that banquet and that crucifixion.

The huge priest fastened his tight cassock after putting on his undershirt and trousers. He buttoned the full-length black smock and descended to the sacristy, where the altar boys helped him into the other vestments. First, the amice, symbolizing the priest's helmet of salvation; next, the alb for innocence and purity; then, the cincture which designated chastity. He paused for a moment in the prayers that accompanied each garment, and he tied the cord of chastity, snugly, about the waist of the alb. He pinned the maniple, the emblem of spiritual power, on his left forearm, just below the elbow.

He lowered his head, murmuring, "Dear Lord, make me worthy to receive Your sacrament."

Then he placed the stole around his neck, crossing the long band on his breast and tucking the flapping ends into the cincture about his waist. Last of all, he shrugged into the chasuble. And as this robe covered all the others, it was a symbol of charity, and was marked by a cross on its back, denoting Christ's human suffering.

" 'Our Father, who art in Heaven, hallowed be . . .' " He whispered the prayer softly, and when he had finished, he added, "Amen." Then he made the sign of the Cross and signaled to the altar boys. Head bowed, he followed them to the altar, where he swiftly checked the furniture of the Mass. He glanced at the tabernacle, thinking how much like the little inn it actually was. For it was within a little inn that Christ was born, and it was from the tabernacle that he would take out the Blessed Sacrament. He looked at the two candles of beeswax symbolizing the body of Christ and at their flickering flame which symbolized His soul. The corporal, the pall, and the purificator of white linen were properly placed. The paten, a small plate upon which the Sacred Host would be placed, gleamed dully.

Father Scarpi said the Confiteor. He stooped low in contrition for his sins. After Dominus Vobiscum, the priest said aloud, "Oremus," and went up to the altar.

He chanted the introit psalm to its full length and concluded by saying, " 'Glory be to the Father and to the Son and to the Holy Ghost, as it was in the beginning, is now and ever shall be, world without end. Amen.' "

After the alleluia verse he turned to the Gospel which was opened to John 16. Then he faced the parishioners.

"You have heard what our Lord said concerning the sorrow that is turned to joy," he said clearly. He went on and spoke of the pain of childbirth which would lead to the joy of an infant. And he spoke of how St. Paul described His own rebirth; the pain of death would lead to eternal life, to God. . . .

The time passed quickly, and before he was aware of it the priest read aloud, " 'Et Verbum caro factum est.' " *And the Word was made flesh.*

Father Scarpi genuflected reverently and finished the beginning of the Gospel of St. John.

" 'Deo Gratias,' " the acolyte murmured.

The priest walked down to the foot of the altar steps, where he recited the prayers after Mass which Pope Pius XI had decreed should be directed for Russia and the Russian people. Then the big curate ascended the altar, took his chalice, bowed to the Cross and descended again. At the foot of the altar he genuflected toward the tabernacle. The altar boy handed him his biretta, and Father Scarpi put it on and followed the acolyte into the sacristy. The Mass was over. Christ once again had allowed himself to be crucified for the faithful.

In a fashionable house overlooking Jamaica Pond, Frank O'Meara was sitting at breakfast. He slowly raised his orange juice and sipped it. He looked at a pudgy man with fat cheeks who was placing a cup of warm cereal on the little table of the breakfast nook.

"Just right, J. J."

"Thanks, boss. I chilled it exactly ten minutes like you always say."

"A man's got to have a good breakfast," Frank explained. "A guy rushes his breakfast and he's due for a breakdown. He's got to get enough proteins without too much carbohydrates. They kill a guy, carbohydrates. A professor said that in a health resort."

Frank was quite familiar with diets and calories. Two years before a doctor had told him that a heavy person was a person who died more quickly than a light person. Frank wanted to be a light person.

Now he examined a spoon carefully. He wiped it on a clean linen napkin. This was an old habit, dating back to his youth when he ate in shabby restaurants. He spooned out a small portion of the cereal and tasted it, smacking his lips.

"Is it okay, boss?" J. J. asked. "I did just what you said."

Frank O'Meara nodded. "Bien. Trez bien." He smiled. "That's French for 'very good,'" he explained, and dug his spoon delicately into the cereal.

After breakfast O'Meara took out a package of cigarettes. He flipped one out. J. J. leaned over and held out a burning match.

"You better start dressing," Frank said. "I want to make the eleven o'clock Mass at the Church of the Blessed Sacrament."

"There's plenty of time," J. J. assured him. He hesitated. "Boss, Sandy Mac's in the library."

75

"He knows better," Frank said coldly. "And on a Sunday too."

"He says it's important. That's why he didn't call. He's been waiting for you to finish breakfast."

Frank got up, flinging his napkin on the table. "Get dressed," he growled. "I'll talk to him."

He went into the library.

A short thin man with pale blue eyes and a scar slashed across his face was holding a book in his hands. He looked up and put the book into a bookcase. "Lotta books," he said.

"Haven't I told you not to bother me on Sunday?" Frank said.

"Listen, Frank." Sandy Mac held up his hands. "I got news on Shannan."

"Does he want out?"

"No. I got a tip an attorney saw him last night."

"Attorney? What the hell—"

"This guy is a legal beagle for that investigating committee."

Frank placed a cigarette in his holder and lit it nervously. "What gives?" he asked bluntly.

Sandy Mac said, "I don't figure Joe to sing, but why don't he want out?"

"He figures on a commute. I don't know how he figures it. What the hell, I think he's crazy when he says he'll beat the rap—"

"Frank," Sandy Mac interrupted quietly, "they're offering him a reprieve if he canaries on you."

"How?"

"Income tax."

"The Capone frame?"

Sandy Mac nodded.

Frank said: "Forget it. I trust Joe."

"Okay, okay." Sandy Mac shrugged. "I'm just passing it on."

Frank didn't say anything for a long time. At last, he sighed. "Pass the word," he said tightly. "If Shannan doesn't want out by next week, he's through."

"You mean—"

"You know what I mean," Frank said.

"It'll take money," Sandy Mac said. "Whether he wants out or not, it'll take money."

"All right, it'll take money. Now get out," Frank said quietly.

Father Scarpi and Father Sconnetti traveled to Revere by subway. At the new Revere Beach Station, the priests boarded a bus going to Malden Street. Victor Scarpi's house was on a high hill off Conant Street.

The priest's old father lived with Victor. Another brother, John, who had become a silent, moody man, often roomed there as well. John Scarpi did murals for churches and institutions. He seldom looked for work, however, and sometimes was idle for long periods. Slightly older than Octavio, John had hoped that his younger brother would go into business with him.

Father Scarpi smiled, remembering the trouble John had taken to teach him the rudiments of drawing and design. But at the time Octavio had been interested in the prize ring.

Strangely, of all the brothers John had been happy at Octavio's decision to enter a seminary. John was the agnostic of the family.

Father Scarpi, looking out of the window of the swaying bus, remembered the consternation which had greeted his decision to become a priest. The strong anticlerical tradition in the family made the idea of his becoming a priest seem somehow undignified.

When the brothers learned of his decision, they gathered together and tried to dissuade him. The occasion for the family gathering had been Octavio's discharge from the army. All the brothers and their wives had met at Salvatore's house in Somerville. They had dinner together and afterward Salvatore nodded and the brothers went down into the cellar, leaving their father and the women upstairs.

Salvatore, the oldest living brother, a man of fifty-five at that time, switched on the cellar light. He had been born in Augusta, and he spoke with a slight accent. He was the smallest of all the brothers, but by virtue of owning a fruit and vegetable market he was the most prosperous. In the last two years of the war he had started a tomato repacking house, and was quite proud of it.

Whenever an old friend he had not seen for some time appeared, he would boast. "Ah, yes, we're progressing. Tomato repacking now. Got a couple farms in Nogales, one in Concord. Vision, foresight," he would say. "My plant will be big, bigger than—why, bigger than the De Mare brothers' outfit. Yes, indeed," Salvatore would say in the dialect. He still made wine in the old style, and the cellar had five barrels of mixed muscato and chianti resting on wooden trestles.

77

Victor, who was then fifty, was a general contractor. He had started out as a fisherman, but during the depression he had switched and worked for the WPA. At the end of the thirties he got enough money together to buy a scoop-shovel and two trucks, and flung himself, headlong, into building. By a shrewd manipulation of rival politicians, he managed to wangle both city and state contracts for construction work and painting.

Anthony, two years younger than Victor, was a tall, lean man with heavy shoulders, long arms, and a quick temper. In his teens he had stabbed a man during a brawl over a pretty little prostitute. He had been given a sentence of three years at the Concord Reformatory. The family was astonished at the light sentence. They had expected him to spend most of his life in prison. It was generally agreed among the older Sicilians that the law and the Courts were institutions to protect the wealthy and oppress the poor. This was known from time immemorial.

During the days in the reformatory, Anthony, a handsome boy with curly hair, learned to read and write in English so well that on his release the immigrants called him l'avvocato, the lawyer, or 'u 'Mericano, the American. In 1918, when he was twenty, the patrolmen of the Milham police force went on strike. Anthony, who was then working in a Milham shoe factory, was approached by a captain of police who told him that since he was strong and could speak English it was his patriotic duty to accept a temporary appointment as a policeman. And so Anthony became a policeman. Somehow, the duty became permanent, and after twenty-seven years on the Milham force he had been made an inspector.

John, the painter, was a tall, sad-eyed bachelor. His brothers called him a dreamer, but John merely smiled when they were irked by his lack of ambition. Many years before, he had brought a girl home, introducing her as his fiancée. For a while his work flourished, but the girl caught pneumonia and died. After that, John seemed purposeless.

On the day that Octavio told the family of his calling, John stood apart from his prosperous brothers. He glanced at Octavio, seeing the distorted, broken nose, the deep-set, shadowed eyes, the high cheekbones. There were innocence and gentleness in his brother's gray eyes. John felt that it was his brother, and yet not his brother, for Octavio was dead. The strong boy who had been his closest companion, who had the power to kill a horse with a single blow, was

78

dead, and in his place was this stranger who now claimed to have seen God. John felt humbled, ashamed, and angry. Humbled by the self-abnegation in Octavio, ashamed because he could not believe as his brother believed, and angered that such a virile man would willingly relinquish realities for what he, John, knew to be the frail dreams of neurotic, monkish men.

Victor and Anthony sat behind an old kitchen table, while Salvatore uncorked a bottle and poured wine into large tumblers. Octavio pushed a stool against the wall and sat down. They drank, and Salvatore, wiping his mouth on the back of his hand, turned to the youngest Scarpi.

" 'Kay," Salvatore said. "We glad you're home. 'Kay. Now, why don' you get a nice girl and get married?"

"Sure," Victor said. "What're you trying to do? Break Pa's heart? You know what he thinks of priests."

Octavio looked at his brother John. "All right, you're the cultured one. The artist, the agnostic. Aren't you going to throw your two cents in?"

"I'm glad," John replied. After a moment he said, "I can only envy you." He turned away.

They heard someone coming down the wooden stairs leading into the cellar.

"Papa," Salvatore said.

Beneditto Scarpi walked into the cellar and stood at the foot of the stairs looking at his sons. He was a lean whipcord of a man, of average height, in his late seventies. He was still fishing each day, then, in the winter of 1945. His eyesight was fading so that he constantly squinted. His skin was gnarled and mottled with age, and colored deep brown by the elements. He walked with a limp that had been caused by a rifle ball lodged deep within his leg. He had got the wound many years ago in Sicily, when, as a young man, he rode with the provincial Maffia.

It had happened that a member of their band, one Domenico Bino, a married man with four children, became enamored of a young girl, and she grew heavy with child. The local head of the society drummed him out of the Maffia, and Beneditto with two others were picked by short straws for the duty of killing the villain. Beneditto carried the rifle his father had used under Garibaldi during the liberation. He rode between his two companions on a stolen mule as they

79

departed on their mission. Beneditto admitted that he did not wish to kill the culprit, and that, in truth, he did not have the heart. One of the riders, his Uncle Tomaso, fingered his huge mustache and glared at him. He should have confessed his attitude before departing for the mission, his uncle informed him sternly. Now that they had started, he would simply have to attend the justice administered to rapists. Still, Uncle Tomaso told him, when the time came for shooting, Beneditto could shoot into the ground and thus salve his conscience.

Domenico Bino, the cause of the disturbance, was an astute man who knew of the swift justice meted out by the Maffia. Earlier that morning he had stolen a splendid stallion of Arab blood from the stables of an estate south of Augusta. He rode the splendid beast back to his house, kissed his wife and children goodbye, and vaulted on the waiting bay.

But just then Uncle Tomaso, Beneditto, and their friend came into view astride their fast-jogging mules.

"Stop, thief!" Uncle Tomaso cried, seeing Domenico Bino on the fleeing stallion. He clambered down from his mule and began firing. Beneditto got down, raised his rifle, and sighted Domenico Bino. Then he lowered the muzzle and shot into the ground. He was knocked down by a numbing blow on his leg, and sat, stunned, watching Bino spur the bay and vanish within a forest of chestnut trees. Later, his Uncle Tomaso pointed out the granite boulder that had caused the ball to ricochet and bury itself in Beneditto's right leg.

Beneditto had never revealed the details of the event. When pressed by his sons or friends, he would only smile sadly and say the wound was incurred in line of duty when he was a Maffiuso.

Now, he walked into the cellar saying, "Che cosa fanno questi birbante?"

"We're not up to anything," Anthony retorted.

But the old fisherman's eyes narrowed. "I knew you when you were wet behind the ears," he said with a crooked smile, tilting his head as he always did when calling for explanations.

John said, "Octavio is going to become a priest."

A sudden silence ensued.

"Prete?" the old man echoed. "Parrino?" He looked at Octavio. "Parrino?" he repeated. "Perche?"

The old man shuffled toward his last-born son, limping. Octavio, towering above the fisherman, looked away.

"My son, look at me. Do you wish to become a priest?"

"Yes, my father."

"So be it!" Beneditto cried, embracing his son. "So be it!"

He took in the five men grouped around him. Three of his sons were not there. Nicolo had been killed by the men of Japan and buried on an island like Sicily. Onofrio had died from that strange malady which atrophied his muscles and made his flesh shrink; and Annunziato was dead, too, his spine broken by a ball from a drunkard's pistol. Annunziato had lain in a hospital bed waiting for death to take him, suffering for fourteen—or was it fifteen?—years in agonizing pain, while he, worthless old man that he was, vecchio e 'maro, complained about the niggardly pain in his own leg.

He sighed. "My sons," he said, "one is never too old to learn. When I was young, as you know, I was in the Maffia." He tapped his leg. "It was necessary then. A Sicel very rarely obtained justice in the Italian courts. Each province banded to administer justice to rapists, greedy landlords, and corrupt officials.

"The Italian judges did not think that deflowering a virgin was such a bad crime. So it was up to the Maffia to punish and drive out the rapists. Because the Italian courts didn't think that peasants had any rights over the landlords, we had to punish landlords to teach them that peasants did have rights. Human rights. But enough. You understand."

He paused. "What is so, is so. In the end the Maffia disbanded; it was broken down by corrupt members. Today, I understand, many American gangs have adopted the name. So be it. What was an honorable society is dragged into the mire."

He smiled wanly at Octavio. Salvatore handed him a tumbler of wine, and he sipped at it.

"On the other hand," he said, "the priests who were dishonorable when I was a boy have been replaced by honorable men. Now that the mail is coming to the States, many men write that the priests suffer with the people. So be it," he added slowly.

He limped to the stairs and, holding on to the rail, turned back to them.

"Times change," he said. "Perhaps because of the poor, suffering Jesus, man may also change." He slowly climbed the stairs.

81

When the bus reached Conant Street, the two curates got off and started up the steep incline toward Victor's house. Father Scarpi wondered what had caused the anxiety in his brother's voice when he had spoken to Victor over the phone.

Partway up the hill, Father Sconnetti held up his hand. "To be young again," he panted.

Father Scarpi looked to the east, where he could see the faint cobweb pattern of the roller-coaster on Revere Beach. Below, in the hollow of the valley, were the geometrically laid-out homes of a municipal project. A fat old beagle waddled down to him, sniffed at the cuffs of his trousers, seemed satisfied, and continued its waddling descent.

As they went on climbing, nearing the little plateau where Victor's house was, Father Scarpi saw his father. The priests were concealed by shrubbery and approached unnoticed.

Father Scarpi saw that his brother John was with the old man.

"Go away," the old man was saying. "Get married, get lost."

He limped over to a spade that was struck upright in the soft loam. Gripping the handle, he dug into the earth. But John took the tool from his father's hands and began digging, turning over topsoil. Later, John would harrow it with a rake and then the old man would plant hothouse plants of tomatoes, string beans, cucumbers, egg-plants, peppers, and winter melon.

"If you want any digging done," John said, "I'll do it."

"Aii!" His father bristled. "Aii, you rooster without a hen, give to me my spade."

"Go on, Pa. Sit down and relax."

"I no relax. I work. When I die, I die working."

John shook his head. "You don't have to do anything but rest," he observed mildly, "and you do everything but."

"Pig of a devil," the old man said, "must I pay heed to one who is newly spawned?"

John, who was now in his forties, chuckled.

"Pa," Father Scarpi cried, and emerged from the brush on the side of the road.

The old man glanced around. "Tell this imbecile," the old man roared, pointing to John, "to stop annoying me. A man can hardly enjoy his old age. They're all afraid I'm going to die," he grumbled. "Do they think I'm immortal? For fifty years on the sea, I dreamed

82

of a patch of land to cultivate, and now they won't let me near a tool. Do they forget that I'm their father?"

At that moment, Victor came out of the house and shook Father Scarpi's hand.

"What's the trouble?" the priest asked Victor.

"It can wait," Victor said evasively. "Rose has gone for a drive. She hasn't returned yet."

Beneditto Scarpi embraced Father Sconnetti. "All right," he said. "Now is the time for a hand of boccie. 'Na bella jugada. Let us make quick."

Father Sconnetti laughed. "Father 'Tavio and John against Mr. Scarpi and myself. Youth against age, brawn against brain. How's that?"

But John wasn't inclined to play, so Beneditto invited his nearest neighbor, a tall leathery-skinned farmer, Compare Fabrizio.

Fabrizio had come from Abruzza years ago, had settled in Revere and had never left it. He subsisted on his poultry and farm, and argued constantly with his wife.

Compare Fabrizio walked nonchalantly from his farm, striving to conceal his eagerness to play boccie.

"Oh, Compare, the priest and I wish to challenge you," Beneditto Scarpi said.

He laughed. "But I can't play against the two of you alone," he said.

"You shall have the honor of playing with my son," the old man replied.

Compare Fabrizi looked Father Scarpi up and down.

"Honor?" he said dubiously. "Is he a champion boccie player?"

"He's a priest," the old man replied proudly, winking at Father Sconnetti.

"A priest?" the Abruzzian peasant asked. "That is of no importance to me. I never go to church."

Father Sconnetti laughed, and Father Scarpi tried to maintain a straight face.

"Well," the big priest said, "if we lose I'll pay for the beer."

Compare Fabrizio made the sign of the Cross. "Charity from a priest? Will miracles never cease?"

They tossed a coin for play, and Father Sconnetti won. He chose to throw the marker. The boccie alley was a pit about six inches deep, more than four feet wide, and about forty feet long. The little priest went over to one end of the alley with Compare Fabrizio paired off against him, and Father Scarpi went to the other end, paired off against his father.

Father Sconnetti tossed the marker, a hard rubber ball about the size of a tennis ball. It stopped rolling about five feet from the end where Father Scarpi was standing.

Then the little curate carefully threw a point ball, a hard sphere about the size of a bowling ball. The idea was to get as close as possible to the marker. It was a good cast, and the ball came within two or three inches of the marker.

"Good toss!" the old man shouted. "Point ball."

"But what point ball?" Compare Fabrizio said scornfully. "Allo partner, how is the ball?"

"Very close," Father Scarpi replied.

"These priests and their litanies," Compare grumbled. He slouched down the alley, his long arms dangling. Carefully he sighted the balls, squinting his eyes and pondering on their positions. "Point?" he said. "Ha!" He returned to the opposite end and, wetting his finger, tested the air for adverse winds.

"But throw the ball!" the old man shouted.

Compare Fabrizio tossed the ball high in the air. "Boccie," he shouted. "Watch out! Boccie!"

The hard rubber sphere smacked into Father Sconnetti's ball, knocking it away, and the point reverted to Compare.

"Have you seen, Priest?" Compare cried. "Have you seen?"

He strutted back and forth, proud as a peacock.

The little priest threw his remaining ball. It rolled between Compare's ball and the marker.

"Ma, che fortuna!" Compare shouted. "What luck! Listen, Priest, if I went to church would I have the same luck?"

He cast his ball. It struck the massed balls, scattering them. Compare ran down the alley like a lean gray wolf pouncing on a hare.

The balls were close together.

"Stripes have a point," the old man chortled with glee.

"Stripes?" Compare cried. "Stripes have nothing. The plain ball is closer to the marker. It's my point."

"Measure," the old man said. "I dare you."

Compare Fabrizio pulled a long blade of grass to measure the distance between balls and the marker. After a moment, he exclaimed, "Sangue de Garibaldi," and threw down the blade of grass in disgust.

"What does Garibaldi have to do with it?" Beneditto Scarpi mocked. "The little priest is a champion."

They continued playing until Father Sconnetti and Beneditto Scarpi had earned the winning score of eleven points.

"Nobody pays for the beer," Beneditto said. "It's on the house."

After he had brought four bottles of beer out of the cooler in the cellar, they each cast a ball for boss and underboss. The ball closest to the marker made its thrower boss, and the ball next closest designated underboss. The boss of the game could drink all the beer, or he could give a bottle to another player if the underboss agreed. The underboss had to ask for a drink, but he could deny a drink to anyone except the boss.

Beneditto Scarpi won underboss and Father Sconnetti won boss. Compare looked at them distrustfully from the corner of his eyes. He knew he wouldn't get a beer unless both men agreed to give him one.

Beneditto offered a bottle to Father Sconnetti and uncapped another for himself. They drank slowly, with evident relish, smacking their lips loudly, making a point of ignoring Father Scarpi and Compare. Compare looked at them wistfully and licked his lips. It was a warm day, and the game had been long.

"Never expect mercy from a priest," he grumbled.

Father Sconnetti laughed and choked on his beer.

"Choke," Compare muttered. "Choke."

"If," said Father Sconnetti to Beneditto thoughtfully, "mind you, I say, if—if I designate a bottle of beer as being free, would you allow a certain farmer to drink?"

"Non po' essere." Beneditto shook his head sadly. "On the other hand," he went on, holding up a bottle of beer, "don't you think we should have one free bottle?"

"Yes," said Father Sconnetti.

"Do you think that ox of a priest there deserves a drink?"

"If you want to give it to him," Sconnetti shrugged.

The old man passed the bottle to Father Scarpi.

"But what am I?" Compare Fabrizio asked. "A Turk?" He bristled.

"I'm a Christian, I am. I've been baptized, confirmed, and sprinkled with holy water. I can see right now that a good Christian hasn't a chance here."

"The last bottle is free," Father Sconnetti announced.

Compare pretended to be deeply hurt. "I'm going to tear down the holy pictures my wife has all over the walls and beat her with them."

"Because Signor Fabrizio is a good Christian," Father Sconnetti said, "may I change my mind and give him the beer?"

"Compare, do you want this beer?" the old man teased.

Fabrizio was afraid to say Yes in the event the old man refused and afraid to say No in the event the old man would agree.

"I don't know." Compare shrugged.

"He doesn't know if he wants the beer," the old man explained to Father Sconnetti gravely.

"Ah, no," Compare Fabrizio cried. "I want it, all right."

"Then take it!" The old fisherman grinned, triumphant.

As they drank their beer a car stopped at the foot of the steep hill, and Victor's daughter got out. A young man was with her, holding her arm. She waved to them across the field that separated the boccie alley from the road, and they entered the house.

Compare Fabrizio tilted his head and drained his bottle, his Adam's apple bobbing. He wiped his lips on the back of his hand and started toward home. "Oh, Scarpi," he said, stopping. "Next time we play I want the little priest as my partner. He must pray harder than you do." He shook his head solemnly and continued on his way.

John came out of the house. He was carrying a suitcase and was dressed in a pair of baggy pants and turtleneck sweater. In the crook of his free arm he had a raincoat and a jacket.

"Where you going?" Father Scarpi asked.

"Got a job in Worcester. Murals." He embraced his father. " 'Bye, Pa."

"Watch yourself," the old fisherman murmured in the dialect.

John shook hands with his brother and Father Sconnetti. He swung away and started down the hill. In a few moments they could hear him starting his car; it trundled down the hill in second gear.

Victor motioned to Father Scarpi, who followed him.

"Come into the house," Victor murmured. "They're waiting for you." Victor seemed nervous.

86

Victor's wife, Lucy, a tall woman with a mass of black hair and flashing dark eyes, was at the door.

"I'm against it," she said. "He's a stranger. 'Nu 'Mericano. I'm against it," she repeated.

Victor shook his head. "Keep quiet, Lucy," he whispered.

Rose Scarpi and the young man she had brought home were seated in the living room. The boy got up and shook hands with Father Scarpi.

Victor cleared his throat. "Father 'Tavio is the religious head of the family," he said. "We'll abide by his decision."

A coffee table in the center of the room held an electric coffee pot and five cups.

"Coffee, Father?" the girl asked.

"Yes." Father Scarpi smiled, wondering what was wrong.

Rose got up and poured the coffee. She was a lovely young girl. Her slim body was graceful as she poured, but her hands trembled.

Lucy said, "They want to be married."

"Fine. That's wonderful," Octavio Scarpi said.

Victor shook his head. "Dana is a Protestant," he said.

Through the picture window Father Scarpi could see his father and Sconnetti. The curate was hefting a boccie ball. He tossed the hard rubber sphere. He could hear Beneditto shouting, "Good toss, nice toss!"

Father Scarpi looked at the boy. "Are you willing to become a Catholic?" he asked.

"Sure." The young man shrugged. "I was never religious in the true sense of the word."

His casual reply saddened the priest. "Do you think you can bring yourself to believe in the doctrines of the Church?"

The boy was holding a cup of coffee to his lips; he lowered it on the table.

"I don't think it'll be difficult," he said. Suddenly, the boy dropped his casual air and leaned forward urgently. "No," he said. "I can't believe in some of the doctrines." He sat back, relieved.

Lucy laughed uneasily, and Rose cried, "Dana Greer!"

Father Scarpi tensed, remembering the brother that Ellen Greer had written of in her diary. He stood up abruptly. "What did you say your name is?" he asked quickly.

"Dana Greer," the boy said.

The priest stared at him. "Did you ever hear of a woman named Ellen Greer?"

After a moment, Dana sighed. "If you mean the girl that Shannan killed, yes." He was silent for a moment; then, "She was my sister."

IX

St. Thomas, in his book on matrimony, states that the grace of God accompanies those who have received that sacrament. He goes on to say that the Church lists many impediments which make an undesirable marriage either illicit or invalid.

Dana Greer, young and impatient, was only dimly aware of these impediments. All he knew was that his sister Ellen seemed to stand between him and what he wanted. He turned away from the priest and gazed out of the window. Through the sparse foliage of the fig tree beside the window, he saw Rose's grandfather casting a boccie ball to the opposite end of the boccie alley.

It was Ellen again, he thought, Ellen turning up like a nightmare to haunt him. He saw Ellen in slacks, her close-cropped hair uncombed, reading a book, her glasses perched loosely on her nose. He heard Ellen say: "Men haven't got souls. Only women have them."

It had taken the Korean War and a hitch in the Navy to get away from Ellen, and now, even when she was dead, she plagued him. She had been mother and father to him for ten years, since he was twelve. Dana could scarcely remember his mother. She had been a big woman with yellow hair; Ellen used to say she dyed her hair. His mother would leave on mysterious trips for a week or two, and when she came back she always had money.

One day Ellen had an argument with his mother. He had been too young to remember what it was about, but the next time his mother went on a trip Ellen moved to another part of the city, taking Dana with her. The next time he'd seen his mother, she was dead.

He remembered how Ellen had been when he was going to high school. They were living in a three-room apartment on Irving Street when he brought Laura home one spring night for dinner. Laura

89

looked more mature than her fourteen years. She had a full mouth and a well developed figure. After dinner, Laura did the dishes and Ellen dried them. Then his sister persuaded them to stay home instead of going to the movies. Ellen went out of her way to be nice to Laura.

They had a good summer. Ellen rented a cottage at Falmouth for July, and took them there with her. At night they would sit on the bench in front of the cottage, watching the surf gallop, white-maned, onto the moonlit beach. After the first week Dana noticed that Laura seemed upset. One day when he came back from a fishing trip he had taken alone, he found Laura gone. Ellen was irritable and moody, and said that the ungrateful girl had left without a word. When Dana tried to follow her, Ellen stormed at him oddly.

In Boston, Dana called Laura, but she was evasive. She wouldn't go to his house, she said, although she wanted to see him. They began to meet secretly. Ellen kept asking about Laura, but Dana would shrug away her questions. Then Ellen found her, and began telephoning to her, writing to her, begging to see her again. Dana never learned whether Laura had resumed acquaintance with Ellen again after Falmouth. One day, when Ellen went to Laura's apartment, and pleaded with her through the closed door, Ellen heard the crash of glass and a cry. Running downstairs, she found Laura on the sidewalk. She had died instantly.

Dana had met Rose while he was still in the Navy. He'd gone to an Italian wedding feast in a Revere Beach hall. A friend of his named Aglitti had taken him. "It's a real party," he'd said to Dana. "I ought to know. Plenty to eat and drink!" At first, Dana had felt uncomfortable among the noisy Sicilians, but he soon joined in their merriment. When he saw a small object roll on the floor, he picked up a plastic medallian. Within the plastic were a miniature Madonna and Child wearing little jeweled crowns. Dana thought it very pretty. A fragment of palm leaf was taped to the back of the medallion, and above the front there were printed the words: "My Mother My Confidence—300 days of indulgence. Pope Benedict XVI. Rose Scarpi."

Aglitti said, "I know her; she's a bridesmaid." He introduced Dana to Rose. She was tall and slim with long brown hair and gray eyes. Her blue gown billowed out as she turned to Dana, holding out a slim white hand. "I believe this is yours," he said, showing her the medallion.

They danced together, and later Dana asked if he could take her home. It was a warm night, and they walked down Malden Street, fingers entwined, laughing at each other for no particular reason. He helped her up the steep hill, and put his arm about her waist. When they reached her house, he bent forward shyly and kissed her.

Dana loved Rose deeply, and felt that she understood him. She was right for him, in every way. He looked at Father Scarpi.

"The bride and groom must be in a state of grace when they receive the sacrament of Matrimony," the priest said. "If you don't think you can believe in the Church, it isn't likely that you would be in a state of grace." He paused, and added, "The Church cannot marry you."

"Uncle 'Tavio!" Rose cried. "Father 'Tavio." She burst into tears, and turned to her mother. "I wanted to be married in church, Mama."

"Rose," the priest said, "if Dana can't believe in the doctrines of the Church, how can he be married in a church?"

"If you won't marry us," Rose said stiffly, "we'll have a civil wedding." She went to Dana and took his hand. She dried her cheeks and lifted her chin.

Father Scarpi took out his tobacco pouch and filled the bowl of his pipe.

Dana said, "I'm not religious, but I know the word 'religion' means to bind people together, to bring to them a love of God and a love of their fellow man. But your Church finds all kinds of rules to keep people apart. I'm no theologian, but what makes a man like you, a man who has renounced sex and marriage, an expert, a mediator, between a man and a woman?"

Father Scarpi stared at the stem of his pipe, annoyed by the boy's familiar argument. Rose began to cry again.

"The Church doesn't make rules to obstruct love," the priest said. "Her rules prompt and assure love." He glanced at the young man. "I'm sorry you feel as you do about the Church."

Dana said, "I love Rose, and I want to marry her."

"Think it over," Father Scarpi answered. "There's time. Pray to Him and He will help you."

On Monday morning a requiem Mass was said over the closed coffin of Vincent Spinale. After the funeral Don Peppino went to the fraternity, where he had an appointment with the professor and Santo Cuniggio. The three men walked into the downtown section of Boston, and down the South End part of Washington Street. When they arrived at a doorway marked *Da Vinci Statuary*, they stopped and, entering a malodorous vestibule, climbed a flight of steel steps.

"Da Vinci," the professor informed his companions, "is a name long associated with art. Perhaps this man is related—of course distantly—to the great Leonardo."

They walked into an office filled with the clatter of a typewriter. A pretty girl behind the typewriter looked up. "May I help you?" she asked.

"Yes," Carmello Poverello assented. "We are on the thought of having a statue made. A small religious one," he added.

The girl nodded and walked into a doorway lettered *Employees Only*. She returned a moment later with a tall lean man, who was wiping his hands on a blue denim apron that was splattered with plaster of Paris.

"I'm Greenberg," he said. "What kind of statue were you interested in?"

"We have the desire to speak with Mr. Da Vinci," the professor replied politely.

Greenberg smiled. "That's me. It's a trade name," he explained.

Don Peppino was surprised. "A Hebrew making a statue of a Catholic saint?"

Cuniggio was startled. "St. Dominic will turn over in his grave."

"But, no," the professor said. "Consider that Michelangelo made a statue of Moses and David. Certainly, then, a Hebrew may do the same with an Augustan saint."

"We can always have the statue blessed afterward," Don Peppino reflected.

"But of a certainty," Poverello agreed. He turned to Greenberg. "We are thinking of a statue of St. Dominic about six feet high."

"You mean life-size."

"Yes. The size as in life. Precisely. How much?" the professor inquired cautiously.

"Well, naturally it would mean working from the ground up,"

Greenberg said. "There would be the clay, the modeling, the casting, the bronzing. You want it in bronze?"

"Yes, in bronze. How much?"

"Ten thousand dollars."

"Dieci mille!" Don Peppino exclaimed. "Oh, pretty boy, we do not wish to buy your shop. We only want a statue."

The professor assented. "We want only a church statue."

"A plaster cast? But I haven't got a mold of this saint you're talking about. I'd still have to get a sculptor to make the clay figure. I'd still have to make a mold for the pouring."

"Wait a minute!" Cuniggio cried. "You give to me a headache. We want to know how much."

"Offhand I'd say two, three thousand," Greenberg replied.

"We are lost!" Cuniggio lamented.

"Silence!" Don Peppino shouted. "You say just now you do not have St. Dominic. What do you have?"

"Well, I can cast St. Anthony, the Virgin Mary—"

"Wait," the professor said. "Let us see the statue of St. Anthony."

"I don't have a cast on hand, but I'll show you a photograph."

The three men took the photograph of St. Anthony and huddled over it conferring volubly. At last they approached Greenberg, who had been standing to one side, smoking.

"For a statue of St. Anthony, how much?" the professor asked.

"One thousand dollars."

"But why does he always talk with many zeros behind his numbers?" Don Peppino complained.

"Instead of painting it brown, will you paint it black and white? You know the habit of the Dominican monk."

"All right," Greenberg agreed.

"One more thing. Will you make a Bible out of plaster and have the saint holding it?"

"Yes."

"But we haven't a thousand dollars," Cuniggio said in the dialect.

"Ask him if he'll take eight hundred," Don Peppino whispered to the professor.

Poverello, ignoring the fishmonger, said: "You must do another thing. You must have lettered at the foot of the statue 'San Domenico de Sicilia.' All right? 'San Domenico de Sicilia.'"

"Write it down," Greenberg said wearily. "Write down everything. You can write, can't you?"

Carmello Poverello drew himself up and with great dignity said, "I am a professor."

"But where's the thousand dollars?" Cuniggio insisted.

"We have a lack of $145 dollars to make up the thousand. We shall make it up as a penance."

"But it was Peppino's fault," Cuniggio said.

"I am hoping," replied the professor, "that he will contribute $100." They looked at the fishmonger, who sighed agreement.

Greenberg watched the professor take out a pencil stub, lick the lead point, and begin to write.

"San Domenico," Poverello wrote, "could convert anyone. It is written that he went among the Turks."

After Spinale's funeral Father Scarpi changed into street clothes. Father Ferrera was out, and Sconnetti was in the inner office. He told the little curate he was going out.

"Please return in time for supper, 'Tavio," Father Sconnetti said teasingly. Father Scarpi nodded and hurried out.

The law offices of White, Fisher and Aaronson were on the twelfth floor of the Law Building on State Street.

"Is Mr. White available?" he asked the receptionist.

"Who is calling, please?"

"Father Scarpi. Tell him I want to speak about Joseph Shannan."

She returned in a few moments and directed the priest into an office.

"What's this about Shannan?" he asked.

White was a tall man with gray hair and a slight paunch.

"I want to know if you think Shannan guilty of the crime he was convicted for," Father Scarpi said.

"Shannan guilty? That's a great question to ask me. Of course not." White looked at the priest. "Why are you interested in Shannan?"

"I'm a friend," the curate replied slowly. "That is, he and my brother were friends." Father Scarpi felt uncomfortable. "My brother —he's dead. I felt—well, I went to see him."

White stood up suddenly. "It was crazy," he said. "Though the man was innocent, he was convicted. Circumstances, however, were against

94

him. But why a vote of first degree, without clemency, within three hours? All through the trial he kept saying: 'They'll acquit me in less than an hour. You'll see.' " White shrugged. "But toward the end, when Abrams kept harping that Shannan had known Al Capone and Luciano, the jury could scarcely hear anything else."

The priest cleared his throat. "Mr. Abrams let me read Ellen Greer's diary. Shannan wanted me to get it for him. Why did you object to Mr. Abrams introducing the diary as evidence?"

"That damn' diary," White muttered. He rubbed the back of his neck. "It was heads you win, tails I lose. The diary was passed on to Abrams by the detective hired by Shannan's wife to get evidence for a divorce. It was probably stolen from the girl's apartment. It brought out two things: one, the girl wanted to get rid of Shannan; two, she was probably a lesbian."

He glanced at the priest, who nodded.

"If she was a lesbian, wouldn't that have been a possible motive for Shannan to kill her? It might have created a certain amount of sympathy for him, but I decided it wouldn't help me as much as it would help Abrams. So I objected."

White paced nervously to a window. After a while he turned to face the priest. "Father, I feel badly about the case. I'm convinced that Shannan is innocent. The killer was the man Shannan saw starting down the stairs when he came out of the elevator, before he went into the girl's apartment. He said the man was sunburned and had bushy hair. Most of the money Shannan gave me, I spent on private agencies to find the man." He held out his hands. "But nothing came out."

"How does the girl's brother fit into the case?" Father Scarpi interrupted.

"The boy saw Shannan leaving the apartment. Joe passed by, not knowing who he was. When Dana went into his sister's flat, she was dead. He saw the blood-smeared knife and called the police."

Father Scarpi looked at White a moment. "I don't know if I should ask you this," the priest said. "Perhaps you'll think I don't have faith in you but—"

"What do you want to know, Father?"

"Would you mind lending me a transcription of the case?"

"Do you think you'll find something, Father?" The lawyer smiled.

"I don't know. Perhaps with prayer."

"All right, Father. I understand, but I can't give it to you now. I'll dig it out and send it to you. All right?"

"That would be fine, Mr. White. I'm at St. Dominic's in the West End."

"My friends call me Larry," the lawyer said, writing the priest's address on his desk calendar. "And Father, in your prayers throw in a few words about us finding the man with the bushy hair. It's too late for an appeal, but I'll ram any new evidence down the governor's throat."

Father Lazzini was in his room, lying on his cot and listening to a small radio on his table. There was a knock at his door, and he shut off the radio. "Come in," he said.

The pastor entered. He sat on the chair which Lazzini offered, and Lazzini sat on the edge of his cot.

"You were not saying the Office, were you?" he said.

"No," Father Lazzini said. "I was listening to the radio. I just bought it last month."

"Ah, yes," Father Ferrera said primly. "Still, in a way, that's what I want to talk about. Have I not given all the curates their monthly stipend at the regular time?"

"Yes." Lazzini nodded, puzzled by the question.

"Why, then," the pastor said querulously, "does Scarpi go about so shabbily? His trousers are shiny, and once I saw a patch on his knee. When he gets into his suitcoat, he is unable to button it; his wrists protrude, and the bib and collar flair out loosely. Now, you know I seldom interfere in the matter of clothing. But one time, as I walked near the altar rails of the lower church," he said, "Scarpi was praying, and there were holes in his boots."

"Perhaps I can explain," Lazzini said. "I was also puzzled. Then Sconnetti told me that at the time of his subdiaconacy, Octavio took a personal vow of poverty. He sends his whole stipend to the archdiocese building fund, and will not accept money. His clothes are gifts from his family. He tells them he prefers laborer's boots. Joe and I sometimes buy him things—handkerchiefs, books that he likes."

"Good heavens, man!" Ferrera exclaimed, "a diocesan priest is not isolated. He should make a decent appearance before his parishioners."

The pastor mused for a while. What a thing to do! A vow of

96

poverty. "Octavio Scarpi," he said as if to himself, "you're a fool." He got out of the chair and walked to the door, where he hesitated. Then he turned around and raising the skirt of his cassock, took a woman's purse from the pocket of his pants. He took out a $20 bill and gave it to Father Lazzini.

"I believe," he said, "that this is enough for a pair of shoes—low shoes, not boots. Will you take care of it, Dante?"

Lazzini nodded and the pastor walked out of the room. Father Lazzini bowed his head. "Misereatur vestri omnipotens Deus," he prayed.

Father Ferrera was praying for Octavio Scarpi. There was a turbulence in the priest that troubled the pastor. Learning of Father Scarpi's vow of poverty was disturbing, too. It was almost impossible for a diocesan priest to maintain such a vow. "Oh, Lord," he prayed, "give him fortitude; make him endure. Don't let him despise his own strength."

The pastor remembered an occasion when Lazzini had challenged Scarpi to a few bouts of hand-wrestling in the outer office. Octavio had been reluctant, but Dante kept heckling the curate, so that finally Octavio accepted, saying he would try once and no more. Lazzini, who was proud of the strength in his shoulders and arms, rolled back the sleeve of his cassock and confidently placed his elbow on the desk. Scarpi sat opposite him and they gripped hands. With a quick effort Lazzini forced Octavio's arm to the desk. He had expected a difficult tussle, and was surprised at his easy victory.

Scarpi acknowledged defeat and got out of his seat, but Dante, winking at the pastor, commented that Sicilians were all show and no strength. Scarpi agreed to one more try.

They gripped hands again, and, with steady pressure, Octavio forced Lazzini's hand down. Dante blinked. "Six out of ten wins determines championship at St. Dominic's," he said. Six times in a row Scarpi duplicated the feat. Lazzini, with some shame and resentment, muttered, "You win."

Suddenly the big priest cried, "What have I done?" and walked out of the office, visibly agitated. Afterward, Father Sconnetti explained that Octavio had taken a vow that he would never engage in body-contact sports. And hours later Ferrera had seen Octavio before the altar of the lower church, weeping quietly.

97

There was a knock at the pastor's study, and Father Scarpi came in. "May I be excused for a few hours this afternoon, Father?"

The pastor did not want to question the curate who stood towering over his desk, his face tense, his hands clenched. But he knew that something was disturbing Octavio Scarpi.

"You may be needed," Father Ferrera said.

"Yes, Father," he said, and walked stiffly out of the office.

A little later the pastor saw Father Scarpi at devotion in the lower church. He waited until the big priest was finished, then went to him.

"Father Scarpi," the pastor said, "if you still want to be excused, you may leave now."

"Thank you, Father."

From his office the pastor watched the big priest leaving the rectory. Father Ferrera had been sitting at his window watching the children playing in the street.

"Scarpi," he murmured, "what are you up to?" He sighed. He knew that as senior curate and pastor he was responsible for the conduct of all the other curates. If a curate defected in his duty, he, Father Ferrera, would be notified and castigated.

The pastor ruffled the bills in his hands. For a painting and plastering of the lower church, $1200. The grocer's bill was $218 for the rectory and $627 for the attached convent. He shut his eyes. Two months' bills. He knew he shouldn't have had the lower church painted. He walked to a little desk near his cot and unlocked the drawer where a frayed and tattered bankbook lay. Father Ferrera thumbed the pages and glanced at the balance: $1367. The archdiocese would pay the sisters' bill. That left him a bill of $1418 to be paid with a $1367 balance. Well, that wasn't too bad. He'd give the contractor $1000 and hold back the grocer's bill until next month. Sufficient unto the day the evil thereof.

The pastor heard the housekeeper tap at the door. "The door's open," he said.

She laid a letter in front of him. It was a special delivery from the Chancery. He slit it open and glanced at the usual greeting. Then the typed words leaped at him: "It has come to our attention that Father Octavio Ignatius Scarpi, second curate, St. Dominic's Church, our diocese, is occupied with matters outside the realm of spiritual necessities.

"We are gravely concerned when any curate engenders, by his precipitate action, the impression that our diocese wishes to intervene in secular affairs."

Father Ferrera shut his eyes for a moment. "Scarpi," he whispered, "Scarpi, what have you done?" He went on reading. "Father Scarpi's interest in Joseph Shannan, a condemned criminal who has all necessary spiritual ministering in the person of the prison chaplain, is deplorable.

"We trust that our brother will assert the necessary authority in correcting Father Scarpi, and in subduing our anxiety."

Father Ferrera glanced at the closing words: "We remain one in Jesus Christ our Lord."

He looked at the familiar scrawled signature and touched the embossed Chancery seal.

Why hadn't they called him, he wondered, instead of using this formal communication? Sighing, he reached for the telephone and dialed the Chancery. He cleared his throat.

"Please connect me with the monsignor," he said. "This is Father Ferrera of St. Dominic's."

"Hold the line, Father." Then: "I'm sorry, Father. The monsignor is not in. Do you wish to leave a message?"·

"No," Father Ferrera replied. "No message." He hung up.

"They are angry," he said aloud.

He began to cough, and when he was able to stand he went to his room, drained of strength.

X

St. Thomas, commenting on truthfulness, says that it is a necessary virtue in man's social life. He points out that when men are dishonest they commit not only individual sin but social transgression as well. For the lie creates distrust, and thus invariably weakens social harmony, sometimes utterly disrupting unity and peace.

But there are times when circumstance forces a person into a lie of omission. As Father Scarpi journeyed toward the State Prison to see Shannan, he decided on such a lie.

The boy's wild laughter irritated Shannan. The kid had been brought into the death block last night from the city jail. He had killed a baby and a baby sitter, and he had laughed and wept all night. The guards said he was putting on an act because he had been declared legally sane and was sentenced to die. Not until dawn had the prison doctor come to give him a hypodermic. Then the kid had stopped laughing and had begun to cry for his mother. Now the kid was laughing again, intermittently.

Shannan had just finished dinner when Father Scarpi was allowed into his cell. The guard took away the tray, counting the utensils carefully. Shannan was sitting on his cot.

"Hello, Joe. How are you?"

"All right," Shannan said. "I can tell you haven't got the diary."

"No, I haven't."

"They wouldn't let you read it?"

"No," Father Scarpi lied.

"It figures. Ah"—Shannan grimaced—"nobody gives a damn."

"God cares," the priest said quietly. "And I care."

"What do you want, a medal?" Shannan was riffling a deck of cards on his cot. With a sudden movement he swept the cards off the bed onto the floor, where they scattered about the curate's feet.

A guard edged to the barred door. "Shannan," he said, "you know it's a privilege to have cards in this cell block. Handle them carefully."

The prisoner ignored him. "God doesn't care, Priest."

"You're wrong, Joe—"

"What do you mean?" Shannan interrupted. "Who're you kidding?"

"Would I be here if I didn't care?" said the priest.

"Words," Shannan said. "You're here because you care, eh? Why do you care? Because your brother was my friend? You're not my brother."

"But you are my brother."

And if Shannan wept, the priest thought, it would be Onofrio weeping; and if Shannan died it would be Onofrio dying again.

"Ah," Shannan said, "you're a priest. What am I getting sore for? You're conning yourself and trying to con me. You'll go back to your church and you'll pray—ah, you're a priest."

"Look," Father Scarpi said urgently. "Look at me, Joe Schianno. I'm a priest. What do you see?" Suddenly the curate snatched off his Roman collar. He unhooked the stays of the tight cassock, exposing his bull neck, his huge chest and shoulder muscles.

"I'm a priest," the giant repeated, "and I'm Octavio Scarpi, a man. But I am nothing if you can't see God in me, or in yourself. Nothing if you can't see God."

Shannan stared at Father Scarpi. He watched the priest replace his collar and try to fasten the stays; only one hook would catch, and the cassock was left partly open.

"Priests don't wear undershirts, huh?"

"That's the racket you think I'm in." Father Scarpi smiled. "I can't buy undershirts, among other things."

After a long time Shannan said: "All right, I've met a priest who hasn't got an angle. All you have is God."

"He's with you as much—maybe more than He's with me."

"Sure," Shannan whispered. "Sure."

"Would you like to pray now?" the priest asked.

"It's too late for praying. Thirty years too late."

"It's never too late for God."

"I don't know the words," Shannan snorted. "Forget it! It's still an act; only, you believe it." He shrugged. "I'm not ashamed of anything."

"I am. I'm sorry for many things. Praying would help me, Joe. If you don't want to pray for yourself, will you try to pray for me—for my sins?" The priest lifted his gown and took out a little black book from the back pocket of his patched and shiny trousers. "This will help you, Joe," he said, and placed the book on the blanket beside Shannan.

"I won't look at it, Father," he said. "I got no time to pray."

"I'll leave it anyway. It'll give me an excuse to see you again. You'll let me see you?"

Shannan got up. "I'll be seeing you, Father," he said.

"If you pray, Joe, don't read the prayer off and forget it. Read it slowly," the priest said. "Take one word, or two, and think about them before going on to the next. That's how I pray sometimes."

"I'm not going to pray!" Shannan said. He turned away.

"Goodbye, Joe."

Shannan did not reply, and Father Scarpi signaled to the guard and left the cell silently.

Shannan could hear him walking down the long corridor. He picked up the book. It was entitled *The Sacrifice of the Mass*. He flung it against the wall, lay down on his cot and stared at the ceiling. After a while he picked up the book and took it to the cell window. Daylight was fading, but he could still see the words. He opened to the page marked by a green ribbon.

Slowly, his lips began to move.

" 'Our Father,' " he whispered, " 'who art in heaven . . .' "

Returning to the rectory, the priest paused in front of Don Peppino Messana's fish store. He heard the reedy sound of a flute and clarinet. People were clustered around the entrance, spilling onto the walk, laughing and talking, eyes flashing, hands moving.

"Father Scarpi!" a boy cried. "There's Father Scarpi!" He plunged through the crowd and took the priest's arm. "You know me. Gaetano! Guy. Don Peppino's son. It's his birthday today." A number of young girls pressed around him, their even white teeth shining. They pulled him into the fish store. A young man with a guitar strummed a fanfare. Don Cicco Franco, who was a musician and barber, held his flute aloft.

"Silence!" he shouted. "Silence! Good priest," he said, "won't you bless this celebration so that the evil eye will be repelled?"

"There's nothing evil here," the curate said, smiling, "except, perhaps, your flute."

"Well, then, bless my friscoletto, or, as is proper, mio flauto."

"Ah, no," the priest said. He held up a glass of wine that Guy had put in his hand. "I'll bless this wine instead." He drank the wine. The people laughed and applauded.

A fat man with a clarinet began a tune in which Don Cicco and the young man with the guitar joined.

The priest looked at the blue tile wall decorated with swarms of canvasback ducks. Large posters advertising imported cheeses, olive oil and anchovies were pasted on the wall. Within shallow pools set in tile beneath the windows of the store live lobsters stired sluggishly and crabs scuttled about, their claws fastened with wooden dowels. Eels writhed in another pool under a pale blue light, and stockfish and baccala were soaking in barrels of water and brine.

"Enter," Donna Nina Messana urged him. "Enter, I pray."

"I'm already in," the priest said, and laughed, "and drinking wine."

"Today my husband is sixty years old," she said, "and it is the forty-second year of our marriage. We are celebrating both dates at once."

"It's wonderful to look back on those forty years, isn't it?"

"The first forty years are the hardest." She wrinkled her nose in laughter. "After that, it's easy."

"Where's Don Peppino?"

"In the back room," Donna Nina replied tartly.

In the smaller back room Father Scarpi found Don Peppino playing three-seven with Neddo Spitoli and two other cronies. Neddo Spitoli, who had worked on a dragger with the priest, stood up to shake his hand.

"Oh, picciotti," he said in the dialect, "here's Father 'Tavio."

The three fishermen stood up and bowed self-consciously. Seeing that he had disturbed them, the priest returned to the front store and sat beside Donna Nina.

The fishmonger's wife regaled him with gossip. A pair of young girls in slacks had shocked her.

"If I had a daughter," she whispered fiercely, eyeing the two girls with evident disapproval, "I would smite with the back of my hand where it hurts most before she would walk about like those two. There is no honor left," she went on, shaking her head woefully. "These girls honor nothing."

But a moment later she nudged the priest. "Ah, Father," she said, "look over there. That beautiful young woman with the red hair. All honor she is, all honor. She is Neddo Spitoli's daughter."

Then Cicco Franco, who was the bandleader, stood on the folding chair in which he had been sitting.

"Ladies and cavaliers," he shouted, holding his arms aloft, "because my wife is not here I am happy. And to show my felicity, I shall play a composition I composed to honor an honorable man, the pesciaiuolo Don Peppino Messana." He raised his flute, then lowered it a moment later. "One must be aware," he said, "that I created this great work after much effort and can only give my music to the world if I have a patron."

"Oh, Peppino," Donna Nina shouted to her husband, "Cicco Franco needs a patron."

After a moment Don Peppino waddled out of the back room.

"All right, Cicco," he said, his huge paunch shaking with laughter, "I'm a patron. What do you want?"

"Well, naturally, on your song," Cicco explained, "much effort was spent. It is called 'Don Peppino's Honorable Serenade.' "

"All right, Chatterer. All right. How much?"

Cicco's glasses slipped down his nose. He gestured vaguely. "For genius there is no price. It is the belly that mourns."

"All right." Don Peppino sighed. "How much does the belly mourn for?"

"Twenty." Cicco squinted at him.

Don Peppino glared.

"Ten?"

Don Peppino shook his head. "Two."

"Five!" Cicco shouted. "Absolutely, positively five."

"Two," Don Peppino roared.

"I shall become a fishmonger," Cicco threatened.

"Give him five," Donna Nina said to her husband. "He'll ruin your business."

Don Peppino gave Cicco the money, and the musician began playing his solo. At regular intervals he would interrupt his composition to drink from a glass of wine.

104

The guitarist was speaking to Neddo Spitoli's red-haired daughter. She seemed nervous and kept glancing over her shoulder.

When Cicco, accompanied by the clarinet player, began a tarantella, the young girls, thinking it droll, danced the native dance. The priest saw the guitarist dancing with the red-haired girl.

Suddenly, Neddo Spitoli plunged out of the back room and, hurling his daughter to one side, grasped the guitarist's coat lapels in fury. Father Scarpi was between them in an instant, forcing them apart.

"How dared this disonorado dance with my daughter?" Neddo shouted. The veins in his neck were like cords. "Did he ask my permission first? Oh, disonorado," he said to the guitarist, "my daughter is a virgin."

"This is America," the guitarist told him heatedly. "This is America."

"Go away," Neddo snarled. "Go away and take your horns with you."

"Come," Father Scarpi said quietly. He took the guitarist by the arm. The young man glared at the proud old fisherman; then he grasped his instrument and went out with the priest, muttering, "This is America."

Father Scarpi looked sadly after the musician as he strode away, the guitar, festooned with gay ribbons, nestled under his arm.

During the evening meal the pastor watched Father Scarpi. He was anxious to settle the Shannan matter, but he hesitated to speak of it at the cena. Perhaps, Father Ferrera thought, if I can keep the priest busy, the matter will die of its own accord.

"Father Scarpi," he said, "didn't you do some kind of art work when you were younger? I seem to remember Father Sconnetti mentioning it."

The big curate nodded. "My brother John had ideas of making an artist of me," he said. "But he didn't get very far. Poor John, he was very idealistic at first, but now he's fallen into the conventional patterns."

"Would you mind doing some painting for the church?" the pastor asked. "It's the backdrop to the Nativity scene," he explained. "Don't you remember, last Christmas, how much the colors had faded? The canvas was so cracked that it looked disgraceful."

105

"Yes, I remember."

After coffee, Father Scarpi and the pastor descended to the basement. Among the crèche figures and beasts, beneath the overturned crib, Father Ferrera found the painting. It had been folded tightly into a square.

Father Scarpi opened it. It was badly creased at the seams where it had been folded. He shook his head. "It would be better to do a new painting."

"Will you do it?" the pastor said.

The priest nodded. "I'd try it on Masonite."

"Won't it be too heavy? You know that the sisters carry the Nativity figures and props upstairs."

"No. It won't be *that* heavy." Father Scarpi hesitated. "But I'd replace this view of old Bethlehem."

"With what?"

"With a scene of the manger itself."

"All right," Father Ferrera said. "That sounds good. Go right ahead."

The priest went into a little room where he took off his cassock and slipped into a sweater. He brought a piece of Masonite to where the pastor was sitting, and marked it off. Then he put it across a pair of horses and sawed it. He took a half-pound of rabbit-skin glue and some whiting from the custodian's locker. As he gazed at the fading scene of the old Eastern town, he saw that the painter must have copied it from a modern photograph, for there were a number of Moslem minarets in the painting.

"I'm going to gesso the surface," he said to the pastor as he started to cut a strapping for a back frame.

"Rest for a moment, Father," the pastor said. "I've got something to say." He began to cough, holding his chest. The priest put the saw down and waited for the coughing to subside.

"I received a letter while you were out." Father Ferrera took off his glasses, blew on the lenses and wiped them. "The Chancery," he went on, "wants to know why you're interested in Joseph Shannan. Nothing to be alarmed about, Father, you understand. I was—ah—well, surprised—about Shannan, I mean. Do you know Shannan, Father? I mean personally. I recall that Shannan was raised in this neighborhood." He was interrupted by a burst of coughing. "It is probably known in the Chancery that you were born here, and it must be thought odd that I have kept you in St. Dominic's. Pastors are careful about such things."

The big priest looked at him, but said nothing.

"Shannan is a controversial figure, Father," the pastor went on. "It would be best not to see the secular authorities about him any more, don't you think? Just what is your interest in him?"

"He was a friend of my brother Onofrio," Father Scarpi said. Then: "No, that isn't the only reason. I'm not able to speak."

"You mean you won't?"

"I can't."

Father Ferrera peered at him over the rims of his spectacles.

"Can it be revealed in a confession?" he asked shrewdly.

"It isn't my sin," Father Scarpi said. "It's the sin of a man who is dead."

After a few moments of silence the pastor said, "I'm sorry that I can't help you." As he got up from his chair, his biretta fell to the floor. Father Scarpi picked it up.

"Thanks," the old priest said, dusting it. He looked up at Father Scarpi. "Octavio," he said, "don't concern yourself with Shannan any longer."

"I feel that I should," the priest said.

"The fact is," the pastor said slowly, "as senior curate I'm responsible for your conduct. If you do anything that seems wrong or unusual, I am notified. Your errors are my errors; your folly is my folly. You know that, Octavio." He sighed. "How does this stubbornness of yours stand in relation to eternity, Father Scarpi? Will it place you one inch closer to God?"

"It is His love that makes me, as you say, stubborn," said the curate.

"Is it, Father? Is it His love?" Pausing to catch his breath, the old priest took off his glasses.

"We priests," he said quietly, "are not protected from worldly things by monastic walls. Our life often seems dull, uninspiring. But it isn't, Father. It never is." He put his glasses back on. "Many times, constant association with the secular world tends to make us lose sight of spiritual values. Are you sure it's our Lord who impels you, or is it some pragmatic idea? Do you know which it is, Father Scarpi? Are you having trouble in justifying your actions? Or does the love of Christ really push you on?"

"Amor Christi," the priest said softly.

"Then, in His name I shall not interfere," the pastor whispered. "May He always guide you—and me."

They were both silent for a moment. Then Father Scarpi said: "Would you mind if I didn't work on the painting tonight? I should like to go for a walk."

The pastor said thoughtfully: "Take a walk. Walks are always good. They clear a man's head."

A few minutes later the priest was walking through the streets of the West End. Young men, arguing and gesturing, stood on the corners; a muffled strumming of guitars and singing voices filtered out of dimly lighted bars. Through unwashed windows Father Scarpi saw the emerald green of billiard tables. He heard the sound of a horse's hoofs, the clattering of iron-rimmed wagon wheels, and looked up to see a boy coming home from market, slapping the reins on the bony rump of a tired beast. He wandered slowly toward the Common.

As a boy Octavio had taken walks through the Common with his father, and had pointed out to the fisherman the trees that had seen the Revolution of 1775, reading off, in a childish treble, the names of different trees.

Peering at the green tablet affixed to a tree trunk, he would say " 'Ulmus hollandica?' That means Dutch elm, Papa. See that one, Pa? That's an Ulmus americana, an American elm. And that's a Tilia vulgaris. That's Latin for common linden."

And his father, limping beside him, would beam with pride at his gifted son, for the old man saw only iron plaques, and the letters on them meant no more to him than the tracks of a tern on the dunes of Provincetown.

It was past eleven when Father Scarpi returned to the rectory. There was no one about. He saw Father Ferrera's copy of Dante's Inferno on the desk, and opened it.

At twelve o'clock, Sconnetti and Lazzini returned. They had attended a play, and had seen Katharine Cornell.

"A lady," the little curate murmured. "A charming lady."

"Father Scarpi," Lazzini asked, winking, "what do you think of a priest who approaches an actress for an autograph?"

"I did no such thing," Sconnetti sputtered.

"Did I say you did? I merely asked 'Tavio a hypothetical question."

"You implied that I did." Sconnetti's eyes flashed, and his hands fluttered up and down. Because he was excited he spoke in Italian.

"But didn't you say you'd like to speak to her?"

"I admit that; I admit that. What harm is there in speaking to a lady? A charming lady poised and cool." His face suddenly became deeply saddened.

Lazzini was about to reply teasingly, but with a look at Sconnetti, he remained silent.

Joseph Sconnetti was thinking that man was made in the image of God but with the lusts of the devil. Once, as Elena spoke to him after a choir rehearsal, he had been fascinated by the sensual way she moved. Somewhere he had seen her before. Was it in an evil dream? he had wondered. Was this the net of his ministry, that he should be obsessed with the lure of the flesh after twenty years in the priesthood? Yet, it wasn't only the flesh.

Sometime ago, Father Sconnetti had confessed his painful temptations to Father Ferrera.

"Father," he had added, "wouldn't it be better if I entered a monastery?"

The old pastor sighed. "Every priest," he said, "has a weakness. It is the Cross they must bear. If we all enter monasteries, who will minister to His people?"

Sconnetti closed his eyes for a moment. Was he alone disturbed this way? 'Tavio, that ox of a man, never hinted at such a disturbance. Dante Lazzini scoffed at the idea of sex. The fat priest would simply laugh.

Father Sconnetti broke the silence. "Will you excuse me. I'm rather tired."

He ascended the staircase leading to his cubicle. After a moment Father Scarpi followed him. When the priest passed Sconnetti's room, he tapped on the door. In a moment he heard, "Good night, 'Tavio."

Father Scarpi gazed at the closed door, shook his head, and entered his own cubicle.

Downstairs, Father Lazzini went into the darkened kitchen, switched on the light and, whistling softly, began hunting for a salad bowl. Finding one, he brought a bag out of his coat pocket, and took out two huge Calabrian onions, a clove of garlic, and three tomatoes. He rubbed the garlic on the wooden bowl, minced the onions, and put them into the bowl. Then he sliced the tomatoes carefully over the onions. He added a sprinkling of oregano, salt and pepper, poured olive oil over the salad, and tossed it competently. He looked for bread, but all he could find was half a loaf of sliced white bread. He frowned. Ah, well, he thought, white bread is better than no bread at all.

Father Scarpi went to bed deeply troubled, and fell into an uneasy slumber. He found himself on a limitless desert, and the shadow he cast upon the yellow sands seemed an endless black line that stretched to the horizon. His mouth and throat were so dry that he couldn't swallow, and his tongue was swollen terribly. Far away he saw an oasis, and ran toward it. When he neared it, the oasis vanished, and a woman stood there instead. She had pale gold hair that fell over her shoulders and covered her breasts. At the sight of her, his thirst died away, and he was struck with an intense desire to touch her. He approached her and felt a length of her hair. As he was about to smooth it away from her face so that he could look at her, the knowledge that he was a priest penetrated the dream, and he awakened.

In the darkness of his cubicle, Scarpi trembled. Had he so little Grace that even his dreams were sinful? Surely God had withdrawn from him to allow an old sin to return! Was it His quiet way of warning him? He switched on the table lamp, got up, went over to the small bookcase on the wall and took out the *Raccolta*. He returned to the bedstead and began to read.

When the first tint of dawn came, he arose stiffly and replaced the book on the shelf. Then he put on his trousers, washed and shaved. He slipped into his cassock, chose a clean collar, and put it on, leaving it, as usual, unfastened.

He recited the Aperi, which precedes the Divine Office: " 'Ut digne . . .' " he murmured. Then he was saying the last few words of the prayer: " '. . . has tibi horas persolvo.' I offer you these hours. I offer you all hours, dear Lord."

He felt that he could not be fit to minister at Mass that morning after his sinful dream. He resolved to fast for the day.

Just then he heard the housekeeper running up the stairs, calling him. "Father Scarpi!" she cried. "Father Scarpi! A miracle! A miracle has happened!"

XI

The *Santa Maria*, Don Salvatore Bacafiggo's fifty-foot dragger, hove into Boston Harbor at five o'clock that morning. At seven o'clock Don Turri heard about the miracle.

Two hours earlier Don Salvatore hadn't been thinking about miracles. The day before he had sold fifteen tons of fish to the Empire Fish Company in Gloucester, and because the crew wanted a couple of days ashore to relax in their homes before the next trip he had steered toward Boston Light. They had anchored at the harbor mouth, and at dawn, Don Turri at the tiller, swung into T Wharf. A stogie clenched between his teeth, he looked down from the pilot-house and eased in beside a lobster boat loaded with traps.

After inspecting the quarter-ropes and the bollards that were attached to the gallows bitt, and making sure that the netting was properly lashed to the whip and stay of the mast, Don Turri went below. The fisherman who doubled as cook handed him a plate of boiled whiting and pastasciutta. The crew ate their breakfast in silence. They knew one another; there was no sense in talking; they ate.

When breakfast was over, the hands drained a gallon of wine and got ready to go to their homes.

Twenty minutes later they were walking up State Street, heading for the West End. The fishermen from the North End had gone through the market district. But Turri preferred to walk by Scollay Square, and if he wasn't too tired he would look at the women.

That morning he glanced at the big whisky sign with the clock. The clock's hands showed 6:45. He drew out his old silver watch, checked the time, and wound it.

Don Turri was sixty-five years old. He had begun fishing when he was eight. He smiled, thinking that in Augusta, his *Santa Maria* would be classified as a large fishing vessel.

When he was a boy he had gone seining for sardines with his father. His father had a seven-foot boat with a sail. If his father were alive and could see the catch he'd sold in Gloucester, the old man would blink his eyes. Don Turri chuckled. But the old man would have seen cod, flounder, tautog, bass, whiting, pollock, and even some bonitas.

Truly, the Virgin Mary had blessed this land with wealth and plenty. There was so much wealth that the ricci could idle away their lives sailing sporting boats and fishing with lines. What a waste of time! Sometimes, when they were dragging in a fish trap, near bluffs of sand dunes, he'd see their sloops dart by with the wind directly abaft and the spinnakers set and pulling. He'd look at the water breaking at their prows, and curling away, and hope they weren't chasing away a big school of fish.

Ah, this America! He sighed proudly. Sicily—now that was something else. Wonderful land, but played out. It was like a fish trap that was dammed and used so constantly that soon a man would cast in his net and find nothing except starfish. In Sicily, women and children used to gather clams, mussels, sea urchins, and periwinkles among the rocks for food. But here many people had never seen some of these seafoods, much less eaten them.

Don Turri had emigrated to the United States when he was fifteen years old, fifty years ago. At that time the poverty-stricken Sicilian aristocracy rode in hired coaches, for which they could not pay. Their removable escutcheons were temporarily fastened on the coach doors.

In those days of mass emigration, lawyers, poets, and artists congregated in the cafés of Augusta to speak of their illiterate, fleeing countrymen. They sat stirring their black demitasse of espresso, discussing the Moorish luxuries of Sicily's Norman kings, commenting on some poem that betrayed Theocritus' Sicilian childhood, or laughing at the petty tyranny of Dionysus, King of Syracuse, when Plato had gone to Sicily to teach the king philosophy. They starved gracefully, these artists, too much in love with their culture, too much impressed by the antiquity of their history and their traditions, to leave Sicily.

Only the peasant left; the peasant and the fisherman, the stonemason, the itinerant farmhand, and the fugitive from some personal vendetta. Don Turri Bacafiggo had fled with them, and now his children's children called him "Grandpa Sal." He knew he would die here, and he was content. God had been good to him.

He walked down Hale Street, but before entering his house he went into the first-floor room that belonged to Don Turrido Bellino. He always paid his respects to Bellino, for when he had come to America the old man had lent him the money to buy the *Santa Maria*, and had shown him where the good fish traps were marked off the shoals so that he had never run aground.

But before he could open the door, Bacafiggo heard a scream. He saw a woman on the street and heard her shouting: "A miracle, a miracle! Donna Maria can hear! The deaf shall listen!"

Early that morning Donna Maria Spinale decided she had lost her bargain with God. Four days ago, as her son Vincent lay dying, the priest had allowed her to stay in the room. Suddenly a bright light had seemed to hover over the priest for a moment, and as it disappeared she was able to hear the priest giving her son the last rites of the Church. She held back a startled cry and listened to sounds she had not heard for fifteen years. She was able to understand the words her son had spoken, for she had come to America when she was a young girl and had gone to school. But the words seemed unbelievable to her at first. Her son a murderer?

She had listened, trembling. So great was her love for her son that, as she heard his confession, she made a desperate plea to God.

"God," she had cried to herself, "God, make my son live and let me remain deaf. For if my son dies, Your gift is of no joy to me. Take back my hearing, and if You want, take my life, but let my son live. As long as he lives, I am content in my deafness and lack of speech."

Thinking that by rejecting God's gift, she could perhaps keep her son alive, she refused to admit that she could hear, and was able to speak. Then, when Vincent died, she was too heartbroken to tell anyone that she could hear again.

Donna Maria had already made breakfast for her daughter Theresa, who worked as a seamstress in a garment factory, and was now heating a little pan of milk, in which she stirred two spoonfuls of powdered cocoa. The cocoa was for her granddaughter, Mary, who attended school at San Domenico. She could hear her son Al snoring,

113

and shut the door of his room. Al was a fisherman, and he would ship out that night.

Theresa came into the kitchen fully dressed to go to work. She sat down for her breakfast of toast and coffee. Mary followed her shortly. Donna Maria embraced Mary warmly.

"You spoil her," Theresa said. "And after the way she behaved about her father!" She looked at Mary. "She doesn't grieve for him. For shame, for shame. Your father!" The child sat opposite Theresa, trembling. Donna Maria put a cup of cocoa before Mary.

"Why don't you say something?" Theresa shouted. "You're sorry— you were wrong. Anything! Don't sit there moping!"

The child burst into tears and got up from her chair. She ran into the room she shared with her grandmother.

"Come back!" Theresa called. She sprang out of her seat and ran after Mary. Donna Maria, wringing her hands, followed. She saw her daughter turn Mary around and slap the child's face.

"Theresa! Stop it!" The words came from Donna Maria, constricted, but plain.

With her hand raised to strike again, Theresa turned and looked at her mother, gaping. Mary lifted her tear-stained face. "Nonna!" she cried. "Nonna!" and ran into Donna Maria's arms.

Theresa stared, her mouth twitching.

"Yes, I can speak, and God has given me back my hearing too," her mother said. Her mouth twisted and she wept softly, hugging the child.

Theresa, sobbing, ran into Al's room. Her brother, quickly slipping into his trousers, ran into the bedroom. "Is it true?" he cried. "E vero?" And, when he was certain, he ran from room to room, flinging up the windows and shouting the news into the streets.

Women cluttered the stairway, and children beat pots and kettles with wooden spoons. A miracle had come to Hale Street! They shouted from their windows to one another, and told their husbands that the Blessed Heart of Jesus was in the street. The bewildered men gathered in the narrow street, arguing and gesturing. Many of them didn't go to work, for it wasn't every day that a miracle happened to a neighbor.

When Bacafiggo heard the story, he resolved to do something. After all, one must respect a miracle.

As chairman of St. Dominic's Fraternity, he rounded up the members, and led them in formal marching order to the building in which the Spinale family lived. Their flat was already jammed with neighbors.

Bacafiggo marched through the crowd shouting, "Make way! Make way for St. Dominic's Fraternity!" It was his intention to lead the members into Donna Maria's home and congratulate her on the miracle. And, naturally, he wanted to see and speak to Donna Maria himself.

But as he was about to enter the building, Donna Maria, accompanied by her Theresa, came down the steps.

"Where are you going?" Bacafiggo asked.

"To church," shouted Theresa over the cries of the crowd. "To St. Dominic's to speak to Father Scarpi."

Church? Why hadn't he thought of that? Naturally, a miracle belongs to Jesus and to His Church, even if the priests are no good. Jesus was not to blame for the priests.

"To church!" Bacafiggo roared. "To church!" He pointed toward St. Dominic's, and the crowd followed, enlarging, as more and more people joined them on the way.

XII

St. Augustine defined a miracle in very few words.

"A miracle," he said, "is something which seldom occurs, something difficult, surpassing the ability of nature, and going so far beyond our hopes as to astonish us."

And St. Thomas said, "We do not marvel at the wonder of a miracle but at its infrequency."

Father Scarpi reflected on the Saint's words as he heard the startled cries of the housekeeper. He ran down the winding staircase, and for the first time he heard the murmur of many voices coming from the street.

Theresa Spinale was in the foyer with her mother, Donna Maria. They were weeping.

"Father," Theresa cried, "Father, my mother can hear! My mother can hear and speak! God! My mother can hear and speak! She saw a light over your head, and she could hear."

The passionate tears of the woman and Theresa's sobbing words made the priest tremble with so great an emotion, that he could not speak. He stared at them, unbelieving. Could it be true? he wondered. But Theresa was babbling how, after fifteen years of deafness, her mother was able to hear again. The deaf and mute woman could hear and speak!

The priest gazed at the old woman, who was wiping away her tears with gnarled, veined hands. She nodded and shuffled closer to him, weeping. Kneeling, she tried to kiss his hand. But the priest gently pulled his hand away from her, helped her to rise, and held her in his arms.

"Father and son," she said awkwardly in the dialect. "Father and

116

son," she repeated. The sounds were muffled but clear enough to be understood.

"My mother says it is you who restored her hearing and power of speech."

"No," the priest cried, "not me, but Almighty God!"

He saw that there were many people outside, and heard the voices shouting of a miracle. He went into the street, and saw that traffic had been stopped by the throng. He asked Father Lazzini to open the church, and he turned to the people and cried out, "Let us thank God." Then he led the old woman into the church, and the crowd followed them. They kneeled before the tabernacle, and the people grew still. The priest said, " 'Our Father, who art in Heaven,' " and the people began to pray with him.

He saw Father Ferrera kneeling beside him, and after the Lord's prayer he heard the pastor whisper: "A miracle. God, make it a miracle. After forty years, a miracle!" Father Ferrera's old body trembled.

Then Elena Mare began to sing the *Ave Maria*. The people within the church, and those in the street, joined her. As the people sang, Father Scarpi struck his breast. "God, I am unworthy," he said. "God, I am unworthy."

Father Sconnetti and Father Lazzini led Theresa Spinale and her mother into the rectory. Father Scarpi followed, walking beside Father Ferrera. There, Theresa told them how Donna Maria had come to speak again. At length, she turned to Father Scarpi, saying, "Father, my mother and I would like to speak to you alone."

Father Ferrera offered them his office, and Father Scarpi led the two women inside.

"Father," the girl said, "my mother was able to hear for the first time when you gave the Last Rites to my brother."

"You mean during the confession?" the priest asked in alarm.

"Yes. As my brother confessed, the sudden light came into the bedroom, and she was able to hear."

"But why didn't she speak then?"

"Because my brother was dying. She resolved not to use the gift from God if my brother died. And she asked God to take back her hearing, and let my brother live. After his death she was too heartbroken to let anyone know she could hear."

Theresa held her mother's hand. "It wasn't until this morning that she admitted she could hear and speak."

The priest felt bewildered. He asked, "Did she understand what he said to me?"

"She's been here for forty-five years, Father. She went to school. She can understand English."

"Then she knows?" the priest asked.

"Yes, Father. This morning she asked who the wrongly condemned man was, and when I told her she insisted on coming here."

"That was good of her," the priest murmured.

The old woman shook her head and said that it was her Christian duty.

"You knew what would happen?" the priest asked.

The old woman nodded.

"Dear lady," he said, "if you speak of this you are admitting that your son was"—the priest hesitated—"a murderer."

"Mio figlio e morto," she said slowly, groping for the words. "The other man is alive. And if he dies for my son's sin, it is a mortal sin for me. My son is dead," she repeated. "May God have mercy on him. I shall pray for him. But this other poor Christian must not die for a crime he did not do."

"We'll have to speak to the district attorney. But first I must see the pastor. Please wait here. I'll return right away."

Father Ferrera was whispering the first psalm of Vespers in the little office of the Blessed Virgin: " 'He has shown might with His arm . . . He has put down the mighty from their thrones. . . .' " He saw the big priest approaching, waiting The pastor said the second psalm, crossed himself, murmured the name of the blessed Trinity, and nodded to Father Scarpi.

"Donna Maria," the priest said hurriedly, "was at a bedside confession while a priest administered Extreme Unction. She refused to leave the room, and the priest allowed her to stay because the dying man was her son and because she was deaf. The priest thought as long as she was deaf—" Father Scarpi faltered. "The dying man confessed to a—terrible crime. Another man has been convicted for this crime. What can a priest do? What should he do?"

Father Ferrera shook his head, understanding at last what had been troubling Octavio Scarpi.

"How can I advise you?" he said. "When it is a question of a man's life or a principle, you know as well as I do that we have no choice. When a man becomes a priest, he becomes one with Christ, and he should view things from the perspective of eternity. You know that, Octavio." He sat down abruptly, took off his glasses, and began folding and opening them absently.

"Still, like Christ on earth, the priest is a man. Perhaps the priest —within principle—should try to save a man's life. But he cannot reveal, or admit hearing, any confesson." He sighed. "I could not stand in that priest's way, Father. God forgive me, I could not.

As Father Scarpi started away, the pastor said, "May you go with God and my prayers."

Three people sat on a long bench in the anteroom of the district attorney's office. One was a young woman with keen eyes that flicked over the room, settling on the typist who sat at a metal desk. Another was an old woman clothed in a drab black mourning dress and wearing a black kerchief in peasant style. Her face was a deep brown, the color of people who have lived in the sun and by the sea for many years. The other person was a big priest whose huge hands were awkwardly folded on his lap.

"Theresa," the priest said to the young woman, "your mother knows why I can't say anything about the confession, doesn't she?"

Theresa nodded. "She understands, Father."

A door opened and a man hurried out. The typist said, "Mr. Abrams will see you now."

A few days before, Abrams had attended a dinner in honor of the attorney general, and had spoken to one of the guests, a monsignor, of Father Scarpi's earlier visit. The monsignor had assured him that the priest was acting in an unofficial capacity and that Abrams wouldn't be annoyed again. "Did he give you much trouble?" the monsignor had asked. "No," Abrams had said, and laughed. A vote was a vote, he had told the monsignor irreverently. And the Catholics were in the majority in the county. When the monsignor had written Scarpi's name in a little notebook, Abrams had been dismayed. He hadn't meant to cause trouble for the big priest, but he hadn't been thinking of a possible chain of command when he spoke.

But apparently the monsignor had only been talking through his skullcap, Abrams thought, for here was the curate again, twice as big as life. He felt irritated by the priest's reappearance.

"Glad to see you, Father," he said, but without offering his hand.

"This is Maria Spinale." The priest brought the old woman forward. "And this is her daughter, Theresa. Mrs. Spinale has something to tell you about Joseph Shannan."

"All right, Mrs. Spinale," Abrams said. "You have the floor."

The old woman stared at him, nervously, then looked at her daughter in appeal.

Theresa went to her mother, and held the old woman's hand.

"My mother is afraid of you." Theresa took a deep breath. "My brother Vincent killed—that girl Ellen Greer!"

Abrams got up. "Young lady," he said, pointing his finger at her, "do you realize what you're saying? You're accusing your brother of murder!"

There was a moment's silence. Then, firmly, Theresa said: "Yes, I do. My brother killed Ellen Greer."

Abrams stared at her; then he spoke into the intercom. "Ruth," he snapped, "come in here! And bring your notebook."

When his secretary came in, he turned to Theresa. "Name?" he asked. "Address?"

After Theresa had answered, he told her to sit down. He took a cigar out of a box on his desk and, stripping off the the cellophane, lighted it.

"All right," he said, "now tell me what happened."

"My brother Vincent," Theresa repeated, "killed Ellen Greer."

"Mr. Abrams—" the priest interrupted.

"Please, Father," Abrams held up his hand. "We have standard methods of interrogation."

"Were you an eyewitness to the killing?" he asked the girl.

"No. My mother heard him—"

"Then why are you doing the talking?" Abrams cut in.

"My mother can't speak very well."

Abrams looked at Maria Spinale. "Can you understand me?" he asked slowly, pointing to himself.

"Yes. I understand."

"Your son told you he killed Miss Greer?"

"Yes, signor." Tears came into her eyes.

"Where is your son?" Abrams asked.

"My son is dead."

Abrams glanced at the priest. "What is this?"

"Apparently Mrs. Spinale's son killed Ellen Greer."

"But now he's dead. How very convenient!" Abrams retorted. "You're not writing that, are you?" he asked his secretary.

"Yes, you didn't say not—"

"All right, all right, cross it out. Hell, leave it in. It won't make any difference." He shrugged.

"Mr. Abrams," the priest said, "am I to understand you're not taking this information seriously?"

"I take all information seriously," Abrams retorted. He shook his head. "Listen, Father! Three men have already confessed to killing Ellen Greer. I took their confessions, although I knew they were crackpots. Here, you want to see them?" He took a few sheets of paper from his desk and threw them on the blotter.

The priest didn't look at them. Abrams got up and walked up and down behind his desk.

"Do you or your mother know why your brother killed Ellen Greer?" he asked abruptly.

Theresa hesitated. She looked at the priest. Finally, she said, "No. We don't know."

"In short, neither you nor your mother saw your brother do the stabbing, and neither you nor your mother knows why he did it. If he did," Abrams added.

When Theresa didn't answer, Abrams said: "All right, Ruth; that'll be all. Tear up those notes."

"Mr. Abrams," Father Scarpi said, "you're saying that the word of these women doesn't mean a thing."

"Frankly, Father," Abrams replied, "it doesn't. Put yourself in my place. A man is convicted of a crime and is waiting for the sentence to be carried out. Then two women come in, tell me that someone else committed the crime, but that that someone is dead.

"They can't say how the crime was done or why. In my place what would you do? What could you do?"

"These women," the priest said tensely, "sacrificed their good name in coming here. Doesn't that bear any weight on the matter?"

"No, it doesn't. All I have is a woman's word that her son, who is dead, told her he killed Ellen Greer. What if she's not telling the truth?" Abrams cried angrily. "What then, Father?"

Theresa rose from her chair and stood before Abrams. She was trembling.

"Are you calling my mother a liar? My mother never told a lie. She's worked hard all her life and she has raised six children. She never grew fat on somebody else's misery like you!"

"Theresa!" the priest cried.

"Let her speak," Abrams said smiling. But, deep within him, he knew that he had heard the words before, perhaps in his own conscience.

"You bet I'll speak!" Theresa stormed. "My mother heard my brother confess when Father Scarpi was giving him the last rites. For fifteen years she was deaf, and when—" She broke off sharply. She realized that in her outburst she had inadvertently betrayed Father Scarpi, and she looked at him, her face stricken.

"Forgive me, Father," she whispered. "Dear God, forgive me."

A deep silence ensued.

Can it be true? Abrams wondered. Can it be true? Was this the one case in ten thousand where the pattern was distorted? The pattern had pointed to Shannan. It had been a clear-cut case as far as it went. There were bound to be discrepancies, of course, unless Shannan confessed before being executed. There always were.

The only irritants in this case had been the two points raised by White: the weeping child and the switch-blade knife. Who was the weeping child? The Greer boy had seen the child, and Shannan said he had heard her. The switch-blade was the kind of knife that fishermen use. Shreds of fish scales had been found on the handle in laboratory tests.

Abrams looked at the priest. "Is that true?" he asked grimly. "Did you hear the man confess to killing the girl?"

But the priest did not answer.

Abrams pushed back his chair and stood up. "I'm asking you again, Father," he said. "Did this man confess to killing Ellen Greer?"

The priest sat mutely gazing at his folded hands, and Abrams shook his head. Shannan must be guilty; there was no alternative pattern. There were no other suspects.

"Is it an oath of silence that prevents you from speaking, Father Scarpi?" he asked. He glanced at the priest and said: "Don't you want to save the man? If you confirm this woman's story you may be able to."

Abrams was on familiar ground; he was the prosecutor again. "Father Scarpi," he cried, "do you or don't you want to help Shannan?" He paused. Then he said, in a harsh, deliberate tone: "If by your silence Joseph Shannan dies, his blood will be on your hands!"

Abrams gazed at the man standing before him. The curate's eyes were fixed, but his huge hands were clenching and unclenching convulsively. Suddenly Abrams leaned over the desk, looked directly into Father Scarpi's eyes, and said, "Damn your lousy principles!"

The curate walked slowly toward Abrams, reached the desk, and gripped the lapels of his suit in his huge hands. The lawyer could feel the great power and strength of the priest. For a long moment the two men gazed at each other silently.

Abruptly Father Scarpi released Abrams, and looked at his own hands strangely, as if they belonged to someone else.

"God forgive me," he whispered. "God forgive me."

Abrams saw tears well into the curate's eyes.

Father Scarpi held out his arms for a moment; then they fell by his side. He turned and groped his way blindly through the door and out of the office.

XIII

Father Scarpi knew that it was difficult to appreciate the beatitude in which our Lord exhorts us to turn the other cheek. As a boy, if he were beset, physically, by another, Octavio would retaliate.

One day, when Octavio was fourteen years old, his father spoke of strength and violence. They were out at sea, working on Don Turrido's dragger, *La Bella Nina*, shearing heads and gutting. The bad years were upon them, and the market was demanding cleaned fish. Whiting was a half-cent a pound with heads, two cents a pound without heads, and two and a half cents a pound headless and gutless. When the dragnets were hauled in, they would slit the net topside and, wading knee deep into the writhing mass, would keep slicing heads off and gutting until dark. Eighteen hours a day was their regular work schedule.

It was summer, and Octavio, who was still of school age, was on vacation. The old fisherman, who venerated scholars, hoped his youngest son would become a learned man. Octavio particularly liked Latin and history.

Don Turrido yelled down from the pilothouse, signaling to Octavio to start the winch so that the crew could haul in the dragnet. The boy threw the lever into gear, watching so that the lines wouldn't tangle. At the same time Don Turrido slowed the dragger down to two or three knots an hour. When the lines were taut, Octavio speeded up the winch and helped the crew haul up the floats and drag-doors.

Don Cicco Testa and Octavio's father, watching the pulleys attached to the forward gallows bitt, waited for the door-shaped drag-weight at the starboard side of the bow. When it appeared from the water, Octavio threw the winch into action, making sure that the

124

cat's-head spool attached to the winch wouldn't be stopped by snarled line. The winch took in slack, bagging the net, hauling it out of the sea and up to the stay on the mast.

Octavio's father and Don Cicco heaved the loaded net over the coaming, where it hung swaying over the deck. It was a good catch. Don Turrido nodded, giving the signal to open the net. Beneditto Scarpi reached under the ponderous weight of the loaded net and slit the bottom. Hundreds of pounds of fish cascaded onto the deck.

The skipper signaled for another dragging. Two hands were stationed at each of the drag-weights. Octavio released the cat's-head and winch, and the hands cast out the floats and doors. Then the four-man crew and Octavio began cutting off heads, shoveling the cleaned fish into the hold.

Beneditto Scarpi was gutting a haddock and talking to Octavio. He said that the use of violence was a shield for fear, and that whoever eschewed violence was of great courage. The fisherman slit the haddock's belly, crooked an index finger into the writhing fish, and tore out the entrails. A wet bandana was wrapped around his head to ward off the hot sun, and his knifeblade was stained red with blood.

"What say you?" Octavio asked in the dialect and, laughing, pointed to his father's knife.

Beneditto looked at his knife sadly, and with a sudden movement hurled it at the creaking mainmast where the blade sank into the wood, quivering.

"Yes," his father admitted. "But did I not say that men use violence to mask their fears? Does not a man fear hunger most of all?"

Beneditto Scarpi splashed through the fish that slithered about his boots and yanked out the knife. His arms fell by his side, and he looked gravely at the sea about him and the sky above.

As the priest left the lawyer's office he recalled his father's words, and he wondered what fear could have blinded him so that he'd wanted to strike Abrams. "Is it Abrams I fear?" he muttered dazedly. "Or is it the man's indifference?"

Plunged into despair, Father Scarpi walked the streets, unaware of where he was going. Abrams was right, the priest decided. Shannan's death would be on his head. Shannan's blood would be on his hands. Was this the peace he had searched for? Was this the peace from the violence that had hounded him all his life? Was the very silence of sacred principles forcing him to commit violence on an innocent man? Was he killing Shannan? And even before the thought was formed, he saw Onofrio falling and dying, Onofrio, who'd been so much like him; quick-tempered, strong, and at times vicious.

Once, Onofrio had—simply in malice it had seemed then—taken away a litter of kittens. Octavio was five or six. He'd spend hours gazing at the litter in a cardboard box behind the stove. They were blind, he'd been told; and he would poke his finger at one of them, rolling it over and laughing when the kitten squirmed back to its mother's side.

One day, coming home from school, he found his brother bending over the cardboard box, stuffing one of the kittens into a burlap bag.

"What're you doing, Oni?"

But Onofrio said nothing and put another kitten into the bag. Octavio threw down his books and picked up the last kitten, clutching it tightly. He ran through the house calling his mother. He found that he was alone in the house, and he ran back into the kitchen, still holding the kitten tightly. He shouted at his brother, hitting at him with his free hand, and demanding to know where he was taking the kittens.

"I got to drown them!" Onofrio shouted. "Drown them!"

Octavio was too young to understand that it might be necessary, and he gazed at his brother, trembling with hatred. Onofrio had gone clumping down the steps, carrying the burlap bag.

Octavio yelled after him: "I hate you, hate you. . . . I'll kill you—you lousy Oni. I'll kill you!"

After a while, still trembling, still weeping, he put the kitten he had been holding tightly in his hand back into the box. But it lay very still. Suddenly, he knew the kitten was dead. "It wasn't me," he whispered. "It was Oni—Oni killed it, not me—Oni!"

It was a long time ago, the priest reflected, remembering his childish hands—strong even then, clutching the kitten. He had a vivid impression of the unsightly child that he had been, tears stinging his chapped lips, scabs from many falls on his knees, and his knee-length stockings, wrinkled, crumpled to his ankles. He became aware that he was walking along the small strip of park that served as an island on Commonwealth Avenue, and he sat on a bench trying to compose himself. Then, because it was a habit to recite the gradual psalms when he was troubled, the priest whispered from the Ninth Psalm: " 'From the depths I have cried to Thee, O Lord; hear my

126

voice. Let Thine ears be attentive to the prayer of Thy servant. If Thou shalt observe iniquities, O Lord, Lord, who shall endure it?' "

Frank O'Meara was sipping at a glass of warm coffee with skim milk in it. He'd read somewhere that skim milk wasn't fattening, and he insisted on using it in his coffee. As a child he'd drunk warm milk in a glass, rolling the glass back and forth to warm his hands during the cold weather. Over the years he had kept the habit.

J. J., who was watching him, cleared his throat and said, "Sandy Mac is in the library."

"Send him in here," said Frank. He closed his eyes for a moment, resting the glass in the palm of his hand. "You know I don't like to leave my coffee."

Sandy Mac came in, and J. J. brought him a cup and saucer. The visitor poured coffee into the cup and drank it black.

"Well?" asked Frank.

Sandy Mac said, "I got a working setup, both ways."

"You sure it'll work?"

"Christ! Would I say so if I wasn't?"

"Okay. It'll work," Frank agreed.

"Of course," Sandy Mac muttered, "it'll be easier if he doesn't want out—"

"No!" Frank said and, getting up, walked nervously back and forth.

Sandy Mac continued: "But I know you'd rather see him sprung. Only, it isn't as easy as, say, the city jail."

"What's the pitch for?" Frank wanted to know. "Is it set up, or isn't it?"

"All right, all right," Sandy Mac grunted, his eyes wavering. "I got two stalkers—"

"Spare me the details," Frank warned. "You know better."

Sandy Mac looked out the window. "All I want to know is how long we wait."

O'Meara stared at him, his fingertips drumming on the tabletop. "Give him two more days," he said curtly. "Then out—one way or another."

"All right," assented the other. "He's your pal."

Owing to the miracle that happened on Hale Street, the Fraternity of St. Dominic, with attached Sorority, gathered to debate on the motion of according membership to other Sicilians. This had come about because Donna Maria, to whom the miracle had been granted, spurned an honorary membership in the organization.

Donna Maria and Theresa, returning from their interview with Abrams, found a deputation from the fraternity awaiting them in their house. Donna Maria, red-eyed from weeping, hotly refused the offer of membership. "Because I was born in Messina," she cried, "I wasn't good enough to belong to your lodge before. Now, I refuse to join it!"

This had so incensed the members that they had called a meeting, and at five o'clock that evening the fellowship gathered and the discussion began.

Don Turri Bacafiggo, in his role as chairman of the fraternity, said: "Fellow honored and honorable members, a great calamity has befallen us. Donna Maria Spinale has refused—incredible as it may sound—an honorary membership in our honored fraternity." A murmur arose. "Perhaps," Bacafiggo went on piously, "the poor suffering Jesus Christ returned her hearing only to deprive her of her intelligence."

"Enough!" a voice cried, and Nunzio Rao, the cobbler and socialist, arose from his chair in the rear where the opposition was seated. "The woman was right in refusing. She was not allowed into the fraternity before, because she is not of Augustan blood; but now that a so-called miracle," he jeered, "has happened to her we want her in the fraternity."

"Who gave you permission to talk?" Bacafiggo roared. "You were one of those who voted for the man who almost ruined the country when he made depression!"

"That man was a Republicano!" Rao shouted. "And I would not be seen dead voting for a Republicano! They are the landowners and the factory owners of the States United."

"Bravo!" Nino Quatrocchi, a fellow cobbler and socialist, applauded. "Bravissimo!"

"Boys," Neddo Spitoli cried, "I've heard enough. I'm not going to sit here and listen to you windbags spout on politics. As far as I'm concerned it's a whorehouse of words." He turned to the lady members and bowed. "Begging your pardon, dear ladies. The question," he went on, "is, Shall we admit other people into the brotherhood, or keep the organization as it is?" He raised his voice so that he might be heard over Bacafiggo's cries of frustration. "I say, let's go see Father Scarpi. After talking to him, we'll vote on the question."

"A priest?" Nunzio Rao cried, horrified. "In this great country there is a demarcation between government and religion."

"What's that got to do with the price of fish in Rockport?" Neddo Spitoli sneered. He didn't like Rao because the cobbler believed in socialism, and it was well known to Neddo that under socialism a man must give up his property to the government and that the wives can make free love to any stranger who walks by. Neddo Spitoli had decided, a long time ago, that nobody was going to make free love to his wife and nobody was going to take away the house he bought in Medford after thirty years of working on the sea. Nobody, not even the Pope himself.

"It's not that I'm in favor of priests," Neddo Spitoli explained. "But this one is an Augustan like ourselves. He understands us."

"I protest!" Nino Quatrocchi and Nunzio Rao cried out in unison.

But the women got up and began to berate them so that the two cobblers sank back into their seats, audibly commenting on ignorance and stupidity.

"I take it, then," Bacafiggo said, snapping the straps of his suspenders, "that the members in favor of consulting the priest on this matter are in the majority. So be it. I'm against it," he grumbled, "but I shall observe the democracy."

"All right then," Nunzio Rao agreed, "I too shall observe the democracy and see the priest."

Don Turri Bacafiggo made a motion that a delegation composed of the two cobblers, the professor, two fishermen, and himself would pay the priest a visit, and there was much applauding. The other members were to remain until the delegation returned so that they would be able to vote on this troublesome matter.

Then Bacafiggo said: "Now, I have the honor of telling you that the statue of San Domenico is on the way from Sicily. Today 'u professore received a telegram from the great Sicilian sculptor Ettorino Sciacco from his studio in Florence that the statue is coming."

"But," Cicco Franco, the barber and flutist, protested, "if the statue is from Sicily what is Sciacco doing in Florence?"

"How do I know?" Don Turri growled. "Don Peppino Messana was present when the professor got the cablegram. Professor, what did the message say, exactly?"

Swearing softly, the professor got up. He stuck a finger in his collar to loosen it, fingered his flowered necktie, and stroked his beard. That idiot Messana, he groaned to himself.

"Ah, ebbene," he said, bowing from the waist. "The cablegram to which the honored chairman refers was received by me this morning. The words were substantially the same. In explanation why the message came from Florence, I have heard that many sculptors own airplanes. Perhaps the Ettorino, after sending the statue, took a quick trip to Florence. There in his Italian studio—for one must realize that these great sculptors have studios in many of the large countries of the world—he sent the cablegram." He bowed again, and the members wildly applauded.

Shortly, the delegation to see Father Scarpi gathered at the entrance of the Fraternity.

Father Scarpi, when he arrived at the rectory, went directly to his cubicle. He switched on the table lamp and saw a shoebox lying on his cot. Beside it, a slip of paper read: "For Father Scarpi—who takes mad vows." He opened the box, took out a pair of shoes, and sat on his bedstead staring at them. "It must have been Sconnetti," he said. And, smiling, he took off his boots and put on the new shoes.

He went out into the corridor and, hearing the muted sound of a violin, knew that Sconnetti was in. He tapped on the door, and the little curate opened it.

"Ah, 'Tavio," Sconnetti said absently, "entrare."

The floor of the room was strewn with sheet music, and Father Sconnetti stood barefooted, violin and bow in hand, before a music stand. "Working on a new bit for the Liturgy. Without a piano," he explained, "I'm helpless."

"I've put on the shoes," said Father Scarpi, raising the cuff of his trousers.

"Ah, now. Well done." Sconnetti tucked the violin under his chin and ran the bow up and down the strings quickly.

"Thanks, Joe."

"Thanks?" repeated the little curate. "Oh, I didn't get you the shoes."

Father Scarpi stared at him. "Who—"

"Dante bought them. The pastor gave him the money."

Father Scarpi went downstairs where he found Father Ferrera in the lower church, kneeling at the altar rail. He waited until the old priest stood up, then went to him.

"I want to thank you for the shoes—"

"Ah, yes, the shoes," Father Ferrera interrupted. "Do they fit? Father Lazzini bought them, you know." The pastor smiled at him. His breath caught, and he began coughing again. He turned away.

The big curate stared at the crucifix on the wall of the lower church, above the altar, no longer remembering the words he'd prepared. He wished he could tell Father Ferrera everything he wanted to say in order to win his esteem and friendship, a blessing he'd been hoping for all his years at St. Dominic's. But he couldn't say anything. It seemed to him as if he could cause the pastor only trouble. He was a big ugly man, he told himself, tongue-tied and a dunce.

"There's a package for you," the pastor said. "In the office. It's a special delivery."

In the pastor's office Father Scarpi found a bulky manila envelope. It was from the law office of White, Fisher, and Aaronson. Realizing it was a transcription of the Shannan case, he picked it up to take to his cubicle. As he stepped into the corridor, he heard Father Lazzini calling for him. The stout priest told him that several men were waiting to see him in the outer office.

Father Scarpi saw a dozen men standing stiffly in front of the wall bench, hats in hand. He recognized Don Turri Bacafiggo and Don Peppino, and greeted them.

"Be comfortable, gentlemen." The priest said "Signori," the greeting of respect given to titled lords. The result of this courtesy was that no one would sit in the available bench, except for one bearded man who closed his eyes with an air of boredom. The curate knew the bearded man was known as the professor, and he'd often wondered what the man was doing among the group of rough and uneducated fishermen and laborers that composed the fraternity of St. Dominic.

"Is it permissible to smoke?" Don Turri asked.

The priest nodded, and the fisherman brought forth a twisted stogie which he broke in half, offering half to Father Scarpi. The curate refused it but thanked Don Turri courteously. Don Turri lighted it, puffing furiously. As if this were a signal, the others began lighting cigars. Father Scarpi went to the nearest window and flung it open.

Don Turri said: "I wish to discuss a matter with you. But as I'm prejudiced, I refuse to speak of it." He cleared his throat. "But, being chairman of the fraternity," he went on, "I shall argue if a certain party mentions the discussion."

"He's referring to me," Nunzio Rao explained. "I'm not a chairman. I'm not a vice chairman. I'm nothing—"

"Hear, hear!" Don Turri broke in, growling. "As if we didn't know."

Rao glared at Bacafiggo and said: "You'll have to pardon him, Don Octavio. He's a fisherman—"

"Wretch!" Don Turri interrupted, roaring. "What are you insinuating? Did you know, you piddling cobbler, you nail-eating scapparo, that all Christ's disciples, save one, were fishermen? And who was that one? I, Turri Bacafiggo, will tell you. He was Judas, and he was a shoe cobbler like you."

"Signori," the priest admonished.

"Scusi, Don Octavio," Bacafiggo muttered.

"I also," Nunzio Rao echoed. "Seeing that the chairman won't speak," he went on, "I shall bring this matter out."

"But make quick," Don Peppino said. "Make quick."

Rao turned back to the priest after gazing coldly at the fishmonger. He said, "I have the honor of informing you that the statue of San Domenico is on the way from Augusta."

"But what are you saying?" Don Turri shouted. "That was to be my honor. You are to bring out the discussion on hand."

"Un minuto," Nunzio Rao cried. "The discussion revolves around St. Dominic." He smiled triumphantly. "The argument is this, Don Octavio. As you know, the fraternity is made up only of members who came from Augusta, or whose fathers came from Augusta. We have been this way for thirty years; but I, for one, am against it."

He paused for a moment and glared around the room. "Here we are," he declared, "in Bostono, in the cradle of liberty and we are biased in our attitude toward others. Let it not be said," he orated, gesturing to the professor, who seemed to be asleep, "that Nunzio Rao was against the democracy. I say we should open our doors to East Coast Sicels, including those of Catania, Syracuse, and Messina."

"Bravo," Nino Quatrocchi applauded. "A Christian gesture."

"Ah, ha," Bacafiggo cried, "now I shall speak! These socialist cobblers would allow anybody in. Next they'll be saying that Italians are on the same level as Sicels and should be also allowed into the lodge. By the beard of Moses, never!"

"But who said anything about Italians?" Rao protested. "I specifically mentioned only East Coast Sicels."

"Give you cobblers a heel," Bacafiggo shouted, "and you'll take the whole shoe."

"Mr. Chairman," the priest asked, "exactly what is the question?"

"The question, honored priest, is this." Bacafiggo paused, then said, "If St. Dominic is the patron saint of Augusta, shouldn't only Augustans be allowed into the lodge?"

"That is not the question," Rao shouted. "The question is, Should or should not the lodge be open to other than Augustans?"

"Gentlemen," the priest reminded them, "St. Dominic may be your patron saint, but he belongs to the world."

"But it was at Augusta," Bacafiggo pointed out, "that he mounted his white charger and defeated the Moslems."

"Gentlemen," Father Scarpi asked, "what is your reason for not admitting other Sicels?"

A member made his way to the curate. "I'm Santo Cuniggio," he said. "If this were not a church, my stories would make your hair curl."

"Well, then give me only general reasons," the priest said.

"But you are a priest, a virgin. Such stories are not for you." Cuniggio sounded distressed.

"Signori," the priest reminded them, "you forget that I hear confessions."

"True," Cuniggio admitted. "Well, then, there's no need telling you that all other Sicels, except those from Augusta, are liars, cheats, and thieves. You already know that, but here's something else. There are houses of ill-repute in all the cities Rao mentioned in his speech. Right, Professor?"

The bearded man with the necktie nodded. "Precisely," he said. "Catania, Messina, and Syracuse all have houses of ill-repute. I have been there," he added.

"Rooster," Rao hissed.

"But what kind of argument is that?" Nino Quatrocchi asked. "There are houses of ill-repute in Augusta too."

"Ah, ha," Bacafiggo chortled. "Tell them, Professor! Tell them."

"Well, then," the professor declaimed, "it is true that there are

133

houses of ill-repute in Augusta. But"—and he paused to emphasize his point—"not one of the, ahem, ladies was born in Augusta. I have been there," he added.

"Can it be true?" Quatrocchi asked faintly.

"What do you mean, 'true'?" said Rao, annoyed by his fellow socialist. "How do I know? But it has nothing to do with the discussion on hand."

"Nothing?" Quatrocchi quavered. "Don't you see, if it's true that we of Augusta are more chaste and our women more virtuous, well, then, we must keep the others—"

"Basta!" Nunzio Rao shouted. "I think we should return to the Fraternity and discuss this question further. We know how the priest stands on the issue."

They decided, after more quibbling, that Rao's idea was a good one, and they began walking out. As they filed by, the priest detained Carmello Poverello.

"What is it, exactly, that you're professor of, Your Honor?" Father Scarpi inquired.

Poverello flushed and, seeing that the others had gone ahead, said: "I am a poet—not Dante, but a poet. Actually, the title was bestowed upon me by—by the Fraternity. But I am an expert on anatomy. . . . an *expert*." At the threshold, he turned back to the priest. "I'm nothing," he said quietly. "A peddler who scratches lines of poetry. But because I am able to read and write—I taught myself—they call me Professor. And many years ago I told them that I was a professor, for I did not wish to disappoint them. It makes them feel good, for they say, 'It is not too bad that I am uneducated, for does not the professor peddle for his bread?' And I read many truths and tell them of these things." He shook his head, smiling. "Do you think I'm wrong?"

"No," the priest replied gently. "I think you are right. Good night, Professor."

Carrying the package from Larry White's office, Father Scarpi went upstairs to his cubicle.

Father Ferrera sat in his office, staring at a white sheet of paper. He had decided to write to the Chancery about Donna Maria Spinale.

He wrote:

134

"Dearly beloved brother in Christ:

"A singular incident occurred in our parish this day. A woman who was deaf regained her hearing and is able to speak intelligibly. There are certain details that make me think this case may require special interpretation. . . ."

He stopped writing and looked at the words. How could mere scratches of the pen convey his feeling? he wondered. Ah, wouldn't it be holy if it were a miracle? But he put the thought away. He shook his head; he wasn't worthy. He was too unworthy for the Lord to extend a miracle to his parish. These things he knew. At night, on his iron lettino, gripping the bedstead as he coughed, he'd try to enumerate his sins. Many had faded from memory, but those that were important would never fade. He was sure of that. Sins that had seemed small at the time he'd committed them, were no longer small, and they loomed larger and larger as the years passed by. He had committed a sin once against his earthly father for which he never felt he could atone.

"Forgive me, Father," he said to himself. "Dear God, forgive me."

He'd been newly ordained and was walking down Cambridge Street when he committed that sin of pride. He was walking beside a diocesan monsignor, Monsignor Rafferty, who had wanted him to act as an interpreter. The monsignor was going to interview a group of newly arrived Italian Franciscan fathers of the Order of Friars Minor, who were to be billeted in the Church of Santa Lucia in the North End. The monsignor was a friendly man who spoke gently of the Church's responsibility to the Italian immigrants. He was Irish, and said that the Irish in Boston did not understand the traditional Sicilian anticlericalism. Father Ferrera spoke of the Sicilian point of view eagerly. He mentioned his own father, then quickly amended that his father was not anticlerical because he was educated, was an engineer of sorts. Actually, his father was a street paver.

As they were walking to their meeting with the immigrant friars, Father Ferrera saw his father working at his job of paving streets. The old man had his head down and held a cobblestone between his knees. He was chipping it to make it fit, and Father Ferrera did not recognize him at first. The monsignor paused to comment on the

135

man's skill, and at that moment the young priest's father raised his head, and Father Ferrera found himself looking at the familiar stern countenance with the flowing mustache. He stood still for a brief moment, shocked by the encounter. His father, seeing him, smiled, but the priest hurried past him without saying a word, pretending to listen attentively to the monsignor. He could never forget the reproach in his father's eyes, and the way the old man's face had grown white with shame.

Soon afterward his father died, and he had never atoned to him. It seemed such a trifling incident, Father Ferrera reflected, such a small sin of pride, and yet he knew it had been sweepingly revoking of God and love. It had never ceased to make him feel unworthy.

Father Scarpi ripped open the manila envelope, and in his eagerness his hands trembled. After seeing Abrams, the priest had telephoned White to tell him of Donna Maria's confession to the district attorney, revealing as much as he could without a further breach of faith. The lawyer had informed Father Scarpi that a transcription of the Shannan case was in the mail on its way to him.

The big curate sat in the straight-backed chair in his cubicle, and, taking out the transcript, began reading. The white glare of the paper hurt his eyes, and the type blurred, making his head ache.

At nine o'clock the housekeeper told him that a parishioner wished to speak to him. It was Don Turri Bacafiggo.

The rough, old fisherman shifted his blue eyes unhappily.

"I do not know if what I am to tell you is an honor." He shrugged. "Maybe yes, maybe no. But I am here to tell you that we voted on the question of membership. The majority voted to allow East Coast Sicels into the lodge."

"I'm glad," the priest said. "It should have been done long ago."

"And your people are of Augusta." Don Turri sighed. "What is this world coming to? I am proud to say I voted against admission. But, as the cobbler says, one must observe the democracy." He shook his head sadly. "Mark my words," he went on, "next the agitators will agitate for the admission of Italians. And after that non-Italians; and the only thing worse than an Italian is a non-Italian.

"This America, the greatest land in the world," he observed, "believes this fable of equality."

The alarm clock on Father Scarpi's writing desk indicated five-thirty when he found the first mention of the child in the testimony. The section was headed: First cross-examination of State's witness Dana Greer (Counselor L. White questioning).

Q. You say you saw a weeping child? A little girl?

A. Yes, sir. She came down the stairs.

(L. White suspends queries. He informs the Bench that there is no child listed in the building. He stresses that the child may be an important witness. The Bench rules that defense is digressing. L. White resumes questioning of witness D. Greer.)

Q. Did the child say anything?

A. No, but she was crying hard.

A few minutes later, the priest found the child mentioned again: State's case against J. Shannan. It was sub-titled: First testimony of Dana Greer. (District Attorney A. Abrams questioning.)

Q. Please tell us everything you did prior to entering the apartment your sister was living in.

Q. I bought a package of cigarettes in the store at the corner, then walked to the building where my sister lived. I buzzed my sister's apartment but no one answered. I buzzed the custodian but no one answered there either. A woman came out. No, first the woman came out, then I buzzed for the janitor.

Q. The custodian didn't reply to your ring?

A. No. Later, I found out that the buzzers were out of commission.

Q. Please go on, Mr. Greer.

A. As I rang for the janitor, a man entered the building and went on the self-service elevator.

Q. Mr. Greer, is that man in this courtroom?

A. Yes, he is.

Q. Will you please walk up to him and point him out?

A. Yes, sir.

(State's witness Dana Greer descends from chair, stops before the defendant, and points his finger at Joseph Shannan.)

Q. Thank you, Mr. Greer. Please go on.

A. It was cold in the vestibule, and as my sister had promised to be home at five o'clock I thought she was detained somewhere. It was then about 5:40, so I thought I'd wait for her in front of her apartment.

137

Q. You were cold in the vestibule and, thinking your sister would return momentarily, you decided to wait upstairs where it was warmer?

A. Yes.

Q. Continue.

A. As I was smoking a cigarette, a child came down the stairs. She was weeping. I finished the cigarette, and went on the elevator. When I got off at the fourth floor, a man came out of my sister's rooms. He had his hatbrim turned down, but I recognized him. It was the man who had gone up a few minutes earlier.

Q. Wait a moment, Mr. Greer. Was it the same man you pointed out a moment ago?

A. Yes, sir.

Q. You saw Joseph Shannan coming out of your sister's apartment?

A. Yes, sir. I did.

Q. Please go on.

A. I saw that the door of my sister's apartment was ajar; the lock was broken. I went in and found my sister on the floor. She was covered with blood. A switchblade knife lay on the floor beside her.

Father Scarpi turned over the pages of the testimony until he came to the page marked: Cross-examination of defendant Joseph Shannan; District Attorney A. Abrams questioning.

Q. Mr. Shannan, did you see anyone before entering Miss Greer's apartment?

A. No, but the lock of the door was broken.

Q. Did you hear anything as you went into Miss Greer's apartment?

A. Yes, I did. I heard a kid crying.

Father Scarpi looked away from the sheet of paper. Why had a weeping child walked downstairs from the fourth floor to the entrance? he wondered. There was an elevator in the building. Why did she walk? Why had she wept? How old a child was she?

Father Scarpi glanced at his watch. It was six o'clock. He put the pages of testimony back into the envelope, and went down to the sacristy, where he dressed to celebrate early-morning Mass.

XIV

When Father Scarpi went into the dining room for breakfast, the pastor and the other curates were waiting. They murmured greetings and Father Ferrera said Grace.

"Is it true that the statue of St. Dominic is on its way?" Father Ferrera asked Father Scarpi.

"I was told it was."

"You made all necessary arrangements, I suppose? I mean, about space in the upper church for the statue and the ceremony?"

"Yes." Father Scarpi nodded. "Everything is ready. I'm to make a speech on the steps of the church after the Saint is taken through the streets by the lodge members."

Father Lazzini saw Sconnetti gazing at him. He flushed, suspecting that Sconnetti disapproved of his appetite, and stopped eating.

"Tell me, Father"—Lazzini winked to Scarpi—"what do you think of a priest who asked an actress for her autograph?"

"I did no such thing," Sconnetti fumed. "That's a lie."

"Gentlemen," the pastor said suddenly. "I must go to my room." He sounded exhausted. "Father Lazzini, please cover for me." He nodded to the curates as he got up from his chair and shuffled out.

The curates were silent for a while. Father Lazzini looked at the food before him, then, with a muttered exclamation, pushed it aside.

"He's not well," Lazzini murmured.

Sconnetti arose. "I'll be in the lower church," he said quietly.

The two remaining priests looked at each other. "Shall we join Joe?" Father Scarpi suggested.

Father Lazzini nodded assent. They went to the lower church, and knelt beside Sconnetti at the altar rails. There, the three of them prayed for the pastor.

At ten o'clock the housekeeper told Father Scarpi that a visitor was downstairs. It was Marie Shannan.

"Hello, Father," she said, twisting a handkerchief around her fingers. Her face was very pale.

"He still won't see me," she said. "After you left the other day, I sat down and thought the whole thing over. I turned it around in my mind. In the beginning, Joe loved me, and I think I loved him." She hesitated. "I know I love him. Now he hates me. He won't see me. Father, is it my fault? He was the one who got himself involved. Not me. Not me," she repeated. "I love him," she added. But it seemed an effort for her to say the words.

Why do men and women destroy each other? the priest wondered. Was it the inconstancy of life itself that did it? The doubt, the insecurity? How does hate spring from love? How can a man detest a woman he has held in his arms, and loved?

Marie Shannan looked at him imploringly. "Father," she said, "take me to him. Please."

Thirty-odd years before Shannan had served time for armed robbery. He was fifteen then, but the prosecutor had thought him older. Because his birth certificate had been lost, the Court decided he was eighteen, and sent him to prison instead of to reform school. It was there that he made contact with the Midwest ring. He had been hired as a truck driver by Al Capone while he was still in prison.

It was at Concord that he learned that the big men never got caught, except by accident. Only young punks without a pay-off got jailed, but not the big men. The big men angled their way into the rackets and the gambling joints, or built up protective associations for bookmakers. A guy could flourish, shaking down gamblers and bookies, and only have hooligans to worry about, not a country full of cops.

Driving a truck for the prohibition gold-mine sounded like a good beginning to Shannan. Only a few Coast Guards and a handful of Federal police were concerned about bootlegging. And if he were tried in a civil court, money could tie up prosecution. Joe got smart fast in those days.

Shannan shut off his portable and stared at the wall of his cell. That was a long time ago, he thought. A long time ago.

At mailtime a guard brought him a thick letter.

"It's from the State House," the man said.

But Shannan knew it wasn't a reprieve. He would have heard, by the grapevine, of any reprieve long before it came. Maybe it was the diary. Three days before Father Henry had asked him if there was anything he'd like, and Shannan had repeated his request for the diary.

Now, as he ripped open the envelope, the words leaped at him: "Certified Copy of Diary. Property of Ellen Greer, deceased." There was a date, a seal, and a scrawled signature.

Shannan began to read.

He was still holding the sheet of paper in his hands when the guard unlocked his cell door. Shannan took the slop bucket from under his cot and carried it to the door to exchange it for a clean one.

The trusty who took it from him had his back to the guard. He looked at Shannan and mouthed, without sound, "Out?"

But Shannan was staring past him remembering Ellen Greer. Suddenly, with a vicious movement, he swept the pages of the diary from his cot to the floor.

The guard slammed the door.

"What's the matter with him?" asked the trusty.

"You know better than to talk while doing your work," the guard said. The trusty turned and walked away.

Shannan gazed at the papers on the floor, his face white, his hands clenched.

All right, he thought. I'll get word to O'Meara. I want out, all right. I want out.

At the prison, Father Scarpi introduced Mrs. Shannan to Father Henry, who got a special pass for her and accompanied them to the death block.

Shannan was standing at the window of his cell. The sheets of paper were strewn on his cot. When the guard opened the door and the curates entered with Mrs. Shannan, Joe stared at his wife. "Get out," he said harshly.

"Joe, give me a chance," she pleaded. "I love you. I'm your wife."

"All of a sudden you love me," Shannan said. "Why? Because they're going to kill me? Don't worry," he said flatly, "everything is yours."

"I don't want your money," she cried. "Do you want me to say I'm to blame? All right, I'm to blame." She began weeping quietly.

"No," he said dully. "Nobody's to blame—except maybe her."

Father Scarpi saw that Shannan was holding some typewritten sheets out to him. The priest glanced at them and his heart bounded.

Father Henry said, "I got in touch with a friend in the Governor's office."

Shannan looked at Father Scarpi. "You read it, didn't you?"

"Joe," the big curate stammered, "forget it. Why don't you forget it?"

"Forget it?" Shannan cried. "How can I forget it?" He glared at the priest, gritting his teeth.

"Joe," Father Scarpi said, "pray to God for help."

"God!" Shannan sneered. "God is a word people use as an excuse. There is no God!"

"Don't say that!" his wife cried. "Don't say that, Joe."

She reached out to touch him, but he turned his back.

"Why did you come?" Shannan asked his wife. "To see me squirm? To hear me say I loved you?" His voice broke, and he paused, gripping the bars of the door. "Okay," he cried hoarsely, turning back to her. "Okay, I loved you. It was you that pushed me away. You said, whatever I touched became rotten. All right, I stopped touching you. How many years ago did that happen, Marie? How many years ago?"

"I'm sorry, Joe. I'm sorry," she sobbed.

"Was it the time," he persisted, "you found out you just wouldn't be invited anywhere, no matter how much money Fix Schianno had?"

"Stop it, Joe," she begged.

"No," he said. "I've got to find out. When did we split, Marie? You knew I got my start bootlegging. You knew I was in the rackets. But you married me. You could've had any one. Why me, Marie? Why me?"

"I loved you," she sobbed. "I still do."

"No," he said. "You don't love me. You're sorry for me. You feel guilty at the way I'm going to die. But you're not to blame, Marie. The only thing your'e guilty of is marrying me in the first place."

He looked at them like an animal baited beyond endurance. "Now get out of here! All of you. Get out!" Suddenly he drew back his fist and smashed it into the wall. Father Scarpi heard the bones splinter, and winced with pity. Shannan looked at his hand and wrist, bewildered. Blood seeped from the lacerated skin and the wrist flopped unnaturally. The priest knew that it was broken.

The guard outside walked to the telephone. "Get the infirmary," he said laconically.

"Joe," Father Scarpi murmured, "Joe." But Shannan shook his head dumbly. The big priest turned, took Marie Shannan's arm, and led her from the cell.

After Octavio Scarpi's mother died, and while their father was at sea, Octavio's oldest brother, Annunziato, cared for them. Nunzio would hurry home from the cigar factory to cook supper. Unfortunately, he gave more thought to their stomachs than to their clothes, and the younger boys were always more or less ragged. Nunzio was tolerant and would overlook their escapades. The rule of their father, however, when he was at home, was strict.

One day, after Octavio had hurt a boy in a street fight, his father gave him a beating. He was ten or twelve then, and his father's heavy hand made his head ring.

That night, the old fisherman came into their room, where Octavio shared a pallet with his brothers John and Nick. The old man shook his son in the darkness.

" 'Tavio," he whispered.

The other boys sat up apprehensively, and Octavio cringed on the pallet.

"I want to speak to 'Tavio, and you, my other sons, must listen," Beneditto Scarpi said.

The old man drew Octavio near him. His rough hand passed over his son's face and he kissed the boy. "Did I strike you too hard, my son?" he asked.

"No, Pa. It doesn't hurt, now."

"My son," he said. "I had a brother named Onofrio, after whom I named my sixth son. My brother was a giant who stood a hand over six feet. He was possessed of great pride and greater strength. When we came to America, my brother and I, we lived in Lawrence. We worked in the woolen mills, and I began to save money to enable your mother to follow me with Nunzio, who was three, and Salvatore who was an infant. But there was a strike, during which a policeman shot and killed a woman by accident. To cover their mistake, the police collared my brother, who was a fearless striker, thinking to blame him for their crime.

"Onofrio," he went on slowly, "could not understand what they wanted. Had he submitted, he would not have been tried, for there were many witnesses who saw the policeman firing the shot that killed the woman." The fisherman paused and blew his nose, overcome by emotion.

"But, because my brother was strong and proud, he fought back. While they were taking him to the police station, he broke the neck of one policeman, strangled the other, and escaped. The police found him some days later, hiding in a cellar, and they shot him down as if he were a mad dog."

He patted Octavio's shoulder awkwardly. "My son," he said, "it's wrong to put your faith in strength. For when the strength leaves, what shall sustain you?"

The fisherman kissed the boy again and went out of the room.

At the rectory, the housekeeper knocked on Father Ferrera's door and handed him a special-delivery letter. It was from the Chancery.

The old priest opened the letter, hoping it would be a reply to his communication about Maria Spinale. But instead, he read: "We are extremely displeased at the continued disobedience of Octavio Scarpi. Our brother cannot have been firm enough in forbidding the curate's interference in secular matters. We must remind our brother that he is as responsible as is the second curate. . . ." The letter's tone was harsh and unequivocal. Father Scarpi must be stopped, the pastor thought. Taking the letter with him, he went downstairs.

When Father Scarpi returned to the rectory he found Father Ferrera waiting for him. The pastor was pale and unsmiling. He passed the letter from the Chancery to Father Scarpi.

"Will you explain this?"

The priest read the letter and handed it back to Father Ferrera. He said nothing.

"Have you broken principle?" Father Ferrera asked.

"No, Father. I haven't."

"Father," the pastor asked, "why are you interested in Shannan?"

"He is innocent."

The pastor stared at his subordinate. He could scarcely rebuke Octavio without rebuking himself. But he knew that he must speak.

"You've decided that he's innocent, but you're not a lawyer; you're a priest," he said harshly. "God forgive me, I encouraged you to continue this folly. I was wrong, Father." He paused to catch his breath. "In the eternity which is to follow, this breath of existence is insignificant," Father Ferrera said softly. "And a hundred years shall seem as a single sigh."

He looked compassionately at the priest towering above him. Then, in a sudden flush of sympathy, he cried: "Octavio, what frustrates you? Is it Shannan's death, or the concept of death itself?"

But Father Scarpi remained silent.

"Father Scarpi," the pastor said at last, "I am ordering you not to concern yourself with Shannan any longer."

The priest said nothing.

Father Ferrera shook his head. "I think you've done a fine job in the parish. But I believe the fact that you were here creates emotional havoc within you. I may have to transfer you to some other parish."

After a long silence, Father Scarpi asked, "May I go now?"

"Yes," the pastor said, "you may go. But before you leave is there anything you would like to say? My boy, my boy, what is troubling you?"

Octavio Scarpi looked at Father Ferrera. "Father," he said, "I must do my duty as He has given me the light to see it, but sometimes I am troubled."

"What is it, Father?" the pastor asked kindly.

"I'm confused," the priest said. "Sometimes, I have the feeling that God has lost His faith in humanity."

"Is this a confession, Father?" the pastor asked.

"No."

"How old are you, exactly, Father Scarpi?"

"Thirty-eight."

Father Ferrera fell silent for a moment. Then: "No matter what you are troubled by, as a curate you cannot indulge in the luxury of philosophy. As a curate you must not interest yourself in theoretical problems of mercy and justice. Leave that to the Jesuit fathers whose specialty it is.

"A curate like yourself does not have the moral right to think for, or of, himself," he went on. "There are too many bewildered people who need your help."

The pastor was gripped by a sudden spasm of coughing, and the priest turned away. The pastor wiped his lips slowly. "There is nothing more to say. You must not concern yourself with Joseph Shannan. That is a direct order, Father Scarpi."

In the basement hospital of the prison, an intern and two male nurses worked on Shannan's wrist. They gave him an injection of cocaine, took some X-rays and, deciding it was a clean break, quickly set the broken bone, and put his wrist in a cast.

When one of the prison officials inquired about Shannan, the intern said that the injury was not serious and that the prisoner could be returned to his quarters the following morning.

By lunchtime the effect of the cocaine had worn off, but he demanded food. A male nurse and an orderly trundled a chrome food truck through the small ward. The orderly placed the dinner on the bed tray and winked at Shannan.

"Still sticking it out?" he whispered.

Shannan shook his head. He knew that the best time for a break would be while he was in the hospital ward. "I want out," he hissed.

The orderly blinked and nodded nervously. "How long you got in the hospital?" he asked. Shannan shrugged.

"Hey, Doc," Shannan said to the male nurse, "how long am I going to be in this smelly place?"

"Don't worry, tough guy; you're going back in the morning."

Shannan looked at the orderly. The man nodded again.

When lunch was over, the orderly removed Shannan's dishes.

"Tonight," Shannan whispered.

The orderly shrugged. "Maybe," he said.

"Take off your pants," the male nurse said, holding out a pair of hospital pajamas. Shannan got up slowly and removed his prison trousers. He slipped into the pajamas the nurse held open. When the nurse gathered up his pants, a book fell to the floor. The nurse picked it up, looking at it. It was the Sacrifice of the Mass that Father Scarpi had left with Shannan.

Shannan muttered: "Give me that; it's mine."

The nurse said nothing and turned the book over to him.

Shannan frowned, defensively. He opened the book with his free hand, turning the tiny pages with his thumb. He remembered that as a boy, he had known all the prayers in Latin. He propped himself up on the pillow, and, covering the portion of the page that was in

English, he tried to read the prayers in Latin. Then he ran across a prayer he recognized.

" 'Ego sum," he whispered, "resurrectio, et vita . . .' " Shannan shook his head and frowned. The big bastard, Onofrio's brother, believed all this, he thought. He crumpled the tiny book in his hand and started to throw it away. But then he checked the impulse, and tucking the book into the sling that supported his broken hand, he lay back and looked at the white ceiling.

XV

Mrs. Salvatore Bacafiggo and Mrs. Neddo Spitoli sat in the outer office waiting for Father Scarpi.

Giovanna Bacafiggo was a short, bowlegged woman with a round full face and wispy gray hair arranged in tight curls. Above the curls she wore a tiny box-like hat with a long pheasant's tail. She was stout, and her enormous bosom was propped up by a tight girdle. A few hours earlier her daughter Bianca had helped her into the corset while she berated the girl for not having found a husband. She had intimated that when she was her daughter's age more than one man had sent his suit to her father. Since Bianca had fastened the girdle, Giovanna hadn't dared to draw a full breath for fear the corset would burst and her bosom go charging out. Because Giovanna wasn't one to tempt the devil, she breathed very slowly, never quite filling her lungs.

Concetta Spitoli sat opposite, with her hands folded primly on her thin thighs. She was gaunt-faced, and much inclined to revery. People would come to her, and tell her their dreams, and Concetta would interpret them, skillfully pointing out their hidden meanings.

Mrs. Spitoli was very rarely called by her husband's name, for she had been known as Concetta Sicca, or Skinny Constance, since she was a little girl in Augusta. Now, as she looked at Mrs. Bacafiggo, she shut her eyes and thanked the Blessed Virgin that she was not fat and ugly.

Mrs. Bacafiggo, glancing at Concetta Sicca out of the corner of her eyes, was also content. How did such a skinny, dried-up thing dare go out on the street? she wondered. Thank the poor suffering Jesus she wasn't skinny and homely!

The two ladies were close friends.

They were the acknowledged leaders of the progressive clique in the lodge. It had been Concetta Sicca who, after five years, declared that the word "fraternity" alluded only to males. Did the men think, she had wanted to know, that they were pulling the wool over her eyes?

She had persuaded all the women in the lodge to address the men as "Sorella," or little sister, until the men signed an armistice and included the words "With Attached Sorority" to the charter of their organization.

When Father Scarpi entered the outer office, he recognized the ladies as members of the lodge, and welcomed them.

"Good day, Mrs. Bacafiggo," he said to Concetta Sicca. She glanced at him to see if he was joking. But, deciding that he was in earnest, she grimaced.

"I'm Mrs. Spitoli," she said. "This is Mrs. Bacafiggo."

"How may I help you?" he asked, bowing.

"We were wondering, Father," Mrs. Spitoli said, "if the novena the church is holding the third week after Pentecost could be for St. Dominic."

"June is the month of the Sacred Heart," the priest replied. "It is more appropriate to direct the novena to that."

"That would be nice," Mrs. Bacafiggo said, but she sounded unconvinced.

"Well, Father," Mrs. Spitoli said, "you know as well as I do that we women started the subscription for the statue of St. Dominic."

"Yes."

"But the men," Mrs. Bacafiggo interposed, "are taking the credit for it. My husband walks around as if he were carrying St. Dominic on his shoulders all the way from Sicily."

The priest maintained a careful silence.

"Now," Mrs. Spitoli went on, glaring at her friend, "if during the Novena of the Sacred Heart you would mention that it's due to the ladies of the lodge that St. Dominic is being brought here, the ladies would appreciate it. After all," she added, "it is the truth."

"Yes," Mrs. Bacafiggo echoed, "it's only the truth."

Tactfully, the priest assured the two ladies that he felt some mention should be made of their success in the subscription drive. The two friends stood up, contentedly, and started to leave.

"I am glad I suggested we come here," said Concetta Spitoli.

Giovanna Bacafiggo forgot her corset and drew a deep breath which she hastily released. "What do you mean, Concetta Sicca? You know that *I* suggested coming to see Octavio Scarpi! It was *my* idea!"

The priest, smiling to himself, watched them go.

At six o'clock the supervisor of the State Prison laundry blew the whistle that dangled over his paunch, the convicts stopped working and filed out of the room. A moment later the lights within the laundry were dimmed.

In the darkness of a huge wash tank a man stirred uncomfortably, splashing the residue of water at the bottom of the tub.

"Everybody here?" he whispered. "Szabo, is that you?" He nudged the nearest figure.

"No, Bat. He's behind me."

"All right, then," Bat Corey said, "let's go. You first, Szabo."

A wide-shouldered man opened the clothes trap and swung out of the tank. He wore the uniform of the prison. Three other inmates emerged after him. The last man said: "Szabo, look under the desk. Giggy, you fish around under the tubs. I'll look in the dryers."

The four men began searching quickly.

"I found them," Bat Corey called out. "Here!" He took out three revolvers and an automatic from an opened dryer.

"All right, you know what to do," Bat said quickly. "Go to the west wall, shoot at the searchlights, and raise hell, but that's all. Don't aim to kill. And if they pin you down, give up."

"Sounds screwy," one of the men snorted, "but my wife can use a couple a grand."

"What about you, Bat?" asked Szabo.

"Never mind me."

"What did you say the signal was?" someone asked.

"The supper bell."

"Should be time for it." Szabo smiled in the dark, thinking that it was the first time inmates were getting paid off simply to do some shooting in the prison.

"Don't try making a break," Corey warned. "Just throw lead until you run out of bullets."

"Level with us," Szabo said. "Is the show to get Fix Shannan out?"

Corey nodded.

"It figures," Szabo said. "We put on the act, and Fix gets liberated."

They waited for a few moments in silence. Then the supper bell rang.

"Here goes nothing," Corey said. He broke a window and vaulted into the dark yard. The other three men followed.

"Good luck, Bat."

Corey watched the three men run toward the west wall; he headed for the infirmary.

When Szabo reached the wall he aimed at the sentry box and pulled the trigger of his .45. Searchlights sprang to life, and the guard on the corner sentry box cut loose with his machine gun. Guards ran through the yard.

Bat waited until they had passed; then he cut across a shaft of light and plunged into the infirmary.

As the hospital guard fumbled for his revolver, Corey leveled his automatic and the guard raised his hands. At that same instant Shannan came out of the ward and struck the guard with the cast on his hand. Shannan took the guard's revolver.

"Let's go," Corey said. They ran out of the infirmary and made for the administration building.

Earlier, two men had walked up to the front gate of the prison and asked the guard for directions. When the machine gun cut loose within the prison grounds, one of the men held an automatic in the guard's side while the other struck him with the butt of his revolver. As the two men walked toward the administration building a black sedan pulled across the narrow entrance to the prison, blocking it. A man wearing a police uniform got out of the car and began re-routing traffic. When the two men reached the door of the administration building, a siren began blasting at half-second intervals. One of the men pushed at the door. It swung open.

"A grand for this door," he said to his companion.

They walked down a long corridor that ended at another door. A guard who was peering out of a barred window held a revolver. One of the intruders shot quickly. The guard spun and fell against the wall.

"Hold it!" the guard said. "I'm hit."

One of the men took the guard's revolver. "Cover him," he said to his companion. He walked to the door that led to the inner yard, took a key out of his pocket, and unlocked the door. He looked at the key.

"Two grand," he said.

A moment later, Shannan burst into the corridor through the open door. As he ran in, gunfire clanged against the iron plates of the door, and Bat Corey, who was behind Shannan, fell without a sound. The intruder slammed the door shut. The other man motioned to Shannan, and they ran back toward the entrance.

A few moments later, they jumped into a moving car which swerved right, toward Boston. Another car came from the opposite direction and, stopping to pick up the man who had been directing traffic, momentarily blocked the prison entrance.

Shannan could still hear the sound of small arms, and the siren kept shrieking at half-second intervals. He looked down at the prison pajamas he was wearing, and began to laugh.

Father Scarpi was in the basement at work on the manger scene when Father Lazzini called down from the head of the stairs, telling him that he was wanted on the phone.

"Father Scarpi speaking," he said into the mouthpiece.

"This is Larry White, Father. Shannan has escaped from prison."

"What!" the priest said. "When?"

"I don't know the particulars," White replied. "I just heard about it myself a few minutes ago."

The priest looked up at the stained-glass window above him. Was this the hand of God?

White said slowly, "Does Shannan know about the confession, Father?"

"No. No, he doesn't," the priest said, and slowly put back the phone.

When Abraham Abrams was called to the phone, he had a highball in his hand. "Abrams speaking," he said.

"This is Captain Boyle of Headquarters. Fix Shannan broke out of prison an hour ago."

The district attorney almost dropped his glass. "Shannan?" Abrams asked. Now he was convinced that Shannan was guilty. Only a guilty man would run away, he thought.

"Yeah, Fix Shannan," Boyle answered. "I called because I remembered that Shannan threatened you after the trial. I'm going to send a couple of plain-clothes men to cover your house."

"Who'd you put in charge of Shannan's capture?"

"I chose a special detail of plain-clothes men and put Dicker of the riot squad in charge."

"Will you switch me to him?"

In a moment a fresh voice was on the wire. "Lieutenant Dicker speaking," it said.

"This is Abrams. I've been told you're on Shannan's escape."

"That's right."

"I want you to have a line tapped. It may help."

"Whose line?" Dicker asked.

"The rectory of St. Dominic's Church in the West End."

"I'm not tapping any rectory lines!" Dicker said.

"I'm tapping it, not you," Abrams retorted. "If you don't want to handle it, I'll get some of my own men on it—"

"All right, all right! But it's a church line—"

"The statutes don't limit where a D.A. can wiretap," Abrams retorted coldly. "I'll send down a man from my office with the equipment. If you get any results let me know."

"Don't kid me, Abrams," Dicker said harshly. "Even you couldn't tap a state line, but they'll let you tap a church." He hung up abruptly.

For what seemed a long while Abrams sat staring at the phone. At last he sighed, lifted the receiver, and began dialing.

At ten o'clock Father Scarpi turned on the desk radio in the outer office. The newscaster opened the program by saying: "Joseph Shannan, convicted murderer, escaped from prison tonight. At the time of the escape, Shannan was in the prison hospital being treated for a broken hand. Police speculate that the injury was sustained as part of an intricate escape plan.

"Details concerning the escape have not been released as yet, but reliable sources indicate it may have been an inside job.

"A guard, Elmer Brice, was wounded while attempting to stop the escape, and a convict, Paul Corey, was fatally shot.

"Joseph Shannan is the killer who was scheduled to die on July 7th for the murder of his girl friend, Ellen Greer. At the time of his trial, the one-time racketeer king boasted of his friendships with Lucky Luciano, who has since been deported to his native Italy, and with Al Capone, the Chicago kingpin of crime who died soon after his release from Alcatraz."

The priest turned off the radio. After a while he felt so restless that he decided to go out for a walk. He headed toward the Common.

Black clouds were massing in the sky as he entered the Common. He sat down on a bench for a few minutes, to try to calm his agitation. A clap of thunder rumbled, and a bolt of lightning cleft the sky. The darkness blackened, and trees loomed before him; their gnarled and twisted branches tossed, and the swaying, leaf-laden limbs thrashed in gusts of wind.

After a while he arose and began to skirt the Frog Pond. Suddenly he heard a cry for help. By the lightning's flash he saw a group of boys who seemed to be whipping a whimpering figure. Startled, Father Scarpi ran around the rim of the shallow pond.

Earlier that night Tommy Rietti had gone to the Black Orchid near the North Station with a few members of his gang. Tommy was sixteen years old. He had quit school three months before to help out in the house. His father had told him he'd been crazy to quit, that now all Tommy had to look forward to was a life of working for his bread until he died. But Tommy had become sick and tired of hearing his mother say that they were poor.

At the cafeteria, Tommy drank coffee and talked to some of his friends. After a while the gang decided to make the rounds in Jerry's car. They went to a café in the South End, where they got mixed up in someone else's fight with a Negro man who was with a white girl. Tommy saw a man take out a knife and he ran up from the side and hit the man flush on the jawbone, knocking him out. They all ran out, then, because they knew that the bartender was phoning the police.

Jerry let them out near the Common because he had to get to work on his night job in a sugar factory. They were walking through the Common, laughing and telling jokes, when Nookie, a thin boy with features that were set in bitter lines, saw an old bearded man lying on a park bench.

"You want to see that wino dance?" he said. He loosened his wide belt and buckle and advanced toward the old man sleeping on the bench. "Get up!" Nookie ordered.

"Leave the old basil alone," Tommy protested.

"What're you, a hero?" Nookie's pale eyes were slitted.

Tommy looked at him and shrugged. "No skin off my nose," he said.

"How the hell can he sleep on that bench?" one of the boys asked.

"They sleep on anything, these winos," Nookie laughed. He struck the man across the waist with his belt. Then some of the other boys took off their belts and began hitting the old man.

"Dance!" Nookie screamed. "Dance!"

The man's rheumy old eyes opened; light fell on his bearded shrunken face. He gazed dully at them, scarcely feeling the blows at first. Then, slowly, he held up his arm in feeble resistance.

"He won't dance! He won't dance," someone shouted.

"I'll make him," Nookie gritted. "Dance, you sonamabitch wino!"

Lightning cut the sky, and the thunder drowned out the sound of Nookie's blows. In the sudden flash of light, Tommy saw a giant with a twisted face and a crooked nose, his eyes wide with anger, lumber around the Frog Pond. The giant tore the strap out of Nookie's hand and flung it away.

"Kill him!" Nookie screamed. "Kill the bastard!"

One of the gang slashed the big man across the face with the buckle of his belt. Enraged, the giant gripped Nookie, lifted him with one hand, and hurled him into the pond. Then he struck another boy with such force that the boy slumped against a tree and sprawled to the ground. Most of the others, frightened by the man's appearance, his size and strength, threw down their belts and fled.

"You too," the man said hoarsely, grasping Tommy. "You too!" His grip tightened about Tommy's throat so that the boy could scarcely breathe.

"Don't hit me!" Tommy gasped. "Don't hit me."

Father Scarpi heard the boy pleading, and he tried to withhold his blow, but the compulsion was automatic, and his clenched right hand struck the boy full in the face. The boy fell in a heap at his feet.

"My God," the priest said softly, "what have I done?" He shook his head, trying to clear it. He looked at the boy, motionless, at his feet. "God forgive me," he said.

The boy he had flung into the pond was splashing out of the shallow water.

"Son," the priest called out, "are you all right?"

"You bastard," the boy swore at him. "You bastard!"

The priest saw him run, sobbing, and holding his arm, through the rain that had begun to fall. The boy he had hurled against the tree rose to his feet and lurched away. Dazed and repentant, Father Scarpi looked down at the inert form of the boy. At some time during the confusion the old man had disappeared.

"Somebody hit me," the boy mumbled.

"I hit you," the priest said.

The boy groaned and peered up at the priest.

"I didn't hit the old guy," he said sullenly. "I was with them but I didn't hit him." Suddenly he whispered, "You're a priest."

"Yes. I'm a priest." Blood ran from the boy's nose. The curate passed him a handkerchief. "Wipe your nose; it's bleeding."

The boy felt his nose gently.

"It's broken," he said fearfully.

Father Scarpi could hear the honking of auto horns on Beacon Street. He glanced at his wrist watch. It was two o'clock.

"What are you doing out so late?" he asked.

"You're not going to pull me in, are you? I got a record. I didn't hit the old guy."

"Where do you live?"

"The West End, Father Scarpi," the boy muttered.

"You know me?"

Tommy nodded. "I go to St. Dominic's."

The priest put his hands over his face. "Why did they beat the old man?" he asked. "God in heaven, why did they beat the old man?"

"They wanted him to dance," Tommy replied, "but he wouldn't dance." Then he said, wonderingly, "But you hit me. And you're a priest!"

"Is that all?" the priest asked vaguely. "Is that all?" The boy was silent. Finally, the priest shouted, "Get out of my sight!" The boy turned and walked away. The priest just sat there and wept bitterly. Not only for the old man, but also for the boy, and for his brother Onofrio, and finally for himself.

XVI

Shannan and a lean man got out of the car at Atlantic Avenue and walked around T Wharf to the left side of the pier.

A man emerged from the shadows.

"Bennie?" he asked.

"Yeah."

"Follow me."

They walked to the edge of the pier, where the man called Bennie descended a wooden ladder. Shannan followed, but the lean man remained on the deck of the wharf and faded into the shadows of the building on the pier. Shannan clambered into a lobster boat and went down into the part of the hold below the pilothouse. Frank O'Meara and another man were sitting on the edge of a cot, smoking.

"How're you, Joe?"

"Good. Thanks to you, Frank."

"It cost some."

"Close to ten grand." O'Meara waved his cigarette holder. "Joe, this is Tami. Remember him?"

Though Shannan didn't remember him, he nodded. "Sure. Hi, Tami."

"Good to see you, Joe." They shook hands.

"Why don't you go topside, Tami? Just to back up the kid on the pier." Frank chuckled. "You know how these young punks are."

When Tami went out of the cramped hold, Frank said, "He bodyguarded for me when Brown was shot. Took a ten-year rap, and all he wanted was enough money to buy this boat. He likes it."

"About the money, Frank: I'll raise it—"

"Christ, you're washed up, Joe. What kind of a shake can you get from one of your guys running the operation?"

"I'll get a good shake if I buy protection from you."

"I'm not selling, Joe."

"All right, then, move in." Shannan sighed. "But I want 200 grand for the works."

"That's everything: numbers, the racing setup, fixed games and floaters, the cannery and the soap factories."

"Not the factories." Shannan shook his head. "They're corporations, and my wife holds the shares."

"All right, I'll give you 175 grand for the gambling operations."

"Where'll I go, Frank?"

"It's a big world." O'Meara shrugged. He didn't care where Shannan went now. He had done his job.

"You're wrong," Shannan said flatly. "The world's small. Like an eight ball."

The two men became thoughtful.

Finally O'Meara broke the silence. "Tami will take you to Florida. From there it's your picnic, Joe, but I'll line up a couple of guys down at the Keys who'll freight you anywhere: Cuba, Panama—anywhere."

Shannan said, "You could have had me killed, Frank."

O'Meara arose. "Never entered my mind," he said. "A man doesn't kill his friends."

"No," Shannan murmured. "He only kills himself. By inches. It's a slow death, Frank."

O'Meara's lips curled. "Forget it," he said. "There's a million fishes in the sea. What's a wife?"

Shannan shook his head. He hadn't been thinking of his wife.

Beneditto Scarpi was helped into the automobile by his granddaughter Rose. He resented her assistance, and pushed away her hand. Did they think he was helpless? he wondered. True, he was no longer young, but his father had lived to see ninety-one years. He wasn't that old yet. His father had even gone to sea at that age. Beneditto had been young, only fifty, when the letter came from a sister saying his father had died. Nowadays, these cake-eaters all died young. They had no teeth. They all went to doctors who fixed teeth. But still they died young and without their teeth.

Now, his granddaughter said she wanted to marry this young cake-eater who was driving the automobile. He liked the cake-eater, but didn't like his surname because he couldn't say it. He would say Gree, and everyone would laugh. He knew they meant no harm. But they should have more respect for an old man.

The other day Rose had told him that Octavio wouldn't marry the couple because the young man was Protestanti. He had been surprised; he thought the boy was a Christian. He had looked at the boy and said to his son Victor, "The boy doesn't look like a Turk."

But Victor had explained to him that the boy was not a Turco; he was a different kind of Christian. Beneditto had heard rumors of such people all his life; because he did not wish to appear ignorant he nodded wisely.

"Does he believe in the poor suffering Jesus?" he had asked.

Yes, he was told, Greer believed in Jesus Christ but not in the Blessed Virgin. This had puzzled Beneditto. How could one believe in Jesus and not believe in His Mother? How could one look at a chick and deny it must have come from a hen? He had refrained from asking questions because the more questions a man asked, the more confusing people got. What tremendous knowledge those scholars must possess! He had been told that his son Octavio knew as much as a schoolteacher, as well as being a priest. After that he was a bit overawed whenever Octavio came to see him.

But then, Octavio had always been bright. He remembered taking Octavio for walks when the boy was seven or eight. They would stroll through the Common, and the boy would read the words on the iron plates on the trees. Beneditto had known then that Octavio was destined for great things. True, he had been a bit disappointed when Octavio wanted to become a priest; but if bon alma Agatha, his mother, were alive, she would be happy. Had she not induced the boy to become a helper at the Mass?

Beneditto liked Greer. Sometimes when Greer was at the house the old Sicilian would say, "O Gree, me uddi?" And the boy understood he needed help, and they would go into the garden, and Greer would help him pull the weeds and kill insects. He was a good boy, Gree. That was why he was taking them to Octavio now.

When they arrived, Beneditto would say to Octavio, "You may be a priest, but I'm your father and I want you to marry these young people in a church as Christians." Octavio wouldn't refuse him. He wouldn't dare.

Rose Scarpi sat beside Dana. She wanted very much to be married in church. She would wear white, and there would be ushers and bridesmaids. She would ask her friend Josie to be the maid of honor. Dana would do whatever she wanted. He loved her. She hoped that soon he would get a better job. But she didn't want him to become a foreman paving roads for her father. He wanted to finish college while he worked nights as a watchman. Then, in two years, they would be all right. If only Father 'Tavio wouldn't be so stubborn. Josie had told her that anybody could get married in church as long as they agreed to bring the children up as Catholics. She had told that to Dana, and now he would speak to Father 'Tavio about it.

Dana Greer braked for a light. His Catalina was running beautifully. He had made a good buy in the car. Ten more payments, he thought, and he could call his soul his own. He wished a soul were as easy to understand as a car. He could open the hood of the Catalina and take the motor apart and put it back together again too. But the soul, what was that?

He couldn't understand the urgency Rose felt about getting married in church. They had almost had an argument over it the other night. He had said: "What's the matter with that quiet wedding we agreed on? All we have to do is get to the first justice of the peace in New Hampshire. No fuss. No bother."

Rose's mother had bristled then. "Listen, Mr. Greer, Rose is my only daughter. She's getting married in church."

"If your mother and sister were alive, Dana," Rose had said, "they'd want you to get married in a church too."

He was a little awed by Rose's mother. She was a woman who wasn't afraid to speak her mind. Besides, he had been ashamed of Rose's reference to his mother and sister. He pushed the thought of Ellen out of his mind. She was dead and he'd forget her. He had told Rose how she had been killed, and Rose had felt sorry for him. Even Rose's mother had hugged him when she heard the story. But of course they didn't know the whole story. They didn't know what Ellen had been.

Dana took the right-hand lane that led toward the lower end of Charles Street. He imagined facing the priest. He'd say: "Give Rose a chance to be happy. And anyway, I understand that I can be married in church." He intended to speak boldly to Father Scarpi.

After the morning Mass, Father Scarpi abstained from breakfast and retired to his cubicle. At eight o'clock, however, the housekeeper called to him to come down. The priest had already told Father Ferrera that he would not attend breakfast, and he wondered at the summons. He found Rose waiting for him at the foot of the staircase. A few yards behind her, Dana Greer stood below the stained-glass window which he was examining self-consciously.

"Rose." The priest smiled.

"We have come to apologize. I'm sorry, and so is Dana."

"You have done no harm," the priest murmured.

"I mean about marrying outside the Church. I didn't mean it." Rose smiled at him. "Grandpa is in the car."

"My father, outside?" he asked. She nodded, and the priest ran bareheaded into the street. Rose and Dana followed him.

Beneditto Scarpi was leaning against the wall of the church with the morning sun streaming full on his weather-beaten face.

"Why didn't Your Honor enter?" the priest asked.

"At my age it is best to feel the sun. It warms my bones."

The old man looked at the priest. "What have you done, my son?" he asked. "Your face looks haggard, and there are pouches beneath your eyes."

"Never mind me," Father Scarpi said, laughing. "But Your Honor, is all well with you?"

"All is well by me," he said. "I am ready to meet my Maker when He so wills it. But I have heard that you disappointed these two young people." He nodded to Rose and Dana.

"The young man bound my hands, my father," Octavio Scarpi replied.

Beneditto studied the cement walk; then he said: "Remember the time we were on Vincenzo Pirandello's dragger, and a storm caught us off Marblehead. Remember how the barca was drifting toward the rocks, and how Vincenzo's son, who was a little older than you, and who loved living—what was his name?"

"Peter," Father Scarpi said. He remembered the skipper's son at the radio trying to contact a vessel for help. He had finally torn the radio apart in a frenzy. Then he had stared at the wires in his hands, saying in amazement, "Can it be true that God will let me die?"

"Yes," Beneditto agreed, "Pietro. You too thought we were lost," he went on slowly. "We prayed, you and me, and Pietro joined us,

161

and even Don Cicco Testa. And after a bit the waves subsided and a Coast Guard cutter saved us. Remember?" He smiled, the folded skin around his eyes quivering. "Cannot God help us again?"

The priest looked at Dana Greer.

"If I say that I've changed my mind since last Sunday," Dana observed quietly, "it wouldn't be true." He turned to Rose, and she reached for his hand.

"Don't be afraid," she whispered. "Tell him, Dana."

"I was brought up a Baptist," he said, "but somehow I stopped going to services. It wouldn't be much for me to turn Catholic, but I'd only be kidding you and myself. But isn't there a way," he asked, "for someone who doesn't believe in formal religion, but who has faith in God, to marry a Catholic?"

The curate glanced at Rose for a moment. "Yes," he said, "there is a way. It is possible to get a dispensation from a Chancery or bishop. But you won't be allowed a regular church ceremony." He looked at Dana. "I could marry you in the chapel or in the sacristy."

Beneditto Scarpi drew himself erect. He spoke to Dana in the dialect. "Marry her," the old man said, "for the Church is the heart of men." The priest saw that his father's eyes were damp. "The sun hurts my eyes," Beneditto explained, blowing his nose into a handkerchief.

"We shall marry in the sacristy," Rose said.

"You must agree to bring up your children as Catholics," Father Scarpi said to Dana.

"Sure," the boy said. "Sure, Father."

"You will forgive your old father?" Beneditto asked. "I know I may have said something that is against the rules of His Church, but I do not think He will consider me evil for it."

"He would never consider you evil, my father." The priest put his arm about his father's thin shoulders.

"I have committed many evil follies," the old man said. "But soon I shall be with the ones who are gone—ah, so many more than those who remain. The other night I dreamed we were together: Annunziato, Nicoletto, Onofrio and—I wept that I had lived so long that I could not remember my wife."

"Don't say that, Nanno," Rose protested. "Don't talk of death."

"You must not talk of it, Rosa." Beneditto grinned. "You must talk of children, like these who are running about." He gestured to

162

the children who were passing, notebooks under their arms, on their way to school.

"See how pretty they are?" he went on. "Listen to their voices. Is it not like music? They are in love with living."

Father Scarpi looked at the little girls who greeted him as they passed by. When a tall long-haired girl turned the corner, bearing a bouquet of red roses, the priest recognized Mary Spinale, and recalled her fear at her father's wake.

Earlier that morning, Donna Maria Spinale remembered that it was fifteen years ago to the day that her husband, Biagio, had passed away. It was during Biagio's illness that she had become deaf. She had heard him crying out with pain, and when she ran into his room she tripped on a chair and fell, hitting her temple on the foot of the bedstead. When she was conscious once again, she was told that her husband was dead. But she couldn't hear the words, and it was discovered that she had become deaf. It was not long afterward that her long silence began.

Every year, for fifteen years, Donna Maria had sent two dollars to the church of San Domenico so that Biagio's name would be mentioned at the eleven o'clock Mass. But this year, after her hearing had been restored, she had forgotten to send the money. When she remembered, a sudden guilt flooded through her. How could she have forgotten her bon alma Biagio? Mother of God! Of all times to forget Biagio! Just when she had been given a double blessing.

"I know, dear Jesus," she prayed, "that when You took away my son You gave me back my hearing so that I would be able to help my granddaughter."

Of this, Donna Maria was positive; she knew, truly, of the wonder of His ways. The child had told her that the house disturbed her, and Donna Maria had promised that they would move. And this year she would do something different in remembrance of her Biagio.

She glanced at her Mary. "Daughter, do your Nonna a favor, like a good girl. On your way to school go to Vena, the florist, and tell him you want a big armful of flowers. You understand?"

"Yes, Nonna, I understand."

What a child, this nipota of hers! Like a little old lady, always serious, always sad.

"Then take the flowers Vena gives you and lay them at the foot

163

of St. Joseph and say a prayer for your grandfather and your father."

Mary looked at her grandmother, then suddenly got up and ran to her and embraced her. She began to weep, and Donna Maria held her close. The old woman wanted to speak comforting words to the troubled child, and she cursed herself for being unable to find them. For too long she had put aside the habit of speech. Hadn't the good Lord returned her hearing so that she could help the little one?

Mary dressed, picked up her school books, and went downstairs. On the street, she looked up and saw her grandmother, and waved to her.

She went into the florist shop and repeated her grandmother's message to Vena. As the florist gathered the roses and wrapped them in waxed paper, he said, "Be careful of the thorns."

She nodded, and ran toward the church.

"Hello, Mary. Are those lovely roses for the church?"

"Yes, Father." Mary hesitated. "My grandma told me to put them in front of St. Joseph."

"May I have one?" Rose smiled.

" 'Na rosa per Rosa," Beneditto said.

"Just a little one?" Rose asked.

"Uh uh." Mary bobbed her head, and took one of the long-stemmed roses from the wax paper.

"What is your name, daughter?" Beneditto spoke in the dialect. But Mary couldn't understand his words, and merely looked at him shyly.

"She's a Spinale," the priest said to his father.

"Child of whom?" asked Beneditto.

Dana looked at Mary curiously. "I could swear I've seen her somewhere before," he said.

Father Scarpi remembered Dana's testimony on the weeping child, and his heart bounded. In a single moment everything fell into place.

"Child," the priest said. "Mary, come to me." The priest touched her soft hair. "This is the child that was weeping when you found your sister, isn't it, Dana?"

Startled, Greer looked at the child and at Father Scarpi. "Yes," he said slowly, "that is the child. But how did you know?"

"I've read the testimony you gave in Court," the priest said. "It is said that Shannan is innocent. I believe this child knows"—the priest hesitated—"who is responsible for . . ." His voice trailed away.

"She came down the stairs crying," Dana said. "And I said, 'Why are you weeping, little girl?' but she didn't answer. She just ran out into the street."

Mary was looking up at them, looking from one to another with fear spreading large in her eyes.

"Why were you weeping?" Dana asked gently.

Mary stared at him in terror. "Father!" she cried. "Father, I'll be late!"

Father Scarpi restrained her, holding her hand gently. "Don't worry, child," he said. "I'll take you in myself." He walked toward the school with her, leaving the others behind.

"Mary," he said quietly, "did the lady take you to her house?"

She nodded and tears welled into her eyes.

"Now, now, we're just talking. You and me. Close your eyes. I won't look at you." Mary closed her eyes tightly, and when he asked if her eyes were closed she nodded again.

"The lady took you to her house. What did she do—what did she say to you?"

"She said—she told me she had a doll for me, a big doll. But she lied, Father!" Mary opened her eyes wide. "There wasn't any doll. Let me go, Father. Let me go!"

But he held her hand and said, "Tell me, child."

She shut her eyes again. "She used to bring me ice cream at the school yard, and I told her I wanted a doll. She said she'd get me a doll, and she told me to call her Ellie. She said we were friends, and she told me she liked me better than all the other girls in the school 'cause I was the prettiest." Mary clutched the roses tighter as she tried to hold back her sobs. "She said the doll talked and walked. I believed her." Mary struggled to get away from the priest.

"Pretend I'm not here," Father Scarpi said. "You're all alone. Just say what happened, please. It's important, Mary. Very important."

"She took me to her house," Mary said with a quick sobbing intake of breath. "On the way I saw a man through a window. He looked like my father. He was in a place where they drink whisky. A place where men go—Sister told me—instead of church. Let me go, Father. I want my Nonna!" Suddenly, she hated Father Scarpi. "You're like him! He made me cry, too!"

"Mary," the priest said. "Mary. Child, pretend you are confessing. Say the Act of Contrition. How does it go, Mary?"

" 'O my God,' " she cried, and a great flood of tears burst from her. Father Scarpi held the child in his arms, his hands trembling. What was worth it? he wondered. God forgive him. " 'I am heartily sorry . . .' " Mary went on dutifully, rushing through the familiar phrases in a broken voice. " 'I dread the loss of heaven and the pains of hell, but most of all . . .' " she sobbed.

"Hush, child," he muttered. "Hush."

"A doll!" Mary burst out. "We went upstairs in an elevator. It was so slow. When I looked for the doll . . . she said it was in the bedroom, and she came in the bedroom after me. But she lied!"

The priest stroked her hair gently. "Then what?" he asked quietly. "Did she say anything then?" he insisted.

"No, no!" She squirmed, trying to escape. Then suddenly, she threw her arms about the priest, and the words burst forth in a torrent: "She took off my dress, and I cried, and there was a pounding on the door, and my father broke it down and he looked wild, and he had a knife in his hand." She shook her head, sobbing. "Then the lady was bleeding, and my father put my clothes on and then he beat me. He yelled and he hit me. He's dead," she said slowly. "But he said that if I told anyone, he would beat me again." The roses in her arms fell to the street as she pulled away from the priest and ran toward the school sobbing.

Father Scarpi gripped the iron railing of the school fence. "God!" he whispered. "Heavenly Father. Let the memory escape her!"

Father Scarpi picked up the scattered roses and walked slowly back to the silent little group that awaited him.

"What said the little one?" asked Beneditto softly.

"She saw one human being slay another," the priest replied.

XVII

Often, when Father Scarpi thought of the law, he thought of Nunzio, his oldest brother.

Annunziato Scarpi had been a stolid man who took care of his motherless brothers. He had taught himself how to read and write, and had spent many hours poring over books and dictionaries. He was shy, and disliked frivolity. Once he had proposed to Giovanina Trionno, a stonecutter's daughter who was very beautiful and very American in that she insisted on being called Jenny. But Jenny was a willful girl, and she told Don Turrido Bellino that the oldest Scarpi was too dry for her. A few years later, Jenny married Salvatore Scarpi, who had joked and serenaded her at the window of their house on Hale Street.

Octavio could remember the immigrants filing into the cigar factory at the corner of Hale Street. Annunziato was a foreman there, and he spoke of cutting and bleaching tobacco leaves. The cigars were rolled by hand, and were put in little boxes of fifty or one hundred. These were packed in large crates that were hoisted to lumbering steel-rimmed wagons drawn by huge draft horses. It was exciting to Octavio, and he would often go to the shipping entrance to watch his brother work.

Nunzio came home one night feeling tired. The factory had shut down and he wasn't working. He saw Octavio sitting on the cement step of the building. Nick was there too, playing his harmonica.

"Why aren't you two in bed?" Nunzio asked them.

"There's nobody home and we don't have keys."

Nunzio searched his pockets. "I forgot mine too," he confessed, "but I'll be damned if I wait for one of the lovers to arrive." He was referring to Salvatore and Victor, who had many amorous adventures.

As they were speaking, Octavio heard a siren sound in Bowdoin Square. "It's the hook and ladder, Nick!" Both boys sprang up and ran down the street.

Nunzio went into the alley beside their house and began to climb the fire escape. They lived on the second floor, and when he reached the windows Nunzio saw that they were all locked.

"Hey, what're you doing up there?" A man below called up to Nunzio. He sounded drunk, and Nunzio didn't bother to answer. He began shaking the windows, hoping to work one of the simple thumb locks loose.

"Get down from there!" the man called.

Nunzio was irritated. "Damn' drunk," he muttered. "Shut up!" he yelled.

At that moment Octavio and Nick came into the yard. They saw Nunzio standing up, leaning over the fire-escape railing. At the same instant they heard the sound of a pistol shot. Nunzio swayed and pitched over the rail.

Octavio ran to where Nunzio lay. He was bending over his brother when he heard Nick shout, and saw him grappling with the stranger. Octavio ran up and knocked the man down, raised him up, and hit him again. When the man lay still, Octavio turned to Nick. "I think Nunzio's dead," he said. They stared at the man who lay sprawled beneath them. Then they saw the man's police badge. Octavio bent down swiftly, ripped off the badge, and with it slashed the man's face deeply, once on each cheek. Then he threw the badge away.

Later in court, the policeman claimed he had used his gun in self-defense. Nick and Octavio were tried for assault and battery and attempt to kill. But because they were sixteen and fourteen, and because it was brought out that the policeman had been drinking while on duty, the case was dismissed.

But Annunziato didn't die. Instead he became paralyzed from the waist down. He lived for fourteen years before he died.

The thought of Nick reminded the priest of the greasy pole contest which had often been staged on the lower end of Hale Street. Nick had won the last contest before the war.

The day before the feast of Saint Lucy, a deputation of fishermen and other citizens had called on the mayor of the city, asking for a permit to close off the street. Then, a lumber yard delivered the pole, the same type as was used for telegraph installations.

A band composed of the barber, a couple of fishermen, four ditch-diggers and two professional idlers gathered and began playing martial airs. The people came down from their apartments and after closing off the street, they dug up cobblestones and burrowed a deep hole. Then as the band played, they planted the pole, which had been spread with thick axle grease. Amateur carpenters buttressed the thirty-foot pole at ground level, while others, working from rooftops, secured the upper portion with fishing cables. They anchored the cables to different roofs at the sides of the street.

Then all the merchants contributed some of their wares. Loaves of bread from the bakers Vassaro and Milestro, a whole ham from Biccheri the butcher, fish from Don Peppino the fish-monger, Mortadella salami and provolone from Sansone the grocer. These delicacies were tied about a hoop fastened to the pole.

By rope and pulley, the hoop was raised to the topmast part of the pole. High in the air, little banners on the hoop unfurled and fluttered in the breeze. The contest began.

The young men of the neighborhood, one by one, attempted to skin the pole. But no one was able to master it until Nick gave it a try. He ripped off his web-belt, climbed upon Salvatore's shoulders, sprang onto the pole, twined his belt around it and began to climb.

"Hey, get him!" someone shouted. "Pull him down! It's Nick Scarpi."

"Jesus, he's going to make it! Nick's going to do it!"

" 'Tavio, he's going to make it," Salvatore shouted. "Nick's going to bring home the bacon!"

Octavio grinned and nodded to Salvatore. The band saluted Nick's triumph, drowning the excited babble of the crowd.

And now Nick too—gay, carefree Nick—was gone.

Years later, after the war, Don Beneditto had asked, "What is the name of that island where my son Nick is buried?"

And Octavio had said, "Guadalcanal."

"I would bring my son back to be buried here."

"The time is long past now," Octavio had said. "He is buried on a warm island, and there is a white cross over him."

"Guadalcanal is an island?"

Octavio had nodded.

"Is it like Sicily?"

"Yes," the priest had lied. "It is like Sicily."

Father Scarpi began to walk toward Merrimac Street, thinking of the law, his brothers, and of Shannan. At the corner he met Dixie Lansone, the bookmaker.

Dixie was short, dark, and stout. He smiled and tipped his cream-colored fedora. "Hello, Father."

"Dixie," the priest asked, "where can I find Mego Manatza?"

Dixie's eyes popped. "You're not going to place a bet, are you?"

"No. I'd just like to speak to him."

Dixie glanced at his wrist watch. "Right now he's probably at his place on Scollay Square."

"Thank you, Dixie."

"For what?" The other shrugged, his fat neck lost in his shoulders. He took out a handful of greenbacks and, unfolding the bills, tried to slip some of them into Father Scarpi's hand. "Here, take this," he said. "For the Church. Give it to the sisters. I used to drive them crazy when I was a kid."

But the priest refused.

"What's the matter?" Dixie protested. "Isn't my money any good?"

"Your money is all right. It's your soul I'm thinking of," the priest said.

"I'll mail it in." Dixie laughed.

"I know." Father Scarpi nodded. "You always do. I meant no offense," he added lamely.

"That's okay." Dixie winked broadly. "There's priests and priests. When Father Polleti was in St. Dominic's, he used to shake us books down for donations, so I got in the habit of giving. Not a bad habit."

As Father Scarpi walked away, Dixie took off his fedora and fanned himself. "You're the only priest in the whole town for my dough!" he called.

Father Scarpi encountered Manatza on the Hanover Street corner of Scollay Square. The bookie was talking to a young man who was leaning against a lamp post.

"Father Scarpi!" Dominic Manatza said when he saw the priest.

170

"How are you? Good to see you." He held out his hand, patting the curate's shoulders. "Still feel strong as ever."

"Mego, I want to get in touch with Shannan. Will you help me?" asked the priest.

"I was speaking about you the other day," Mego went on, looking about furtively. "I said you were the strongest man in Boston. Remember the time you belted a horse dead and I won five C notes from Dixie? Remember?"

"Mego," Father Scarpi repeated, "it's important. Will you find him for me?"

Manatza sighed and, turning to the young man who was with him, spoke in low tones for a moment.

Then Manatza nodded to the priest and led him silently to a house on Sudbury Street, and up a flight of stairs to a door marked "Investments. Dick Manning." He unlocked the door, and they walked down a long corridor and into an inner office. A man was sprawled in an easy chair, asleep. Manatza shook him. "Wake up," he growled. "You're getting paid to guard this room."

The man sprang up. "Sure, Mego. Sure."

Manatza smiled. "Ah, go back to sleep." He grimaced and pulled down the brim of the man's hat. "His son plays football for the Harvards," Mego explained. "He works nights, and days he works for me so he can send his son to college."

They entered a room where two men were working at a table cluttered with phones. One of the phones rang, and the man who answered said briskly: "Investments. Good morning . . . Okay. Marengo, Dainty Dancer, and Uncle Jay. One, two, three. Wait a minute." He placed his hand over the mouthpiece. "Get me credit on Big Al."

His companion opened a ledger, and ran his finger down a page. "B rating. Okay. Let it ride."

Manatza led the priest into a small room without windows.

"We'll be alone here," Mego said.

Father Scarpi sat down wearily.

"You look tired, Father," Mego observed gently. "You're pushing too hard."

"Not hard enough." The priest smiled. "I haven't found Shannan."

"That's what I mean," Mego protested.

"Mego," he said, "it can be proved he didn't kill that girl. I want to tell him."

Mego sighed. "I haven't got a crystal ball. I can't find him just like that." He snapped his fingers. "You're on the level? I mean about proving he's innocent? Sure, you couldn't be otherwise." Mego lighted a cigar. "When I was a kid, I couldn't afford a good cigar. Now that I can, I'm not allowed to have them. Doc says I got a bum ticker." Mego took off his hat, and the priest looked surprised at his shock of dead-white hair.

"Yes, Father. I'm getting old," Mego said. "I've been thinking of retiring. There's no sense in all this any more. My son is in California teaching electronics. My girl is married to some shyster in New York. When my wife died—ah, hell, here I am crying again. . . . About Shannan"—he paused and closed his eyes—"I'll find him."

Father Scarpi stood up, and Mego walked with him to the corridor.

"I'll be in the rectory, waiting for your call."

"Okay," Manatza said quietly. "Okay, Father."

"Keep the Faith," the priest murmured.

"That's all I have left," Manatza replied softly.

When Father Scarpi got back to the rectory, Father Lazzini and Sconnetti were in the foyer packing some suitcases. They gestured unhappily toward the office.

Puzzled, Father Scarpi tapped on the half opened door, and entered. The pastor was seated before the desk writing on two ledgers spread in front of him. Bills were strewn all about. An army trunk was in one corner of the room. The priest had seen it before in Father Ferrera's room, at the foot of his bed.

The pastor removed his glasses with a familiar gesture and wiped them. He was very pale and his myopic eyes were bloodshot.

"I am leaving," he said slowly, as if he could not quite believe it.

"Leaving?" the priest echoed.

The pastor passed a telegram over the desk to him.

Father Scarpi read: "Imperative you make preparations to hand over your office immediately. Report to Boston Sanatorium at once. Request remaining curates to undergo X-rays as soon as possible. Father Francis Morello will succeed you. God bless you."

"Sanatorium?"

"Yes," the pastor sighed. "I went there for an examination last Wednesday." He looked at Father Scarpi, smiling sadly.

"When are you leaving, Father?" the priest asked.

"This evening. You won't forget to have those X-rays taken, will you?"

Father Scarpi shook his head.

The pastor took a small parcel from his pocket. "It's tobacco for your pipe," he explained. "I've always wanted to smoke, but I could never overcome my distaste for the odor of burning tobacco." He smiled gently.

Father Scarpi took the package. "Thanks, Father," he said. He knew that the pastor must have gone out to buy it after receiving the telegram. Father Scarpi looked down at his hands helplessly. "Father," he said, "please forgive me for the trouble I've caused you. I'm an unruly person." His large hands opened and closed. "Please forgive me," he repeated. "I have disobeyed you."

"You were long past forgiven, my son. Perhaps we were both a bit stiff-necked," he went on quietly, "both a bit quick-tempered. May God forgive us."

"Amen," Father Scarpi murmured.

Father Francis Morello was a little priest with an abrupt manner. He had been an assisting curate at St. Jerome's in the North End for fifteen years. The parishioners had not liked him because of his sharp tongue and his obsession for cleanliness. He had been known to break into a sermon to castigate the parishioners for slovenliness. Once, because he thought a bride's gown was too revealing, he held up the ceremony until the trembling girl had arranged the veil in such fashion that it would conceal her upper bosom.

Father Morello was precise and deliberate. He was sure of himself; he was sure of God; and he was sure that all of his parishioners were sinful. And to him, all junior curates were suspect until they had been priests at least fifteen years. In this conviction he was guided by his own experience.

Father Morello was now fifty-five years old; he had been a curate for thirty years and an archpriest for fifteen. He was a bit disappointed at his new appointment as pastor in the West End. The district was flooded with Sicilians, and all of them were calfoni: fruit peddlers, laborers, fishermen.

From the first moment he entered St. Dominic's rectory, he was sure the place needed discipline. No one was on hand to welcome him. Two priests were packing suitcases in the vestibule. He recognized the fat one as a priest named Lazzini. He had heard the man was a glutton. He'd put a stop to that.

Father Lazzini, seeing him at the door, straightened and smiled. "Hello, Father Morello."

The new pastor nodded. "Where's Father Ferrera?" he asked.

"In the office waiting for you, Father."

Father Morello grunted and, knocking brusquely on the office door, strode in.

Dominic Manatza disliked his task. He was an independent bookmaker who didn't like to mix with the bigtime men. He minded his own business. At the first of the month he paid off 10 per cent of his net to Sandy Mac for protection, and never had any trouble. His help and overhead and payoffs required 55 per cent. But that left him 35 per cent from an average of $5,000 a month.

Fix Schianno. Mego wanted nothing to do with him. Mego was small. He liked it that way. A small businessman: that's all God made him.

More than thirty years before Mego and Schianno had hustled speckled tomatoes on Washington Street. Mego had acted as lookout for the police, and Schianno had worked the pushcart. If a policeman were sighted Mego would try to bribe him while Schianno trundled the cart away. They weren't supposed to sell fruit or vegetables on the busy thoroughfare.

Sometimes the police had fooled them and cut off Schianno's getaway with the pushcart. Then Schianno would dump the load on the street and yell: "All right, you bastards, all right! There's your fruit!"

One day Schianno had gotten a revolver. He was through peddling, he had said. From then on he'd make a living with a gun. Mego had tried to argue him out of it, and he had mentioned God.

"God?" Schianno had said. "What're you kidding me? What God?" The next thing Mego heard, Schianno was serving time at Concord for armed robbery.

Now Manatza shook his head. "Fix Schianno," he whispered. He poured coffee into a mug, and laced it with a shot of Metaxes. The brandy and coffee made Manatza feel better. The doctor had warned him that drinking was bad for his heart, and he took his brandy in coffee so that he couldn't see it. Every Saturday he'd go to the doctor and get a shot that was supposed to help his heart.

Mego picked up the telephone. One man would know where Joe Shannan was: Frank O'Meara. He dialed his contact, Sandy Mac.

A voice on the phone said, "Yeah?"

"This is Manatza. I want to talk to Sandy Mac."

After a short while he heard a fresh voice. "Mego? What's up?"

"I think you owe me a favor."

"Yeah? What kind?"

"Like contacting Joe Shannan for me."

Abrams sat behind his desk looking at Dana Greer. He felt a mixture of shock and anger at the young man's news. Was it evidence? He knew it was. Damned good evidence. An eyewitness to the slaying.

"You're sure," he asked.

Dana Greer stood before him, angered by the resistance he felt in the lawyer.

As soon as Father Scarpi had left him alone with Rose, he had told her all he knew about Ellen. Somehow, the priest's concern about Shannan, and his passion for the truth, had made him want to clear the air. Dana wanted no secrets between Rose and himself. He had planned to speak boldly to Father Scarpi about marrying Rose. There had been no need for it; he saw that he had meant only to speak arrogantly. Now he stood before Abrams's desk, speaking with fierce conviction. Now he felt truly bold.

"For God's sake, man! Shannan's innocent. You're a public servant. What's the first thing to do?"

"The first thing," Abrams replied slowly, "is to get Shannan back in prison."

Father Ferrera departed that same evening, before dinner. The curates stood on the sidewalk, waving. But the old priest didn't look back. The taxi turned a corner, and they lowered their arms and looked at each other.

"The saint is gone," Father Sconnetti murmured. He blew his nose. "The saint is gone," he repeated, looking at Father Scarpi.

There were tears in the eyes of the huge priest.

They returned to the rectory. Dinner was ready, but Father Scarpi ascended directly to his cubicle. He was reading from St. Augustine when Father Lazzini entered.

"You'd better attend dinner, 'Tavio."

"I'm still observing my fast," he said.

"I know. I told Father Morello you were. But he insists you attend dinner." He shrugged and looked at the floor. "I've heard of Father Morello," he said. "You had better come down."

Father Morello looked at the priest as he entered the dining room. What a hulking ox of a man! he thought. He was sure that the big priest was slow-witted; all big men were. Father Lazzini introduced them, and Father Scarpi sat down.

"I am told that you are observing a personal fast," Father Morello declared.

The priest nodded.

The new pastor was irritated by the curate's silence. "Well, speak up!" he snapped. "Are you or are you not observing a fast?"

"Yes," Father Scarpi said. "I am."

"Good," Father Morello said loudly. He stared at Father Lazzini. "There are others that should do the same."

Father Lazzini pushed his plate away, and the new pastor began eating with great deliberation. The Virginia ham and potatoes were excellent. Father Morello commented on the dinner.

"Wonderful cook," he said chewing a big slice of ham. "She's not Italian, I gather."

"Irish," Father Lazzini explained. "She's been in St. Dominic's since she was a little girl, when the parish was largely Irish."

The pastor waved his fork at Father Scarpi. "How long have you been a priest?" he asked.

"Three years."

"Three years! Are you sure you're happy?"

The priest looked up, startled, but said nothing. After a few minutes he asked to be excused.

Father Morello did not like the curate's attitude. He was not humble enough for a junior curate.

"You may not be excused," he said. "It is my first day here, and if we are to function as an efficient team we must get to know one another better."

Father Sconnetti started to speak, but thought better of it.

"I do not know how many of the problems confronting this church

176

were discussed by the former pastor, but you all must be aware that we are in bad straits financially. Lack of economy. Bad management. Apparently, the former pastor was slipshod in his business dealings. That will cease."

He paused, looking at them. "This church must be the foremost in this area. I shall see to it."

Bit by bit he extracted information from the priests. He was appalled that Father Scarpi's duties were so undemanding.

"In the future, Father Scarpi," he said, "you will be present at all events scheduled in the main church." He knew that such a request was so ambiguous that the curate would hesitate to do anything without first consulting him. "All curates must take turns remaining in the church on duty. When I am scheduled, Father Scarpi will remain in the rectory." His eyes shifted from one priest to another. "Any questions?"

The curates were silent.

Father Morello smiled. "You may go to your room now, if you wish, Father Scarpi."

Joseph Shannan heard footsteps topside. He slipped out of the wall hammock where he'd been dozing and touched the .38 in his waistband. In the dark of the forward hold he could hear the sound of creaking wood more clearly. Then he heard a key in the lock of the trapdoor that led down from the pilothouse. It was Tami.

Shannan put the revolver away.

Tami snapped on the battery light and looked at Shannan. "Sandy Mac is here," he said.

Shannan shrugged, but he laid his revolver beside him and covered it with the blanket. Tami watched him but said nothing. Sandy Mac climbed down into the narrow compartment.

"Hello, Joe."

"Hello, Sandy."

They shook hands, looking at each other with expressionless faces. Sandy said that he was glad that Joe had made it, and Shannan replied that he had had a lot of help, including, he knew, that of Sandy himself.

Sandy Mac said, "A priest wants to talk with you, a Father Scarpi."

Tami broke in: "I know him. Father 'Tavio. He used to fish on Bellino's *Nina* with me. A long time ago," he added.

177

"He came to see me before," Shannan said. "I knew his brother. What's he want?"

Sandy Mac shrugged. "The word's around that he says you're innocent."

Shannan was puzzled. Why should the priest say that? he wondered. Thinking of his previous talks with the curate, he realized that Father Scarpi had never mentioned his guilt or his innocence.

"What do you think?" he asked Sandy.

"You're the boss," the scar-faced man murmured.

"You, Tami?"

" 'Tavio was a good kid, quick-tempered and strong as a bull, but a good kid," Tami repeated.

Shannan put his hand in the pocket of his coat where the Missal lay that Father Scarpi had given him. "Set up a contact point away from the wharf," he said. "I'll meet him."

"Joe"—Sandy Mac looked at him—"Frank says that if you meet the priest you're on your own."

Shannan shrugged, nodding. But when Sandy Mac flipped back his suitcoat and offered him an automatic, Shannan shook his head, turned over the blanket, and pointed to his revolver.

"I'll blow my head in," he said quietly, "before they hook me again."

Father Scarpi was too nervous to remain in his cubicle. After he finished reciting the Divine Office for the day, he went downstairs to the foyer in the outer office and, taking a copy of *The City of God* from the rectory library, tried to read it.

At eight-thirty the phone rang.

"Father Scarpi," a voice said. "I want to talk to Father Scarpi."

"Speaking," the curate said.

"This is Dom Manatza. He's willing to meet you."

"Where?" he asked, relief flooding his words. "Where can I meet him?"

"You know where the Lynn bus depot is? In the middle of Haymarket Square?"

"Yes."

"Okay, a guy will pick you up there at nine-thirty."

"Nine-thirty."

"Don't ask the guy anything. He'll know where to take you. Got that, Father?"

"Yes. Thanks, Mego."

Manatza hesitated. "Okay, Father. So long."

"Goodbye. And thank you."

Father Morello was sitting at his desk with Father Lazzini. He saw Father Scarpi pass the the door, and called out, "Where are you going, Father?"

"Just for a walk, Father."

"I'm afraid I'll have to refuse you, Father Scarpi," he said. "It's almost nine, now. And in the future the junior curate will be allowed to leave only after asking permission."

"Father, I must go."

Father Morello raised his eyebrows. "What's wrong, Father? Did someone die who is dear to you?" He smiled. "No," he added, "I am afraid not." He paused. "Not unless you have a good reason."

"I prefer not to go into it."

Father Morello turned to Father Lazzini. "Was this common practice, Father? Did the Father defy the pastor before?"

"Father Ferrera often encouraged walking. He used to say it was good for us," said Father Lazzini.

Father Morello continued to look at the huge priest. There was an urgency in the curate that frightened him. Frightened by a junior curate? he asked himself. That is absurd. He tried to stare down Father Scarpi, but could not. Father Morello turned away.

"You are not going out." He cleared his throat. "I am pastor here," he said. "Is this how you observe obedience, Father?" His voice became petulant. "Go back to your room!"

But the big curate started to walk toward the front door.

"Father Scarpi," the new pastor cried, "if you walk out of that door I'll report you to the bishop. I'll have you transferred!"

The priest turned and looked at Father Morello. "I wish you would," he said gravely, then turned his back to them and walked out of the rectory.

Abrams was listening to a newscast when the telephone rang.

"Mr. Abrams? Lieutenant Dicker."

"Hello? Yes, yes, Dicker."

"The tap paid off. We think the priest's going to meet him now."

"Now? What time? Where?"

"They got a pickup arranged for nine-thirty at Haymarket Square."

Abrams estimated. "I'll meet you there, Lieutenant. And no shooting. You understand, Dicker? No shooting! Don't harm that priest. I'll personally hang the man that harms the priest. No shooting. Dicker, Dicker . . ."

The connection was broken.

Father Scarpi arrived at the bus depot at nine o'clock. But it was nine-thirty before a man dressed in faded denims and a blue shirt approached him. There was a smell of fish about him.

"Father Scarpi?" he asked.

The priest nodded.

"Come with me."

They walked across Haymarket Square into North Washington Street. The man told the priest to climb into the back of a fish truck that was parked there. As Father Scarpi did so he made out a couple of slabs of ice and a few cod on a wet gunnysack.

The man gunned the motor, circled the rotary, and headed down Portland Street. He turned left at the Causeway, and then drove to the corner of Norman Street, where he stopped.

"Okay," the driver said. "This is where you get off."

The curate got out of the vehicle, and the man drove away. It had begun to rain.

He was standing in front of a vacant store. As he gazed up at the brownstone building, a man crossed to him from the opposite side of the street. A few boys were playing kick-the-can on the far corner. Somewhere nearby a radio was blaring.

"Hello, Father," the man said.

The priest recognized him. They were about the same age, and they had worked on the *Bella Nina* together.

"Hello, Tami," the priest said. He had heard that Tami had been in prison for murder.

Tami gestured, and the priest followed him down a flight of steps. Tami unlocked the door, and they stepped into the basement of the vacant store. They threaded their way through a narrow corridor cluttered with bushel baskets and garbage cans, and then descended another flight of stairs into a subcellar. Tami swung the beam of a flashlight on a door at the far end. Approaching it, he tapped once, twice, and once again. A moment later the priest heard Joe Shannan's voice.

"Who is it?"

"Tami."

The door was opened, and the priest walked into a small room with a cot at one side of it. Shannan was standing up. His right hand was in a sling.

"Hello," Shannan said. "I traded one cell for another."

Special Officer Michael Tetrelli was twenty-nine years old. He was the youngest man in the hand-picked detail on the Shannan case. Though it was unusual for such a young man to be included in the special squad, Mike deserved the honor. In less than five years he had worked his way up from a beat to the plain clothes division.

At first, Mike thought he had been dumb. He had looked the other way if he saw a slight infraction of the law, but soon he became more clever. He began pulling everyone in, drunks, one-rappers on suspicion, petty thieves, motorists who got out of line. The law was the law, he'd say; the rules were made to be enforced. The men in his division used to say that Tetrelli would pull in his own mother if he had to.

Mike was a sober, diligent, quiet guy. A little nervous, but quiet. When he was in double harness, his mate might notice that Mike was inclined to jump if a car back-fired; but the jumpiness was a souvenir from Korea, and Mike got 15 per cent disability from the Veterans Administration for a nervous condition.

Lieutenant Dicker directed his men down the steps leading to the basement of the vacant store on Norman Street. He signaled to Mike to go first because he had the automatic rifle. Dicker didn't think much of fully automatic weapons, but Sergeant Tennessy had insisted on bringing it along.

"Tetrelli," Dicker said, "no shooting unless I give the word. There's a priest in there."

Mike nodded.

Father Scarpi pointed to the cast on Shannan's wrist.

"How's the hand?" he asked.

"So, so," Shannan murmured.

181

The priest said, "I wanted to see you because there's a good—"

"You know something?" Shannan interrupted. "I'm glad to see you. I don't know why—it's a crazy feeling I got. It's like seeing my own family."

"I'm thankful," the curate said. For the first time in many hours, he smiled. "You're like a brother to me, Joe," he added.

"You know that book you gave me, the one about the Mass? I got—" Shannan stopped speaking abruptly, went to the door and, placing his ear against it, listened intently. Then he relaxed, and returned to the other two.

"You know," Joe said, "I must be getting jumpy. For a moment I thought I heard something. Ah, what am I saying? Forget it." He smiled at the priest. "If I can't trust you, who can I trust?" He lit a cigarette. "What do you want to see me about?"

"You've got to give yourself up, Joe. There's evidence for a new trial."

"Are you kidding me? Do you think they'd give me another chance? Ah, no, Father. You're kidding yourself. Because you're good, doesn't mean that everybody is the same."

Unmistakably, now, there was a sound outside the door. Shannan paled, and stared at the priest.

"Shannan!" a voice called. "Come out with your hands empty!"

Tami flattened himself against the side wall. "Jesus! The priest fingered us."

"You bastard," Shannan said softly. "You lousy no-good bastard." He took the revolver from his belt and pointed it at Father Scarpi.

"Joe," Tami cried, "deal me out!"

"Don't be a fool, Shannan!" the priest urged. "Give yourself up. I swear to you there's evidence—"

Suddenly Shannan whirled and fired two shots through the thin panels of the door. "Come and get me, you bastards!" he yelled.

As the priest lunged for Shannan's arm, an automatic rifle began chattering, shredding the door. A sudden violent blow in the left shoulder spun the priest around. The automatic ceased as suddenly as it had begun.

Shannan was clutching at his chest and coughing. Blood spread darkly to the floor.

A man shouted: "Who fired that chopper? You damn' fool! What the hell did you shoot for?"

Father Scarpi knelt beside Shannan. "Joe," he whispered. "Joe, I didn't know. God! Make him believe I didn't know! Joe," he said thickly, "do you believe me? Can you hear me?"

Shannan's eyelids moved. "Yes," he gasped. "Bless me . . . Father . . . for I have sin—sinned." He groped blindly for the priest's hand; then, suddenly, his head rolled over, and he was dead.

The plain-clothesmen who had entered the room stared silently at the priest and Shannan.

Father Scarpi, cradling Shannan's body with one huge arm, murmured, " 'I am the resurrection and the life: he that believeth in me, although he be dead, shall live: And everyone who liveth and believeth in me shall not die for ever.' " Blood was flowing onto his cassock from the wound in his shoulder. He lowered Shannan's head to the floor and stared at his hands.

"Dear Lord," he said, "I have no unction, and I do not know whether I am fit to minister. But I shall minister to him, for he repented his sins."

As the priest placed his fingers together awkwardly, his lips moved. " 'Ego te absolvo . . .' " he whispered.

At last the priest stood up with difficulty and left the room, without seeming to notice the policemen who stood aside for him.

Outside, a young policeman in street dress was standing against the wall. He held a Thompson sub-machine gun in his hands, and was mumbling incoherently, his pale face twitching spasmodically. Lieutenant Dicker stood near him.

"The gun," Lieutenant Dicker was saying softly. "Give it to me, Tetrelli. Like a nice guy, eh? Just hand it over."

The priest stared at them. He began walking, as if in a dream, toward the man with the Thompson. He walked past Dicker and, raising his huge hands, plucked the gun out of the man's fingers. He lifted the machine gun over his head by the barrel and smashed it onto the sidewalk. The wooden stock cracked like kindling faggots. The barrel bent. Then, balling his right hand into a fist, he struck the mumbling policeman. The man's head seemed to twist, and he crashed into a wall and fell to the street.

Dicker tried to restrain the priest but he brushed the policeman aside. Blood trailed steadily from his arm. He reached up, fumbling for his collar. He grasped it in his hand and tore it off, ripping the stays of his cassock.

"God!" he gasped. He flung the collar of his office away from him and, lurching a few feet farther, crashed into a store window. The display window shattered. He rolled on the sharp splinters of glass and fell, headlong, into the street.

The window was wired to a burglar alarm signal. The alarm began to clang.

XVIII

Father Sconnetti knew that sins of passion were not as bad as sins of malice, but the thought was little comfort. When Elena telephoned, his heart bounded, and he could not keep his voice from trembling. No, he said, he wasn't busy. In fact, he was alone in the rectory office. That is, he stammered, Father Lazzini had retired for the night; Father Morello was out; and Father Scarpi had left earlier.

Actually, Father Sconnetti had been greatly disturbed to learn of Octavio's defiance of the new pastor, and he was waiting in the office for the big priest to return. Now he was beset with thoughts of Elena; her charm was locked within his spirit. He had told her she wouldn't be disturbing him at all by coming; and yet he stood there, trembling in agitation. He clutched at the crucifix on his breast.

"It's absurd," he muttered to himself. "I am a priest. If these things disturb me, I shall not be able to minister."

When Elena arrived she was very gracious to him. "How nice of you . . . Father." Her lips pouted.

The priest sprang to his feet and walked back and forth in agitation. "Not at all," he stammered. "Not at all. I was—yes, am—alone. Don't you see?" His collar seemed to strangle him, and he began to perspire. He cleared his throat. "It's warm, isn't it? Shall I open the door—breath of air?"

"Warm?" she inquired. "Heavens, no! I'm cold."

He stood staring at her as she opened a sheet of music. He shut his eyes and turned his head away. She seemed unconscious of his unease, and sat down, waiting for him to sit beside her.

"You'll have to explain about the Introit," she said.

"Ah, yes, the Introit," he mumbled. "Well, don't you see—that is, it's standard procedure. The Roman Gradual," he went on, "points out that singers—the choir—should start the Introit at the time the celebrant"—he looked at her shoulders, marveling at her skin—"approaches the altar. It is a processional hymn you know—to be sung while the priest goes from the sacristy to the altar."

"And I should make the tempo majestic?" asked Elena.

"Yes—majestic," he agreed, gazing on her.

"Well, then," she said as she took his hand and gently pulled him toward her, pointing at the score, "just where would I . . ."

Father Sconnetti found himself sitting at her side, her words blurring in his mind. Elena edged closer, brushing his shoulder by accident. He could smell a delicate perfume in her hair, and soon he lost track of what she was saying.

"Cuore Gesu!" he said to himself. He suddenly remembered words he'd seen countless times: "Whoever shall look on a woman to lust after her has already committed adultery with her in his heart."

"Perdonare'mi, Cuore sacro!" he cried, bounding to his feet, distracted beyond control.

"What is it, Father?" she asked. "Have you forgotten something?"

"That's it. Ecco!" he said quickly, lying badly. "I have forgotten a wedding—"

"A wedding?" she said, surprised.

"Did I say wedding? Ah, no, not a wedding. It's a—a problem. You know, a difficulty. Someone needs me. I—I beg you to excuse me."

Father Sconnetti fled from the office to his cubicle, where he knelt in prayer. At last, long after he heard the front door shut, he returned to the office to wait for Father Scarpi, praying for strength while he paced back and forth.

It was almost twelve o'clock when the telephone rang. He picked it up nervously.

"Chiesa de San Domenico," he said.

"St. Dominic's Church?"

"Yes. Father Sconnetti speaking."

"My name is Abrams. I'm calling about Father Scarpi—"

"Yes, yes. What about him?"

"He's had an accident. He's in the General Hospital."

"I'll be there," Father Sconnetti said.

Abrams met the little curate at the front desk of the hospital. He introduced himself and told Sconnetti what had happened.

186

"How is he?" Father Sconnetti asked.

"He was wounded in the shoulder. The doctors say it isn't too bad. No bones—that is, no important bones—were broken." He paused. "I thought I should call the church," he added.

"Ah, yes. Thank you. That was kind of you. I shall wait until they let me see him."

"You won't have long," said Abrams. "He's coming out of it now."

A swimming face sharpened near Father Scarpi and grew still. At last he recognized Father Sconnetti, who sat beside the bed, his head bowed.

"Are you in my dreams, my friend?" he said.

"'Tavio, my brother!" Sconnetti cried. The little priest gripped his hand.

"Don't pray for me, Joe," he said harshly.

Sconnetti shook his head. "I know about Shannan," he said.

"He died in my arms."

"Abrams said it was an accident."

"Everything is an accident—living, dying," Octavio murmured. He closed his eyes. It was an accident, Abrams had told Sconnetti. Shannan was dead, but it had been no accident. He was responsible. He, Octavio Scarpi, was guilty. He had tried to escape the violence that dominated his life by embracing God. But there was no God. He looked at Father Sconnetti. "No," he said.

"But there is a design in all things," Father Sconnetti said.

"You think there's a reason why Shannan was killed?" Scarpi said. "Is there a reason in the way the police persecuted him? Stalking him down like a wild animal? Where is the design?"

"Octavio," Sconnetti murmured, "God forgive me, I've disturbed you in your illness. I'll go."

"No, Joe. Please don't go. I want to talk to you. You're my friend." He moistened his lips. "Do you know me, Joe? Do you know what kind of man I am? I'm a beast. Oh, I'm not fit to speak to you."

"Ah, no, Octavio. You're hurt now, and sick . . . You'll feel better tomorrow."

"I'll never feel better. That's where I was wrong. I thought the evil in me would be made good by God. I know now that I was wrong. Do you know what I've done?" he gasped. "I have committed rape. Me! I have committed rape! Do you understand? All my life I've hurt

187

people, maimed them, broken them. A thousand times I've confessed the things I've done, but I can't forget them. They're in me, torturing me all the time!"

"Let me hear your confession, 'Tavio. Perhaps it would help."

"No." Octavio winced with pain. "Hear me as a friend. Judge me as a friend, not as a priest. I've broken men's bodies and tortured helpless women. Two nights ago, I hurt a boy. I broke his nose. What kind of man am I that I would beat a boy? Everything I touch, I destroy. Whoever I try to help, I hurt. What does it mean, Joe? What kind of design is that?"

" 'Tavio, 'Tavio! Don't hurt yourself. I cannot judge you. As priest or man, I cannot judge you. Do you think I'm faultless? Don't you think," he asked softly, "I've sinned, and still sin?"

"Don't you see that Shannan is dead because of me?"

" 'Tavio, put your trust in our Lord and—"

"I can't do that." Scarpi spoke harshly. "Don't you see?" he gasped. "I've lost faith! I've lost faith, Joe!" he cried.

"My brother," Sconnetti said, "don't say that. Compose yourself. Many of us have doubted before. I too—"

"But have you ever committed rape?" Octavio Scarpi said. "Did you ever beat men for money? Did you ever kill your brother? Faith! There is no faith! There is no God!"

Octavio Scarpi fell back on his pillow; his hospital gown was stained with blood. He turned his head away and sobbed.

Father Sconnetti put his hands over his eyes. His thin shoulders shook. Tears burst from him. He walked over to the door and leaned his head against the cool metal.

" 'Tavio," he cried, "my poor brother!"

XIX

Beneditto Scarpi gazed at his sons as they sat together in the beer parlor. They were his sons, he reflected, but they were also strangers. He had known this fact for many years, but today it had come upon him in such fashion that he could not ignore it. How much of one another did men know? he wondered. How much did men know of other men? He shook his head.

There was Salvatore. How much did he know about him? He had even forgotten how old Salvatore was. Salvatore had grandchildren. And Anthony, sitting opposite him, draining a glass of beer. What did he know of him? Victor he should know. Beneditto lived with Victor. But even with Victor, he wasn't sure. These men acted sure of knowing him. They gave him money that he didn't need. They were at ease with him.

John, who was sitting next to him in the booth, he knew best of all. That was because John admitted the folly of living and, instead of giving him money, usually took money from Beneditto. John had been working in another town when Beneditto sent for all his sons.

"You know," Victor was saying, "if Lucy hadn't held me back I'd be well off today. Back in 1942 I could've bought a number of houses at cost. Today . . ."

Victor and Lucy, Beneditto reflected. Lucy ordered Victor around. Get the bread, she'd say, and Victor would get the bread. Lucy had been the daughter of an insurance man; her father had not thought a Scarpi was good enough for her. The old man fumed, remembering that. Without realizing it, he grunted.

"What's the matter, Pa?" John asked.

"Don't you see the old man's glass is empty?" Anthony said. He had called his father the old man for many years. He thought of

189

Beneditto as a very old, very nice old man. Anthony's wife, Aggy, didn't like Beneditto. Anthony had wanted his father to live with him, but his wife had been against it. His wife was Irish. She couldn't understand Beneditto, and she had said that he would be lonely in their house because she could not speak Italian to him. Beneditto had then gone to Victor's to live.

"Hey, girlie." Salvatore signaled to the waitress.

The tall blond waitress nodded.

"Good-looking woman," Salvatore grunted. "I ordered a beer," he explained to his father.

"But I didn't want one." Beneditto shrugged. His son Salvatore always knew what was best. He was prosperous. One of his daughters was married to an engineer, another to a lawyer. Salvatore was branching from selling to packaging tomatoes. He had told Beneditto that someday the name of Scarpi would be a big name in the tomato business. But who wanted to be remembered with a tomato? Beneditto wondered.

The waitress placed the beer on the table. "All right, Pa," John said. "We're all together now and we all have a drink. What's up?"

Beneditto cleared his throat. "My sons," he said, "as you know, an accident befell Octavio."

"I know all about that," Anthony broke in. "If Tetrelli was in my division I'd hang the bastard."

"For Christ's sake," Victor said, "let Pa talk."

"But it is not of that I speak," Beneditto went on. "My son the priest has been living in Victor's house for three days now. But he turns his face from me and does not speak from his heart. He is like a machine that moves about automatically. For that reason, and because I am old, I wish to gather the family about me for one last time. I think," he said, "that I shall die soon."

"Jesus! Will you listen to the old man talk?"

"Aw, Pa, don't be foolish."

"My father," Salvatore said, "I shall call the company the Beneditto Scarpi Company. And the product shall be known as Beneditto Tomatoes. That is good, because Beneditto means 'blessed.'"

"What do you want us to do, Pa?" John asked.

"I want you to bring your families to Victor's next Sunday. We shall be all together, perhaps for the last time. On my death your wives will come between you."

The brothers looked at one another, knowing the truth in the words of the old fisherman.

"I know," Beneditto calmly continued, "that your wives will threaten and scorn you for such a proposal. But you are the sons of an old fisherman named Scarpi, and you will obey the last wish of the old man."

"I'll be there if I have to drag Aggy by the hair," Anthony muttered.

Beneditto was pleased; his sons would be there with their American children. And he would be happy hearing their babble. Perhaps the American lawyer who was married to Salvatore's daughter would be there. If so, he would startle the young man by recounting his days in the Maffia. The last time, the young lawyer had been surprised. That pleased Beneditto. He liked to shock young people. Especially lawyers.

But he could never understand priests. The night before he had seen his son without his collar.

"Are you allowed to go about without a collar?" he had asked.

"Sometimes," Octavio replied. But his manner worried Beneditto. His son spoke with despair.

As Victor drove them back to his house, John said: "You would not have had Rose send me a telegram merely for a gathering. Your Honor does not see the others, but you see me often."

"Yes," Beneditto agreed softly, "there is another reason."

Victor said, "What is it, Pa?"

"My son, the priest, speaks as though he were no longer a priest."

Frank O'Meara was sitting beside J. J. in the front seat of the car. He kept muttering to himself.

"What's the matter, boss?"

"As long as we're here, take me into the West End," Frank said.

O'Meara had been born in the West End. Sometimes he liked to drive through the narrow, twisting streets, looking at the familiar landmarks of his boyhood.

"Stop in front of the church," he ordered J. J. O'Meara often went into St. Dominic's. He had been baptized and had made his first Communion there. Now he felt a desire to light a candle for Joe Shannan.

A few moments later he entered the church, dipped his fingers into the fount of holy water at the entrance, and made the sign of the

Cross. He walked down the long aisle of the empty church and, after genuflecting, knelt at the altar rails in front of the old and chipped statue of Joseph. He said an Our Father and two Hail Marys, then lighted a red candle for his mother, a blue one for his father, and a green one for Shannan.

Father Sconnetti was in the rectory foyer, reciting Vespers of the Divine Office. A knock at the door startled him. "Come in," he said.

A boy opened the door. The priest saw that his nose had been broken, and that the ridge was covered with adhesive tape.

"My name is Tommy Rietti," the boy said nervously. "I wanted to talk to Father Scarpi."

"He's not here." The curate sighed. "Can I help you?"

"No . . . no."

The boy hesitated and started to leave, but at the door he turned. "Father Scarpi broke my nose," he said.

The priest remembered Father Scarpi speaking of it in the hospital. "Father Scarpi is very strong," he murmured. "I think he feels . . . sorry, very sorry. He didn't mean it. You see, my son," the little priest said, speaking more to himself than to the boy, "Father Scarpi's heart dies within him when he harms anyone."

"That's why—why I came. Today, after I thought about it . . . Well, what's a nose?" Tommy asked quickly. "Something made me come. I wanted to tell him he should've broken my head. I was wrong."

Father Sconnetti uttered a swift prayer. "Do you wish to make a confession?" he asked.

Tommy was silent a moment, looking at the priest. "I haven't . . . Can you hear me now?"

Father Sconnetti led the way, and Tommy followed him down the winding staircase to the lower church.

XX

Octavio Scarpi, from force of habit, awoke early. He estimated the hour to be between five and six in the morning—Sunday morning. He swung out of bed and, suddenly realizing that he was in his brother's house and not in his cubicle, sank back slowly. He looked outside and saw a clear blue sky.

The desire to say Mass arose in him. He whispered " 'Introibo ad altare Dei.' " But he could not go to the altar of God. He felt an oppressive sense of loss.

He found himself unconsciously starting to recite the matins of the Divine Office, and forced himself to stop.

Shaking his head, he struggled into a gray sweatshirt. He put on a too short pair of denims that belonged to Victor. Stealing silently down the stairs, he went into the garden by the kitchen door. The fat beagle yawned at him, and he nudged the dog gently with his foot. Then he unlocked the front gate and walked onto the dew-laden grass with the beagle ambling along behind him.

Further down the road, he saw Compare Fabrizio rasping a sickle. The old peasant was leaning against the wall of the house he had built with his own hands and was pushing the rasp in little strokes against the edge of the hand sickle.

"Good morning, Lord Fabrizio," Octavio greeted him.

" 'Morning, Priest," Compare grunted. He wanted the churchman to know he wasn't impressed by his visit to Victor Scarpi's.

"It's a beautiful morning," Octavio went on.

"Every morning is beautiful—so long as one is alive," Compare retorted. There was a short silence, upon which Fabrizio glanced suspiciously at Octavio. "Aren't you going to say anything?" he asked.

"What is there to say?" Octavio wanted to know.

"Have you not heard me right?" Compare asked. "Will you not say that death is the beginning of eternal life? That's what all you priests say," Compare scoffed.

"Has Your Honor any fresh eggs this morning?" Octavio asked.

"All in good time," Fabrizio grunted. "First, I must cut fodder for my rabbits." He began cutting beargrass in a patch of fallowing land. After gathering an armful, he brought it to the rabbit hutch, where large sienna-colored rabbits quivered and twitched their whiskers as he approached them.

A rooster was crowing, and Compare threw a pebble at it.

"Aren't you frightened by a savage like me?" he boasted, and chuckled. "Come, we shall go into the house to breakfast."

"But the eggs," Octavio said.

"All in good time," Compare roared.

A short, slight woman with wispy gray hair met them at the entrance. She bowed to Octavio, "Enter, pray," she nodded. "My house is always open to God and the hungry."

"When was this your house?" her husband shouted. "Indeed! And I didn't notice your God helping me mix cement when I erected it, nor did He aid me with the carpentry."

"Pray, Father, pay no heed to the Turk," she whispered.

"I didn't think He'd help me with the masonry," Compare went on, "but I thought He'd help me with the carpentry. He's a carpenter, isn't He?"

"He goes on like this for hours," his wife said. "Pay no attention, pray."

"Where is my breakfast, female?" her husband inquired.

"Ready, my Lord." The old woman winked at Octavio.

They sat down to a breakfast of quick-boiled mustard greens, with the sheen of a few drops of olive oil on them, poached eggs, slabs of caecicavaddo cheese, and mugs of steaming black coffee.

Octavio ate heartily.

"Because you haven't tried to convert me," Compare declared, "I shall lace your coffee with my own brandy. Female," he ordered, "get the brandy."

The woman disappeared and returned with a bottle of peach brandy. Compare poured liberal amounts of it into the coffee, and Octavio sipped the hot brew.

Later, the woman took him into her bedroom. The walls were

covered with pictures of the Virgin Mary. Some of the pictures were very old and faded. Above the bed was a large sepia-toned lithograph of Raphael's Madonna of the Chair. There was a portrait of a soldier on an old walnut bureau, and at the foot of the portrait a candle flickered in the well of a glass jar. There was a faded label on the jar and, peering closer, Octavio made out the legend *Pure Strawberry*.

"My son," she said slowly, "my baby Affio. He died near Salerno, during the war." She nodded to the kitchen where her husband was still at breakfast. "He never speaks of him, and will not allow me to speak. When the President sent us a letter with a medal in it, he threw it away. Then he cursed God, and forbade me to attend the Mass. He says God is a devil, and the devil is God." She began to sob.

Octavio felt weak. He put his arms around the old woman's shoulders.

"But he is a good man," she whispered. "He has never raised his hand to me. He loved the boy too greatly. Do you understand, Father?" She dried her tears. "I am not now weeping for my son. I weep for my husband."

Shortly afterward, Compare took Octavio to the henhouse. He stopped to survey the weather-beaten framework of the chicken coop.

"I shall give Him one more chance to help with the carpentry," Compare said. "When I rebuild this structure, I shall say: 'God, I'm giving you one more chance to help me. If you refuse to help me, then I will never read the Bible.'"

Octavio turned to him. "Do you think you'll keep your word?"

"It'll be easy," the old farmer retorted. "I can't read!" He chortled.

But Octavio didn't laugh, and Compare's face grew sober.

The old peasant glanced at the house. Then he reached high up to a beam of the henhouse and retrieved a leather bag. With trembling hands he loosened the thongs and took out a square box. Octavio had seen such a box many times.

"My son was presented this," Compare whispered. "I don't want her to know I have it, for then she will cry." He brought out a Purple Heart medal.

"Is it not a great honor?" the old man asked. "This of course is the medal of courage."

"It is a great honor," Octavio said.

The old man's eyes were wet as he retied the thongs and replaced the leather bag.

He gathered a dozen eggs for Octavio, and accepted sixty-five cents for them. Still holding the egg bag in his hand, he edged closer to Octavio.

"Priest, will you do me a favor? In secret?"

"It would be a privilege," Octavio said.

"Will you say a prayer for my son's soul? Just a short one? Being a priest, your prayer will have great effect."

Octavio looked away. How could he disappoint the old man? How could he tell him he was unfit to be a priest? At last he said, "I shall, indeed, pray for his soul."

As they approached the house, Compare said to Octavio in loud tones: "You priests are great ones! You eat me out of house and home, and in payment you give me a quarter. A quarter!"

Compare's wife rushed out of the house.

"What have you done?" she wailed. "What have you done?"

"I charged him for his breakfast," Compare said. "Did you think I would not charge him because he is a priest?"

His wife looked at Octavio and saw him wink. She shook her head slowly.

Octavio walked up the hill carrying the eggs. Behind him, Compare was still ranting to his wife. He smiled. Hearing a clinking in the bag, he opened it. The money he had paid Compare was in the bag with the eggs.

He sat down at the side of the road and buried his head in his hands.

When Octavio returned to the house, he found his father pumping water from the well into a wooden bucket.

Beneditto looked at his son, but said nothing as he washed himself, using yellow laundry soap. He rinsed his face with cold water and then dried himself. The towel was startlingly white against the deep brown of his thin arms.

At last he asked, "Why do you not dress for church?"

"I do not feel well," the priest said.

"What grieves you?" Beneditto asked gently. Octavio walked into the yard without answering, and the old man followed him. "Speak out from your heart," he whispered.

196

Victor's wife came out of the kitchen bearing a pot of coffee and two cups which she placed on a small wooden table beneath the grape arbor.

"I have not been to church since your first Mass," Beneditto said as he stirred his coffee. "I have it in my heart to go with you this morning."

Octavio toyed absently with a spoon.

"Morning," said John, coming into the little arbor. He looked at his father. The old man shook his head cautiously. "Ready for Mass, Father 'Tavio?" he asked his brother.

Octavio spoke to his father. "You are still growing raisin grapes, I see," he said. "Are you going to do any grafting today?"

"Ah," Beneditto declared, "that must be done when the moon is new." He turned to John. "What Mass will you attend?"

"When did you start going to Mass?" Octavio asked his brother.

"Oh, I go quite often," John said. "I don't think it helps . . . but I go. Sometimes."

"Ebbene?" Beneditto said. "Let us all attend the eight o'clock Mass at St. Anthony's."

Knowing that he could not easily refuse, Octavio nodded.

They drove down Malden Street in John's car and waited in the courtyard until time for the service. Men in their Sunday finery and girls in flowered cottons stood nearby.

Feeling ill at ease because he was without collar, Octavio edged behind the statue of Christopher Columbus in the huge courtyard. On the opposite side of the court he saw the bronze cast of St. Anthony, after whom the church was named.

Suddenly, Octavio remembered being ordained. The bishop had said, " 'Be pleased, O Lord, to consecrate and sanctify these hands.' " He had felt the bishop's hand resting on his head. " 'That whatsoever they shall bless may be blessed, and whatsoever they shall consecrate, be consecrated and sanctified, in the name of Our Lord Jesus Christ.' "

After the rite, the bishop had smiled at him sadly. Earlier, Octavio had gone to him for advice. He had knelt and kissed the prelate's ring. Then he had asked the bishop if it were not better for him to enter a monastery.

"Why do you wish to enter a monastery, my son?"

Octavio had bowed his head. "I'm too ugly to minister to the people."

197

"Ugly?" the bishop had said. "How does ugliness apply to you, my son? Ugliness is a state of character. You are far from ugly. You are a mediator between God and man, a chalice to the people. Some chalices are ornate and some are plain. Does it make any difference as long as both kinds are blessed by God?"

As they entered the church, Octavio remembered the bishop's words, but now, he thought, he was unfit. The chalice which the bishop had referred to was his soul; and how could the Consecration take place in an impure soul?

Octavio heard the priest intone the Introit. It was from Psalm twenty-six and he repeated it: " 'Hear, O Lord, my voice with which I have cried to Thee: be Thou my helper, forsake me not, nor do Thou despise me, O God my Savior.' "

He watched the priest, hearing him sing the preface to the Consecration and Oblation: " 'Sursum Corda.' "

The choir replied with ringing voices, " 'Habemus ad Dominum.' "

" 'Gratias agamus Domino Deo nostro,' " sang the celebrant.

" 'Dignum et justum est,' " the choir answered.

Octavio shut his eyes. "Why should anyone thank the Lord?" he asked himself. And a voice, seeming to rise out of his heart, whispered, "For eternal life."

"Ah, no," Octavio cried aloud. ". . . non sum dignus."

He stood up, dazed, and stared blankly about the church.

"Sit down!" John said. "Sit down!" pulling at him.

But Octavio gave an incoherent sob and, forcing his way out of the pew, walked quickly from the church.

Carmello Poverello, the professor, gravely studied the huge crate that had been delivered to the fraternity the day before. The truckers, with the aid of a hoist, had placed the crate in the vestibule of an empty tenement building that belonged to Don Turri Bellino. It had been decided to open the crate there, and many members of the fraternity were gathered for the occasion.

Different committees were busy preparing for the festival, which was to be held on the following Sunday. Tomorrow the men from an electric specialty company would begin the decoration of Hale Street. An artist was to paint a large canvas of St. Dominic mounted on a horse. This was to be placed before the figure of the saint until the time came to reveal the statue.

198

Neddo Spitoli and some of the younger fishermen were busy ripping off the boarded crate. At last, the statue was uncovered. The members sighed, the women weeping tears of joy.

The saint looked gently out upon them. The mantle was painted black, the habit white, in the manner of Dominican friars. One saffron-colored plaster hand held a plaster Bible, and the other, a laurel wreath.

"You will notice," the professor pointed out, "that there is writing on the pedestal."

Nino Quatrocchi took out his glasses and, after much hawing of breath, proceeded to wipe the lens. He slipped them on his nose and peered at the lettering. "It says," he stated pontifically, "San Domenico de Sicilia."

"It should have said Augusta," Bacafiggo stormed.

"Oh, stop your ranting, Turri," his wife said. "At long last, San Domenico has come from Sicily."

The professor glanced skyward, and Don Peppino Messana began coughing.

Don Turri then decided to go to St. Dominic's Church to tell Father Scarpi of the arrival of the statue. There he met Father Sconnetti in the outer office.

"I wish to speak to the Augustan priest," the fisherman said.

"Father Scarpi has had an accident—that is, he's ill," the little priest informed him.

"Ill?" Bacafiggo was disturbed. "He'll be all right for the festival and procession next Sunday, won't he?"

"I don't know," Sconnetti said miserably. "Perhaps."

Perhaps? But the fisherman wanted to know. These things must be carefully planned, he explained, biting the ends of his drooping mustaches. Sighing, Father Sconnetti asked him to wait, and went to tell the pastor that Don Turri was there.

Father Morello came bustling into the outer office, where Don Turri was belching clouds of smoke from his stogie. The pastor flung open a window.

"I'm glad you came." Father Morello spoke quickly. "I'll be glad to officiate at the donation of the statue." His words were uttered in carefully cultivated Italian. "It shall be a gesture—my gesture of respect for my parishioners."

"And who, may I ask," said Don Turri, "requested you to make this—this gesture?" The fisherman, stogie clamped in a tight jaw, waved his arms.

"Knowing that Father Scarpi cannot be present," Father Morello said, as if speaking to a child, "I have arranged to take his place. A pastor must be where he is needed."

"Listen to me well, preacher!" Bacafiggo retorted. "I need you like my boat needs a hole at the water line. I haven't gone to church for forty years, and I can hold out for another forty. Either we get the Augustan priest, the son of Don Beneditto Scarpi, or we keep the statue of San Domenico."

Father Morello smiled indulgently.

"You can't set yourself above the Church, my son, my countryman. You will come to me when the time arrives. You'll change your mind."

"I'll change my mind, will I? Like hell I will!" Bacafiggo shouted. "Even if the Pope wanted me to change my mind, I'd tell him to jump in Boston Harbor. And I'm not your son!" he railed. "I'm a Sicel!"

Father Morello felt himself growing angry, but he restrained himself, and watched in silence as the hot-tempered fisherman walked away.

"Calfoni," he muttered to Father Sconnetti. "A common Sicilian fisherman."

When Don Turri Bacafiggo returned to the Fraternity, a special meeting was held. After a hasty vote it was decided that the statue would be kept in the niche in the first-floor corridor of the clubhouse. The women, almost as a body, voted in favor of Father Morello. But the men had always seen to it that the women were numerically, if not vocally, in the minority.

Before closing the meeting Bacafiggo said: "By Garibaldi, who brought taxes to Augusta, if that pastor waits for us to go to him, he'll be waiting until the second coming of Jesus—begging your pardon, ladies."

"Bravo!" Nunzio Rao applauded. "Bravo!"

It was the first time in the history of the Fraternity that the cobbler had applauded Don Turri Bacafiggo.

XXI

As Octavio, Beneditto, and John rode back to Victor's house, no word passed among them.

Dana and Rose met them coming up the steep path, and Rose kissed Octavio. Dana shook hands shyly.

"Surprise!" someone shouted. "Surprise, surprise!"

A group of small children rushed down the hill crying, "Father 'Tavio! Father 'Tavio!" A little girl climbed up his free arm and clung to his neck. "Are you hurt, Father 'Tavio?" a boy asked. Octavio looked at his nieces and nephews, and saw that his brothers and their families were gathered at the front gate.

Anthony Scarpi came down the path and they embraced. Salvatore kissed the priest. "My brother, my Father," the oldest brother said. Jennie, Salvatore's wife, embraced him, and Aggy held his arm. Octavio was overwhelmed by their joy at seeing him.

The older people entered the house, where Victor had opened a gallon of cool dry Burgundy and was pouring the wine into large tumblers. The men remained in the living room drinking, and the women retired to the kitchen.

"Remember when we were kids," Victor said, "when Pa would return from a trip with Don Turrido, and he would look at us and make a stab at calling us by our right names? He always called Octavio, Onofrio. Then he would call Onofrio, Nick, and Nick he would call Octavio. He used to call me Anthony, and he'd call Tony, Turri. After a while he knew he was mixing our names up; so he got the idea of calling to us and saying, "Hey son, what's your name?" Then we'd have to tell him, and he'd say, "Come here, Nick, if it was Nick. That way he got around ever having to learn our names!"

Salvatore laughed, nodding.

"The old man was always good for a laugh," Anthony said. "I remember the time I was learning to write letters when I was in that special school." Anthony winked. He had never told his wife Agnes he had been in prison as a boy. "I used to send the old man letters. We were allowed three letters a month. Just a few years ago he showed them to me. He had saved them all these years. You still got the letters?" Anthony asked his father.

"Yes," the old fisherman said. "They are saved. It is a great thing to read and write. I am able only to inscribe my name as it was needed when I acquired citizenship."

The women were very busy in the kitchen. Lucy was basting a leg of lamb; and Agnes had prepared two apple and three squash pies and was waiting for the lamb to roast so that she could have room in the oven to bake the pies. Jennie, Salvatore's wife, was cooking dishes of the Old Country. She had brought dough and made scacciata, a meat pie filled with beef, pork, and onions; the thick crust of the pie was even now beginning to brown. Ida, Jennie's oldest daughter, was boiling some vedura in a big pot. She had mixed the cicoria and broccoli-rabie in the container. Agnese, Anthony's daughter, was making a large antipasto.

After their wine, the men went into the garden. Beneditto pointed out where he had planted fagiuolini, escarole, and zucchini. Then they went into the yard where Salvatore's younger daughters, Dominica and Santa, were caring for the romping, shouting children. Rose and Dana were sitting under the grape arbor, and near them, Anthony's unmarried daughter, Natalie, was reading the Sunday paper.

Most of the younger women smoked, but not in their grandfather's presence. Beneditto had visited brothels, both in Sicily and America, when he was a young man, and he had reached the conclusion that only prostitutes smoked.

When Salvatore's son-in-law, the lawyer, arrived, Don Beneditto joked with him about the Maffia. The lawyer kept shaking his head and muttering, "Incredible, incredible!" After a while, Anthony and Victor started a boccie game in which they were joined by Beneditto and the lawyer.

John and Salvatore cleared a space in the garden beneath some stunted cherry and peach trees, and fashioned a long dining table by nailing long planks on several wooden trestles. Octavio tried to help but they would not let him, insisting that he should not exert himself. When the table was ready, the women, led by Lucy, hurried out and set it. Then Jennie began to bring out the dishes.

Meanwhile, the younger women fed their children on the small table beneath the grape arbor. Afterward, the daughters and daughters-in-law called to their husbands and sat at the adults' table.

The old fisherman was seated at the head of the table, and Octavio was placed on his right.

A little girl with red hair approached Octavio. She was three or four years old. "Hello," she lisped, and then looked at a fair-haired young woman sitting nearby.

The young woman formed the word "Father" with her lips.

"Father," the little girl said. "Hello, Father." She ran to the young woman and hid behind her, giggling.

"Who was that child?" Octavio asked Beneditto.

The old man looked sheepish, and shrugged his shoulders. "A man my age," he said, "is not expected to remember all their names."

"That's my daughter, Virginia," the young woman said. "And I'm Agnes."

"That's my grandchild," Anthony said.

"To think," Beneditto said to Octavio in the dialect, "that your mother and I started all this." He wiped his eyes.

Victor asked Octavio to say grace, but Octavio demurred. He said that his father, as head of the family, should have the honor. Victor agreed, and urged Beneditto to say the blessing.

"But what can I say?" the old fisherman protested. "I know not the prayer for blessing. I am not a man of God." He paused, gazing sadly at his son. "When I was a boy we threw rocks at the priests of our church," he went on. "That was because we had but little to eat, and the priests had much."

"What's he saying?" the lawyer asked his wife.

"He is recalling the hard times of his boyhood," she said.

"This is America," Anthony broke in. "Say the grace, my father."

The brothers forced Beneditto up from his chair.

"Children," the old man stammered, "my children. God bless you all. And now let us eat this food that the poor suffering Jesus has made possible through His love for us, who are His children."

"Amen," Octavio whispered. Each one touched his forehead and breast and shoulders and began eating the pasta con salsa de carne.

It was a joyful day, marred for Beneditto Scarpi only by the silence of his son the priest.

That evening, after all the others had left for their homes, Beneditto sat with Victor, John, and Octavio in the living room. As he sat looking at his sons, the old fisherman prepared to speak with the priest. But Octavio suddenly arose, muttered good night, and started toward the stairs. John called to him, but the priest shook his head, and disappeared upstairs.

When he was in his room, Octavio took off his gray sweatshirt and looked at his bandaged arm. One week had gone by since his discharge from the hospital.

He snapped off the light and lay on his bed fully clothed. He could hear the sounds of night outside. Bullfrogs croaked monotonously from the stagnant little pond behind the house. Crickets and cicadas chirped plaintively and steadily. Staring into the darkness of the room, Octavio tried to identify the sounds to take his mind away from his own misery, until at last he fell into an uneasy sleep.

All that week Octavio kept silence. John tried to draw him out, but Octavio refused to speak. At night he roamed the countryside, and when he became thoroughly fatigued, he would lie down in the damp fields and lay his cheek against the cool grass.

On the following Saturday, Octavio reached his decision. He would return to St. Dominic's the next day and, after apologizing to Father Morello, he would renounce the priesthood.

He looked out the window of his room into the darkness of the night, where the old pear tree glimmered whitely. Then he went silently down the back stairs and walked across the garden to the pear tree. He leaned his head against it and began to weep. Suddenly, a rage came over him. He struck the tree with his fist, and then tore the sling from his arm and ripped the bandages from his shoulder. He saw the blood welling from his wound.

In a moment, John was beside him.

" 'Tavio!" John cried, taking his brother's hand. "Brother," he whispered.

Beneditto emerged from the grape arbor. "My son," he said softly, "it would help if you shared your despair."

"I am not fit to be a priest, my father," he groaned. "My hands are cursed."

"How so?" Beneditto asked. "How are your hands cursed?"

"You know," Octavio said, "that I killed my brother Onofrio. I hated him, and I killed him. I thought because of that, and many other sins, that I would dedicate my life to God. But when God shut his ears to my prayers, I reproached Him." He laughed bitterly. "Perhaps if He appeared to me I would try to hurt even Him." Octavio stared at his hands. "These are to blame; I am to blame. My strength is the curse of the Devil. I'm no good! I'm evil. No matter how hard—"

He broke off and, cupping his face in his hands, leaned against the pear tree.

"What do you say?" Beneditto cried. "Onofrio died the death of drying muscles and the shriveling flesh. What think you—that your blow killed him? Ah, no! Lived he not many weeks after you had struck him?"

"You're mad!" John cried. "You know Oni died from muscular dystrophy."

"I don't know," Octavio whispered. "I don't know."

The old fisherman sat down on the bench near the well, his knees trembling. He took out a red checkered handkerchief and blew his nose.

"Is this a thing you have accused yourself of these many years?" Beneditto asked quietly. "My son, my son." He shook his head sadly. "There is guilt in all of us, but at times the feeling of guilt is more evil than the act that brought it on."

He stood up and walked to his son. "You have accused yourself of Onofrio's death," the old man went on softly, "and I have blamed myself for your mother's death." Beneditto turned to John. "Yes," he said, "I am the cause of her having fourteen infants in eighteen years. Think you that I am immune to these guilts; that they do not disturb me in the lonely hours of night?"

"But you are not a priest, my father," said Octavio.

"Don't you think priests can know guilts?" John asked harshly. "Don't you think they're human? Because you think the beating you gave Onofrio killed him, do you propose to break away from the priesthood? I won't let you!" he cried.

"What difference does it make to you if I leave the clergy?" Octavio asked John. "You're an atheist."

"What I am doesn't matter. It's you that matters. You are another man's hope," John said. "Would you deprive your parishioners of their hopes just for your own feelings of guilt?"

"You don't understand," Octavio cried. "I tried to help an innocent man and he was killed. God was mocking me, making me aware of my lack of grace—"

"For the love of God!" John interrupted. But Octavio suddenly whirled and ran, plunging across the lawn, across the road, and into a wide meadow. Beneditto and John stood looking after him, and made no attempt to follow.

He wandered for a long time in the starless, moonless night. At last, he sank down, exhausted by the pain of his wound and loss of blood, and lay stretched upon the ground like one crucified.

He did not know how long he had lain there before he became aware of a ray of silvery light that stood like a presence before him.

"John," he whispered. "John, is that—"

Suddenly the light grew blinding in its intensity, and Octavio cried out:

"Lord! Lord, I have sought Thy face for so long!"

When John and Beneditto found him, he was lying peacefully asleep, and his wound had ceased to bleed.

" 'Tavio," John said, shaking him gently, " 'Tavio, are you all right? Wake up."

Octavio roused reluctantly, like one saying farewell to a beloved friend.

"I saw," he said slowly, "I dreamed . . ." He passed his hand over his eyes.

"Father Sconnetti called," John said quickly, "to tell you that Father Ferrera is dying. He has been given Extreme Unction, and he has asked to see you."

The sanatorium was situated on a gentle incline, some two hundred feet from the main road. Leaving John to wait for him in the car, Octavio went inside. When the man at the desk gave him a pass, Octavio asked if Father Sconnetti had arrived, but the man shook his head.

206

Octavio took the elevator to the third floor, where a nurse directed him to Father Ferrera's room. The old priest had his face turned to the window.

When he saw Octavio, he smiled wanly.

"How do you feel, Father?" Octavio asked.

"Happy," the old priest murmured. "How is everything at St. Dominic's?"

"Good. Everything is progressing as you had hoped."

"I forgive you your lie," Father Ferrera said quietly. "Sconnetti told me some of the things that—that happened." The old pastor paused. His forehead was beaded with sweat. "He seemed troubled, and I asked him to call you."

"Did he say I've been away?"

Father Ferrera nodded slowly. "He told me of Shannan, and how you were wounded." His glasses fell off and he felt for them on the bedclothes. Octavio picked them up.

"Put them on the table," Father Ferrera said.

Neither man spoke for a while. Then Father Ferrera asked: "What troubles you, my son? Would you refuse to confess to me as you refused Father Sconnetti? Tell me, my son. Speak out."

Octavio lowered his head, moved by Father Ferrera's concern. "Bless me, Father, for I have sinned," he whispered. Slowly, at first, but then quickly, almost incoherently, he began recounting his sins. He spoke for a long time. He spoke of the German girl, of the white horse he had killed, of Shannan, of his bitter failure to save him. He told of his acts of disobedience, his defiance of Father Morello, his sins of pride, his loss of control, his brutality. He spoke of his brother Nunzio's being shot and how he had scarred the policeman's face. He explained in a passionately broken voice how he had beaten his brother Onofrio.

And finally he spoke of his doubt of God's mercy, his denial of God. Then he could speak no longer, and he sat down exhausted, and buried his face in his huge hands.

Father Ferrera reached out and touched his head. The old priest said: "You have honored me. A priest must have courage to belittle himself." He smiled wistfully.

"When I was a young man," Father Ferrera went on, speaking with difficulty, "I heard that the Catholic priests of the East often marry. I can remember being shocked by the knowledge. And they're

207

just as fine priests as we are." He began coughing; the frame of his body trembled. "You say you dreamed of this girl you wronged. Thank God that He has honored you to suffer for your sin. Pray to God, so that He will be as good to other poor sinners."

He paused, breathing quickly. Then suddenly he asked: "Were you truly interested in saving Shannan, Father 'Tavio? Was it Shannan's death that dismayed you? Or were you still thinking of Onofrio? Your brother dying again while you were still trying to atone for his first death—was that it? You thought saving Shannan was a means of atonement," he said softly, "but when he was killed—" The old priest broke off, coughing violently.

"It was yourself you felt sorry for, 'Tavio," Father Ferrera said. "You say you doubted God's mercy," he went on, shaking his head slowly. "But you based the doubt on your own failings. Because you didn't succeed, you concluded that God has no mercy. Isn't that right?"

Father Scarpi started to speak, but the old priest held up his hand. "The Christian must understand that failure is the eternal cycle of this life—but that failure becomes the resurrection. The Holy Ghost was on Shannan even as he died. Octavio, you are blind indeed. Shannan was saved even as he died!"

Octavio looked away from the old priest. There was a long silence.

"Man must doubt. . . . and question," Father Ferrera said gently. "That is the nature God gave him. But he must believe that God is merciful, even as he doubts His mercy. Man is limited in the space and time of his fleshly life, but God is endless, infinite. Beyond knowledge, beyond doubt, are vision, revelation. . . . awe, and a wonderful. . . . mystery." He was speaking with great difficulty now. "Omnia," the old priest gasped, "exeunt in. . . , mysterium."

The old priest's frail hand gripped Octavio's thick wrist.

" 'Ecce Agnus Dei. . . . who takes away the sins of the world!' " Father Ferrera murmured.

The pastor's face had grown very pale; his lips became darker. His breathing was quick and shallow. Octavio started up to call the nurse, but Father Ferrera stopped him.

"Please, don't disturb her." He smiled sadly. "You say you are too violent, too strong, too impure. You remind me of another man. A monk. This monk struck his brother. And there is a story that one day he vaulted a fence and killed a bull by twisting the neck of the poor beast. He said the same words. 'I am too strong,' he said. 'Like an ox. God does not care for me.' His name was St. Thomas of Aquinas." Father Ferrera coughed again.

"Don't speak," Father Scarpi whispered. "Don't exert yourself."

"You are forgiven," the old priest murmured. "Jesus has forgiven you."

Suddenly, with great effort, he raised himself in the bed. His thin hand traced the sign of the Cross in the air. " 'Ego te absolvo . . .' " he gasped. " 'Dominus vobiscum.' " He fell back on the bed, and blood streamed from his mouth. He struggled to speak, and Father Scarpi placed his ear close to his lips.

"The wonder—of God," said the old priest. "And—And His mercy." Father Ferrera's eyes closed in death.

Octavio knelt at the bedside and gave vent to his grief.

XXII

Hale Street was decorated with archlike bowers of colored bulbs and streaming ribbons. Peddlers hawked balloons and children ran up and down the little street. Vassaro, the baker, was vending huge cuts of pizza con alici and drinking tumblers of wine. Old Rosa Mangacabri was seated on an orange crate in front of a small table where she sold cicire and semenza salata.

Little boys set off firecrackers; and Santo Cuniggio yelled at them to keep their distance, for tonight he would give them the display of their lives: batteries of roman candles, fountains of gold in the black sky; the red, white, and blue of the great American flag—"la nostra bandiera," he shouted. He weaved unsteadily, filled with the laughter of wine.

The statue of St. Dominic was concealed behind a large canvas of the saint on horseback. Nunzio Scalpone's son Affio had painted the scene, and now Nunzio walked back and forth, proudly snapping his suspenders.

The panel depicted the saint astride a snorting white charger with flaring, red nostrils. The horse, its teeth bared, was on its hind legs, and St. Dominic, in his monk's habit, serenely straddled the beast. The white skirt of the habit was raised, showing the muscular legs of the saint. In one hand St. Dominic held the Bible and in the other a laurel wreath. A black mantle swirled out behind the monk.

"Truly a majestic figure, is he not?" Scalpone asked Don Turrido Bellino, who was intently studying the panel.

The old fisherman continued to look at the painting. With his eyes still fixed on the figure of St. Dominic, he said, "There is something wrong."

"Wrong?" Nunzio Scalpone bristled.

Don Turri Bacafiggo, who was standing beside the old man, did not understand. "In what way is it wrong, Your Honor?" he asked politely.

"Surely," Bellino replied, "if St. Dominic was able to chase the Turks out of Augusta with a Bible and a laurel wreath, the Turks could not have been very brave."

Don Peppino Messana, who was standing in front of Don Turrido, turned about. "Your Honor does not quite grasp the significance." The fishmonger bowed. "Carmello Poverello, the professor, was explaining it a moment earlier. This scene, if you please, probably never happened. The artist is showing the superiority of the Bible over the savage pagans."

"You mean," Neddo Spitoli asked horrified, "that St. Dominic never mounted a white horse and didn't chase the Turks out of Augusta?"

"Ah, no!" Nunzio Scalpone exclaimed.

"I didn't mean that exactly." Don Peppino was worried. "I'll go find the professor and have him explain it."

"Someday," Bacafiggo muttered, "I shall take the professor on a fishing trip and throw him overboard."

Rosa Mangacabri shuffled up close to the panel and squinted at it. "Is it not beautiful?" she asked shrilly. "Is it not true?"

"There is a sadness amidst this festivity," Don Turrido observed. "The big priest will not be here."

"This morning my daughter called the home of his brother in Revere," Neddo Spitoli said. "But the priest had left to visit someone in a hospital."

"I shall not be able to confess, now," Don Turrido muttered.

The old fisherman started to walk up Hale Street, followed by a group of younger fishermen and other members of the fraternity.

As Father Scarpi crossed the lobby of the hospital with his head bowed, he heard his name called. Turning, he saw Father Sconnetti. He shook hands with his friend.

"The pastor is dead," he said.

"He lived long enough to see you?" Octavio nodded, and Father Sconnetti shut his eyes for a moment. He was wearing his horn-rimmed glasses. "Last night the hospital chaplain showed me the chapel here where Father Ferrera prayed. He used to visit it against his doctor's orders. Shall we go there?" he asked.

The big priest stared at his hands. "Lead me," he said.

Father Sconnetti looked at his friend with joy.

As John drove them back to the West End, Father Sconnetti said, "I should tell you that Father Morello has requested your transfer." He paused, looking out of the window of the car. "Your orders came through last night. You've been reassigned and a new curate has taken over your cubicle. We're expecting him tomorrow. Father Lazzini and I packed your belongings."

Father Scarpi sighed. "Mea culpa," he said. "I shall miss the West End."

Father Sconnetti pressed his arm. They were silent for a while. Then, Father Sconnetti told him of the situation that had developed concerning the statue of St. Dominic. "I wish that something could be done," he said.

"John," Father Scarpi said, "will you let us off at Hale Street?"

The little street was closed to traffic, and a band was playing on a raised stand opposite the canvas that hid the statue from view.

A voice came over a loud-speaker. "Friends, this is a glad day for all of us. Today we shall parade with the new statue of St. Dominic."

"As if we didn't know!" Don Cicco Franco shouted. He glanced around and saw Octavio Scarpi. "Paesani!" Don Cicco shouted. "Amici! The priest is here! The priest!"

Heads turned. "The priest!" Bacafiggo roared. "The priest of miracles!"

A group of young fishermen ran to Father Scarpi and escorted him to the raised platform. Hundreds of hands touched his old black suitcoat and the gray sweatshirt he wore. No one seemed to notice that he wore no collar. The band began playing a march.

Octavio raised his arm, and the band broke off suddenly. The crowd grew still.

"My people," he said slowly, "on this festive day my heart is heavy. I have heard that you have offended the new pastor of St. Dominic's. I have heard," he went on sadly, "that you refuse to give the statue to our church. I know that this cannot be true. You are too honorable for that. The statue of St. Dominic belongs in the church of his name.

"We priests," he continued, "are sometimes in error. I pray that you forgive us our trespasses. I know that our fathers in Sicily sometimes suffered at the hands of priests. I pray that you forgive and forget these past errors too.

"A good priest," he said, "a hundred good priests, do not make the Church. And a thousand bad priests cannot destroy the Church. The Church is not a building of brick and stone and wood. You are the Church. Every face before me is the Church. For the Church is the whole soul of God's people.

"I do not think," he went on quietly, "that I shall be with you after today. I am not worthy of this parish, nor, perhaps, of any parish. I am not worthy to bless the statue of St. Dominic. I am not worthy to look at the statue. But someday, with God's help, I may be worthy. When that day comes, I shall want to look on St. Dominic's statue in St. Dominic's Church.

"My heart is too heavy at my own lack of grace to speak further. May Jesus look down and send His blessings. God bless you, my people, my children, my fathers. Addio."

He climbed down from the platform. There was no applause. A woman began sobbing.

Turrido Bellino whispered to a young fisherman. The boy raced after the priest. He was carrying a package that old Bellino had given him. The boy caught up to him at the corner.

"This is a gift from the Brotherhood," he said, handing the package to Father Scarpi. "We bought it last week for today. Don Turrido says to tell you we understand. He told me to go ask Father Morello to speak at the ceremony . . . Father," the boy quickly added, "God bless you." He darted off toward the church.

Octavio opened the package. Within it were a dozen Roman collars. He handed the cardboard box to Father Sconnetti and turned away, walking slowly into a nearby tenement.

Father Sconnetti fingered the collars: they were all marked size 18½. Loops had been sewn at the ends of the collars to make them even larger.

Father Sconnetti followed Octavio and found him leaning against a banister in the darkened hallway.

" 'Tavio," Father Sconnetti said gently, putting the box into his hands.

Octavio took the box almost absently; his expression was remote.

213

But when he lifted one of the collars, his hands trembled and his voice was unsteady.

"They are God's people," he said.

Father Sconnetti's eyes filled with tears as he watched Father Scarpi slowly lift the collar to his neck and fasten it securely.

The next morning, a group of fishermen walked through the streets of the West End. When they passed St. Dominic's Church, they tipped their caps. Don Turri Bacafiggo took out his old watch and checked the time with the clock above the whisky sign at Scollay Square.

At the corner of Cross and Hanover streets they met some of the North End fishermen. One of them said, "Oh, Turri, did you get the wine?"

Bacafiggo jerked a thumb toward Neddo Spitoli, who patted the gallon under his arm.

"What do you think?" Don Turri asked.

They sauntered across Atlantic Avenue and clumped onto T Wharf. Draggers and lobster boats were tied to the old pilings. Crews were readying their barcas for the trip out.

Don Turri gazed at his *Santa Maria*, tied between *La Famiglia de Boston* and the *Sant' Angelina*.

"Avanti picciotti," he growled. "Neddo, take the wheel! Santo, make ready the holds!"

Two old fishermen sat cross-legged on a net spread on the pier, watching the *Santa Maria* cast off. The old men were running twine, mending rips in the dragnet. A gallon of Zinfandel was at their elbows. One of the menders took a long swig from the gallon, rolled the wine around on his tongue, and swallowed it. Wiping his lips on the back of his hand, he glanced at the sun. Summer was upon them.

Sea gulls circled the harbor, and screamed as they trailed the *Santa Maria* out to sea.

THE AMERICAN CATHOLIC TRADITION

An Arno Press Collection

Callahan, Nelson J., editor. **The Diary of Richard L. Burtsell, Priest of New York.** 1978

Curran, Robert Emmett. **Michael Augustine Corrigan and the Shaping of Conservative Catholicism in America, 1878-1902.** 1978

Ewens, Mary. **The Role of the Nun in Nineteenth-Century America** (Doctoral Thesis, The University of Minnesota, 1971). 1978

McNeal, Patricia F. **The American Catholic Peace Movement 1928-1972** (Doctoral Dissertation, Temple University, 1974). 1978

Meiring, Bernard Julius. **Educational Aspects of the Legislation of the Councils of Baltimore, 1829-1884** (Doctoral Dissertation, University of California, Berkeley, 1963). 1978

Murnion, Philip J., **The Catholic Priest and the Changing Structure of Pastoral Ministry, New York, 1920-1970** (Doctoral Dissertation, Columbia University, 1972). 1978

White, James A., **The Era of Good Intentions: A Survey of American Catholics' Writing Between the Years 1880-1915** (Doctoral Thesis, University of Notre Dame, 1957). 1978

Dyrud, Keith P., Michael Novak and Rudolph J. Vecoli, editors. **The Other Catholics.** 1978

Gleason, Philip, editor. **Documentary Reports on Early American Catholicism.** 1978

Bugg, Lelia Hardin, editor. **The People of Our Parish.** 1900

Cadden, John Paul. **The Historiography of the American Catholic Church: 1785-1943.** 1944

Caruso, Joseph. **The Priest.** 1956

Congress of Colored Catholics of the United States. **Three Catholic Afro-American Congresses.** [1893]

Day, Dorothy. **From Union Square to Rome.** 1940

Deshon, George. **Guide for Catholic Young Women.** 1897

Dorsey, Anna H[anson]. **The Flemmings.** [1869]

Egan, Maurice Francis. **The Disappearance of John Longworthy.** 1890

Ellard, Gerald. **Christian Life and Worship.** 1948

England, John. **The Works of the Right Rev. John England, First Bishop of Charleston.** 1849. 5 vols.

Fichter, Joseph H. **Dynamics of a City Church**. 1951

Furfey, Paul Hanly. **Fire on the Earth**. 1936

Garraghan, Gilbert J. **The Jesuits of the Middle United States**. 1938. 3 vols.

Gibbons, James. **The Faith of Our Fathers**. 1877

Hecker, I[saac] T[homas]. **Questions of the Soul**. 1855

Houtart, François. **Aspects Sociologiques Du Catholicisme Américain**. 1957

[Hughes, William H.] **Souvenir Volume. Three Great Events in the History of the Catholic Church in the United States**. 1889

[Huntington, Jedediah Vincent]. **Alban: A Tale of the New World**. 1851

Kelley, Francis C., editor. The First American Catholic Missionary Congress. 1909

Labbé, Dolores Egger. **Jim Crow Comes to Church**. 1971

LaFarge, John. **Interracial Justice**. 1937

Malone, Sylvester L. **Dr. Edward McGlynn**. 1918

The Mission-Book of the Congregation of the Most Holy Redeemer. 1862

O'Hara, Edwin V. **The Church and the Country Community**. 1927

Pise, Charles Constantine. **Father Rowland**. 1829

Ryan, Alvan S., editor. **The Brownson Reader**. 1955

Ryan, John A., **Distributive Justice**. 1916

Sadlier, [Mary Anne]. **Confessions of an Apostate**. 1903

Sermons Preached at the Church of St. Paul the Apostle, New York, During the Year 1863. 1864

Shea, John Gilmary. **A History of the Catholic Church Within the Limits of the United States**. 1886/1888/1890/1892. 4 Vols.

Shuster, George N. **The Catholic Spirit in America**. 1928

Spalding, J[ohn] L[ancaster]. **The Religious Mission of the Irish People and Catholic Colonization**. 1880

Sullivan, Richard. **Summer After Summer**. 1942

[Sullivan, William L.] **The Priest**. 1911

Thorp, Willard. **Catholic Novelists in Defense of Their Faith, 1829-1865**. 1968

Tincker, Mary Agnes. **San Salvador**. 1892

Weninger, Franz Xaver. **Die Heilige Mission** *and* **Praktische Winke Für Missionare**. 1885. 2 Vols. in 1

Wissel, Joseph. **The Redemptorist on the American Missions**. 1920. 3 Vols. in 2

The World's Columbian Catholic Congresses and Educational Exhibit. 1893

Zahm, J[ohn] A[ugustine]. **Evolution and Dogma**. 1896